Cédric

A Novel by

William Grovère

Cédric (2nd Ed.)

A Novel by William Grovère

First published (1st Edition) 2022, ISBN: 978-1-6632-4208-2

ISBN: 979-8-218-99754-0

To my five grandchildren:

Faith, Logan, Jack, Travis, Avery—

Cedric's contemporaries—

Acknowledgements

With grateful appreciation to my neighbor Kim, who suggested the idea to go back in time to tell Cèdric's story. Special thanks to Tom, Sandrine, and Bridget for reading chapter by chapter and providing essential feedback. And most of all, I thank my wife, Sylvia, who listened to me read the text out loud, line by line, with crucial editing help. Most of all, I want to thank her for caring for me during a health crisis that might otherwise have derailed the publication of this book.

Special thanks to my sister-in-law, Gigipaws for the cover painting of the Cédric's steam engine.

Cédric

A novel by

William Grovère

Table of Contents

Preface

Cédric is a biography. Not an ordinary biography about some historical figure but a biography about a future fictional character who could be living among us as a boy today. Cédric was an unusually gifted innovator with an intellect that could not be contained within the bounds of conventional thinking. Like Galileo Galilei, he spent his life at odds with the guardians of orthodoxy and was perpetually out of phase with the world. Cédric, the scientist, was introduced to the reader in previous William Grovère novels, *Sea Change*. *The Timecharger* and *La Charlière*, which took place in the 2070s and 2080s after Cédric's untimely death in 2062. He had written a scientific treatise as a college undergraduate, *Dark Matter and the Time-Dependent Speed of Light*, on July 28, 2029, that caused a stir and landed him in hot water. The complete text appears in chapter 3 of *The Timecharger*. (The abstract appears in chapter 23 of *Cédric*.) It contains theories that challenge the commonly held belief that the speed of light is a universal constant. Cédric's hypothesis that the speed of light has been increasing since the birth of our galaxy leads to a host of remarkable discoveries and inventions. Variable light speed theories are not new, but in our current era, just as with geocentrism in Galileo's time, the orthodoxy of fixed light speed is difficult to challenge in the domain of peer-reviewed scientific nonfiction. In the realm of science fiction, however, Cédric's theories impacted the course of history fifty years hence in much the same way that quantum theory impacted it one hundred years ago. The consequences of his theories brought about the discovery of microfusion and the timecharging effect. A subsequent treatise, *Gravitron Theory and the Dynamics of Gravitational Fields Induced by Supermassive Objects in Motion*, originally written in 2062, and finally released to the public posthumously in 2085, gave rise to the discovery of antigravity. These ideas, whether scientifically credible or not, provide the stage on which the action in William Grovère novels take place. This novel, *Cédric,* is the prequel and goes back in time to tell the story of this remarkable scientist.

Chapter 1: Broken

Cédric Rothschild stood at the railing of the fourth-floor terrasse to take in the view as he waited for his father. The terrasse had a commanding view of the Seine in both directions at the point where it divides to go around the private island of this exclusive western suburb of Paris. Childhood recollections flooded over him, and he could smell the faint pungent odor of the pony stables nearby where he had learned to ride. The fond memories of being chased around the apartment by Annie, his American nanny, cheered him up. His father's penthouse apartment radiated conspicuous elegance. The red roses around the perimeter were magnificent, and a gardener was busy trimming every dead and dying leaf to bring each plant to perfection. He had not been home for two years. The apprehension of the encounter seized him suddenly. Being summoned by his father could only mean bad things.

"Cédric!" came the booming voice from behind him. The harsh tone was all too familiar. Cédric turned to acknowledge his father's arrival without saying a word.

"I got another call from the chancellor," his father said.

Cédric still said nothing. He knew the nature of his summons. This wasn't the first time his father had ordered him back to Paris to account for his behavior at the university.

“Your mother and I are really disappointed,” his father said.

“Geraldine is not my mother,” Cédric shot back.

“She will be as soon as the divorce is settled,” his father said, motioning for him to be seated on the lounge chairs, where a pitcher of ice water and glasses awaited them.

“So, you are going to divorce my mother so you can marry your mistress?” responded Cédric.

“Where in the world did you learn to talk to me like that?” his father said in disgust. “You must stop carrying on your unauthorized research. You have upset the department head again.” Cédric’s father leaned forward to pour himself a glass of water as he tried to compose himself, continuing, “They are quite confident that they have identified the dark matter particle using the new collider, and your insistence that dark matter is a fantasy is making Dr. Hendriksen and the entire High-Energy Physics Department very unhappy.”

“He’s just a glory-seeking airhead,” responded Cédric.

“That’s exactly what I mean, Cédric. You disrespect everyone you don’t agree with. You can’t go through life like that.”

“Why does he care?” responded Cédric. “He’s not paying for my research. I am paying for it entirely out of my own pocket.”

Cédric’s father cleared his throat. “Yes, about that. I have decided to cut your allowance to cover just tuition and living expenses.”

"What?" shot back Cédric. "You can't do that! My experiment is almost finished. It will demonstrate compellingly that the speed of light is not constant."

Cédric's father leaned back in the chair and crossed his legs in a vain attempt to lighten the mood. Then, after an awkward silence, he said, "Dr. Hendriksen is looking for a bright young scientist to join his research team. He has asked specifically for you."

Cédric said sarcastically, "How many millions of euros did you pledge to the university this time to pull that off?"

His father poured him a glass of water and handed it to him. "No thanks," he said, standing to leave.

"Sit down, Cédric," his father commanded. "We are not finished."

Cédric sat back down. "You can't cut me off now," he protested. "I am less than six weeks from finishing the experiment and defending my thesis."

His father said, "The university is not going to grant you a PhD for your rogue work. They say it's total foolishness."

Cédric insisted, "They will think differently once I demonstrate that the speed of light slows down in the vicinity of a massive object."

His father looked down in dismay. "You know, Cédric. They only let you into the university because of my endowment to the library. Your grades were not good enough. I had to pull strings."

This last jap cut deeply. His father always got in the final word by putting people down. Cédric's entire life had been spent trying to live up to his father's expectations, but no matter what he did, it was never enough. Cédric stood up and walked away. The tears only began to flow when he passed the doorman and exited to the street.

Cédric passed through every stage of emotion on his return trip to England—from anguish to anger to rage—before finally settling into sadness and dark depression by the time he entered his apartment near the university. He lay on his bed staring at the ceiling. It was late, but he could not sleep. At last, he went to his desk and composed an email to his father.

Dear Father,

I apologize for storming out on you. That was very bad form on my part, and I am sorry. Please forgive me. You have always been good to me, and I know you have always been concerned for what is in my best interest. I know of your disappointment that I chose physics rather than law, and I was defensive because I had a pretty good idea why you wanted to talk to me in person. I knew that Dr. Hendriksen had gone to the chancellor to try to silence me, but you need to know that he is an arrogant charlatan. He is only interested in personal glory and recognition and sees identifying the dark matter particle as his way to achieve it. I understand that he secured tens of millions of pounds in research grants for the university at a time when the Physics Department was faltering. However, it irks me that he would go to the chancellor to exert pressure on you to suppress my work. Obviously, my theories are very threatening to him, but he refuses to engage me directly for fear of the consequences to his professional standing. In fact, I am not alone in my views. I have support from one of my thesis advisers, a professor in astrophysics, but in secrecy because we both know he would be blackballed by the university if he were to endorse the unorthodox views I have been promoting. I am a gadfly to Dr. Hendriksen, and I recognize that my own arrogance could be my undoing. I promise to tone down my rhetoric. I hope your faith in me has not been damaged beyond repair.

Your devoted son,
Cédric

Cédric went to Sheffield the following day to try to acquire a critical part for his experiment. He found himself in a run-down part of the city that had once been a thriving center for manufacturing with numerous machine shops. But now, only a few remained open, and the general atmosphere was dark and oppressive. He requested that the taxi, which had brought him from the train station to the address he had been given, wait for him. He retrieved the slip of paper from his pocket to verify the name on the sign over the door: "Fred's Exotic Metals Supply." He rang the bell next to the door and heard the click of the lock signifying for him to enter.

"Are you Fred?" he asked.

The man standing behind the counter in the lobby responded, "That would be me. How can I help you?"

Cédric answered, "I have been told that I might be able to obtain a uranium tube here." He reached into his pocket and unfolded the paper with a sketch of the part he wanted to purchase and showed it to the man. “I would prefer depleted uranium, but I am having difficulty finding a source. Unprocessed uranium will serve my purpose just as well. Even though it is slightly radioactive, I will shield it in lead blocks in my experiment at the university.”

“You surely know unprocessed uranium is contraband,” said the man. “You need government authorization. Do you have a certificate for purchase?”

Cédric pulled a wad of bills from his pocket and unfolded them without looking up.

“Let me take a look at that drawing,” said the man, studying the sketch carefully and then looking up. “That sure looks a lot like a Fergusson transmutation tube.”

Cédric smiled knowingly without saying a word.

“All right then,” he said, turning. “Wait here. I will be right back.”

He returned after a couple of minutes and placed the object on the counter in front of Cédric, a lead cannister about fifteen centimeters long and five centimeters in diameter. “Fergusson has been out of business for quite some time. I got stuck with an inventory of these things. That will be twelve thousand pounds.” He said this in such a way that he expected Cédric to just walk away empty-handed, but Cédric started peeling off the banknotes.

“Will this do?” he said, handing the bills over and picking up the canister that he estimated to weigh about a kilogram. He began unscrewing the endcap to inspect the contents.

“You can’t open it in here!” said the man in alarm. “You will set off my scintillation detectors. You can rest assured. The tube is inside the lead shroud. Don’t unscrew the endcap until you are in a safe location.”

“How do I know the tube is actually inside the lead shroud then?” asked Cédric.

The man cocked his head slightly to signal his annoyance. “Trust me, it’s in there. But if your uranium tube isn’t inside, bring it back, and I will refund your money.”

Cédric slipped the cannister into his knapsack and nodded. “We both know I was never here,” he said, turning to go out the door. He took the taxi back to the train station.

The maglev back to Candlebridge took a little over an hour. Cédric bolted from the train station, walking briskly the few blocks to his lab, enjoying the pleasant July evening air and the exhilaration of finally being able to complete his experiment. It was nine o’clock on Friday by the time he arrived at his building. It was locked up, as most of his fellow students were in the local pubs getting inebriated for the weekend. Hopefully, he would have the building to himself. He punched in the door code and went inside. The hallway lights came on automatically. His lab was at the far end on the right. He passed by Dr. Hendriksen’s lab, which was thankfully dark. The adrenaline coursing through his body was intense, eradicating any sense of the passage of time as entered his lab and began turning on the various pieces of equipment to allow them to warm up. He removed the cannister from his knapsack and admired it for a moment before unscrewing the endcap and pouring out the contents, a shiny uranium tube, ten centimeters long and one centimeter in outer diameter, with a small one-millimeter diameter hole passing through the center. It was perfect. He opened the vacuum chamber and slid the tube into a hole in a lead block inside to verify the fit before placing the tube back inside the lead cannister and screwing the endcap back on.

The first order of business was to confirm the alignment of the laser. He had fabricated the laser himself to deliver a precise femtosecond pulse when activated. The laser pulse went through a beam splitter with one half of the beam passing through a phase inverter. When the two pulses were recombined at the detector, their arrivals could be observed with extraordinary precision. Only when each of the two beams traveled precisely the same distance in vacuum would they cancel each other, and no signal would be detected. Thus, Cédric had developed an ingenious calibration method for the precision measurement his experiment demanded. He removed the lead block from the chamber and engaged the turbomolecular pump to achieve the necessary high vacuum. If either beam were to strike even a single gas molecule in the chamber during transit, it would be refracted. Piezoelectric actuators allowed Cédric to position the mirrors inside the chamber to a locational tolerance of one angstrom. He began firing the laser while adjusting the position of one of the mirrors until the light from both beams canceled and no signal was detected. From this, he knew that the two path lengths were the same. More importantly, this meant that the two beams traveled the same distance in the same length of time. In other words, he knew that the speed of light in both beams was the same.

Once he was satisfied with the alignment, he released the vacuum, placing the lead block back in the chamber, positioning it so that one of the laser pulses would travel through the center of the one-centimeter diameter hole bored through it. Again, he pumped down the chamber and repeated the experiment. There was a difference in the arrival times of the two pulses, with the lead block in place, but the effect was so slight as not to be statistically significant. He released the vacuum, and this time he removed the uranium tube from the cannister and carefully slid it into the hole in the lead block. Based on his calculations, he expected the effect to be more pronounced because the density of uranium is almost twice that of lead, and the hole through it was much smaller. He closed the chamber door and pumped it down one more time. He stared at the button to activate the laser. This was the moment of truth. He would know in just seconds if his variable light speed theory had merit or was simply fantasy. He held his breath and pushed the button. He nearly fainted when the difference in arrival times was two nanoseconds. The speed of light passing through the hole in the uranium tube was measurably and unmistakably slower. He now had incontrovertible evidence that the speed of light was not constant in a vacuum. It was slowed down in the presence of mass. He let out a delighted, "Yes!" and jumped out of his chair and began hopping up and down. He performed the entire procedure three more times to confirm repeatability, each time carefully recording the results in his laboratory notebook. He had worked through the night and had lost track of time.

That was when the door to his lab opened, and a contingent of police entered. "Mr. Cédric Rothschild, you are under arrest!" They seized him and handcuffed him behind his back.

As they were leading him out, Dr. Hendriksen entered the lab with some campus security guards. He was fumbling with a Geiger counter, trying to detect the radioactive signal. He popped open the vacuum chamber and scanned the interior. "That's it," he said triumphantly. "Unmistakable. It's alpha decay from uranium-235!"

Chapter 2: Denial

The door to Professor Cecil Edwards's office was open a crack, which indicated that he was available for serious matters but not for idle chat. Cédric rapped at the door and pushed it in to get permission to enter. Dr. Edwards was at his desk and signaled for him to come in.

"It worked," Cédric exclaimed jubilantly. "It really worked. I slowed down the speed of light. The laser pulse going through the uranium tube arrived two nanoseconds late. That means the speed of light going through the tube was just five million meters per second, just a fraction of the accepted value in vacuum. Do you realize the implications?"

Dr. Edwards lowered his reading glasses to the tip of his nose and looked intently at Cédric, who was pacing and doing pirouettes. "I heard you were arrested this morning," he said.

"It was nothing," replied Cédric, "just a little misunderstanding. The police let me go as soon as we got out of the building."

"A misunderstanding?" Dr. Edwards replied. "Your laboratory has been designated a crime scene."

"That's why I came by," said Cédric. "My keycard has been deactivated, and I was hoping you would let me into my lab."

"Did you hear what I just said? Your lab is a crime scene. I can't let you in."

Cédric paused while the remark sank in. "I only want to fetch my lab notebook so I can finish writing up the experiment," he said.

"Cédric, the lab is sealed, and everything in it has been confiscated until after the investigation."

"Investigation? What investigation?" shot back Cédric. "The school dropped the charges."

"The criminal charges, yes, but, Cédric, you are under suspension pending expulsion from the university."

The jubilation emptied from Cédric along with the color in his face. "What are you talking about?"

Dr. Edwards indicated for him to be seated and said, "Cédric, you smuggled radioactive contraband into the building!"

"What? A hundred and fifty grams of unprocessed uranium?" Cédric responded. "A few alpha particles. What's the big deal?"

"You set off all the radiation detectors in the building, causing a campus-wide emergency."

"Come on, Dr. Edwards. We both know it was a trivial infraction of school policy," said Cédric.

"That could get you expelled," responded Dr. Edwards.

Cédric stood up and walked over to the window. Turning and pointing, he said, "Do you see that building across the quad? That's the Rothschild Library. My father donated that. Do you really think they will kick me out of the school? Six more weeks, and I will defend my thesis. Then they will be done with me for good."

Dr. Edwards exhaled and stared down at his desk. "Are you not aware that the department rejected your dissertation?"

"My father said something to that effect a couple of days ago, but I thought it was just another of one of his attempts to threaten and discourage me. Dr. Edwards, sir, they can't reject my dissertation now that I have the undeniable proof. Five thousand meters per second! Really! You can't possibly be serious!"

Cédric was overcome by panic as he began pacing the office. "Surely you won't let this happen."

"It's out of my hands," replied Dr. Edwards. "It's not a departmental matter. It has gone all the way to the chancellor's office."

"Hendriksen!" said Cédric angrily. "That sewer rat is behind this. He's the one who told me where I could purchase that uranium tube. This is nothing more than a setup."

"Can you prove that?" asked Dr. Edwards.

Cédric thought about this for a moment and said, "He handed me a slip of paper with the name and address in Sheffield. Look, I still have it." He reached into his pocket for the note, but it was gone. "Oh no. The police must have discarded it when they had me empty my pockets during the arrest."

Both men sat in silence as the gravity of the situation settled in. Finally, Cédric asked, "How about the manuscript? When do you think it will be ready to be submitted to the journal?"

"I'm sorry, Cédric," replied Dr. Edwards. "You know that I am in basic agreement with many of your theories, and I have checked the mathematics, but no journal would publish your paper without a well-known coauthor. And even then, I doubt seriously that it would get past the reviewers."

Cédric said, "You are a highly regarded astrophysicist. I was hoping that you would join me as a coauthor."

"You have taken on the entire scientific community by claiming that the speed of light is not a universal constant," said Dr. Edwards.

"That's not exactly what I claimed," responded Cédric. "I am only claiming that the speed of light is dependent on time. At the exact same time at two different points in space, the speed of light is the same. It's just not possible to measure the speed of light at one point in space without traveling to the other point to measure it again, and that takes time."

The two sat quietly again for a while. "So, you don't endorse my theories?" said Cédric rhetorically. "Don't you see? I just proved it. Local time depends on mass. Energy conservation demands it. I have just succeeded in comparing the speed of light in two different time frames."

"If I were to endorse your theories," replied Dr. Edwards, "it would cost me my job. I would be forced to resign from the university."

"I understand," said Cédric, standing to walk out of the office dejectedly.

"Wait. I have something I want to give you," said Dr. Edwards, turning and pulling a volume from the bookshelf behind him and handing it to Cédric.

Cédric read the title aloud, *"Mere Christianity."* Passing it back, he said, "No thanks. I don't really have any interest in spiritual stuff."

Handing it back to Cédric again, Dr. Edwards said, "No. Please take it. I think you're going to need it. The book was written by an Oxford intellectual named C. S. Lewis who was a lighthouse to Great Britain during the darkest days of the Second World War."

Cédric walked somberly from the physics building toward his apartment just off campus. His anguish was turning into consuming rage in the only way he knew how to deal with such a monumental injustice. No sooner had he walked past the Rothschild Library than a sudden cloudburst caught him by surprise, and he was completely soaked by the rain in a matter of seconds. He dashed to his apartment through rivulets that quickly became ankle-deep rivers in the streets. Once inside his apartment, he stripped out of his wet clothes. The book that Dr.

Edwards had given him was completely ruined. He tossed it in the waste basket and headed to the bedroom to find something dry to put on. Then he sat down at his computer to compose the following exposé:

Dark Matter

There is a very dark matter going on at Candlebridge University among the research faculty. In particular, a certain Dr. H. has been extorting millions of pounds from an unsuspecting British public to carry out fraudulent research. Were this not bad enough, this same Dr. H. has gone to extreme lengths to suppress the work of others at the university that would discredit him. Dr. H. is a charlatan hiding behind his research grants and notoriety. His only pursuit is international fame and personal glory. His arrogance knows no bounds. He even named the fictitious dark matter particle he claims to be on the verge of discovering the "Hendri" particle. No such particle exists, and he knows this. But, in order to keep his charade from being found out, he actually went to the trouble to set up a fellow scientist for expulsion from the school who disagrees with him. I call on the House of Lords and those who oversee the scientific endeavors of all the otherwise honest scientists in England to investigate this egregious dark matter at Candlebridge University.

Signed: A concerned graduate student, July 6, 2036

Cédric checked the exposé several times to be sure the language was sufficiently inflammatory and then sent it to the London newspaper well known for relishing and publishing such scandalous material.

Chapter 3: Closure

Candlebridge was a quaint English hamlet midway between London and Manchester. Legend had it that there had been a tavern across the river from the main thoroughfare, and the proprietor had constructed a covered bridge that he had lined with candles during winter to entice travelers to stop in. The bridge was long gone, but the village had otherwise changed almost imperceptibly since the seventeenth century. Now, the ancient town of Candlebridge was completely encircled by the sprawling modern glass and brick buildings of the university, which ensured that the village would remain small. Cédric's apartment was just above a pub in the town center. This had been his home for the past three years, and he was very fortunate to have it. Most of the student housing was located outside the perimeter of the university, requiring the use of bicycles and a network of shuttle buses to get around. For Cédric, everything he needed was within a short walking distance.

He had gone to bed early the previous night to try catch up on the sleep he had missed the night of his triumphant, successful experiment and subsequent arrest early the next morning. It was Sunday, and he had planned to sleep in when he was awakened by the thunderous clanging of the church bells down the street calling parishioners to seven o'clock mass. Ordinarily, he did not leave his windows open at night, because of the boisterous partying of the students in the pub below who had had too much to drink, and the thick tobacco smoke that wafted up to his apartment. But it was unseasonably warm on that night in July. Shuttered windows were not an option, and every sound outside was amplified by the still, humid air. A gang of noisy magpies just outside his window made it clear that there was no point in trying to go back to sleep. He dressed and headed to the café across the street to see if by any chance the morning newspapers had been dropped off.

There it was. Right on the front page, his diatribe, "Dark Matter." A wave of exhilaration flooded over him as he removed the free paper from the rack and headed inside for morning coffee to savor his work in print. The editorial commentary read, "A disgruntled graduate student has really stirred up a hornet's nest this time. Such a brazen attack on Candlebridge University will surely not go unnoticed." Cédric said to himself, "Disgruntled, they say? When they start looking into this matter, the truth will come out." He checked for messages on his phone and saw one from the chancellor's office requesting his presence at 9:00 a.m. on Monday to "commence an investigation." "Perfect," Cédric said aloud as he headed outside with his double espresso to prepare his defense.

"The chancellor will see you now," said the receptionist in the expansive top-floor suite of the administration building. Cédric had arrived five minutes early and waited impatiently until half past nine. He had assumed that he would be meeting one-on-one with the chancellor, but rather, he was ushered into the boardroom where a dozen august-looking university officials were sitting around a large, oval table. The room was completely quiet, and all eyes were boring in on him. The only person Cédric recognized was the dean of the Science and Engineering College. He realized immediately that he had just walked into an ambush.

"Please have a seat, Mr. Rothschild," said the chancellor, pointing to the empty chair at the head of the table. The newspaper that Cédric recognized immediately was on the table in front of him. The chancellor picked it up and, pointing to the front-page article, asked with an angry voice that shook the room, "Who might this disgruntled graduate student be, Mr. Rothschild?" He put the newspaper back down and folded his hands on the table, taking a deep breath to regain his composure. "Do you have any idea what you have just done? The trouble you have caused?"

Cédric sat quietly waiting for his opportunity to begin his defense.

"You have embarrassed this university and besmirched our fine reputation. You have done unimaginable damage."

"Let me explain," said Cédric.

"No! You let me explain," said the chancellor. "I was on the phone with your father for much of yesterday. His heartbreak regarding this matter is unimaginable. You have embarrassed him and disgraced the Rothschild name." He paused to take a drink of water, then continued. "In an emergency session of the

Disciplinary Council, we have unanimously decided to separate you from this university."

Cédric sat upright in his chair and said, "You're kicking me out of the school? You can't do that! Do you have any idea what my recent discovery will do for the reputation of this university?" Cédric was fuming. "And you are going to allow a sewer rat and fraud to discredit my work and then cover it up with whitewash?" He stood up, and his rage was in full display. "Give me my laboratory notebook and my lasers, and I will gladly be out of here!"

The chancellor looked over at the science and engineering dean and said, "This is a reasonable request. Can you arrange for Mr. Rothschild to remove his personal effects from the laboratory?"

"Perhaps once the Environmental, Health, and Safety Department is finished with the decontamination," the dean responded.

"Decontamination!" exploded Cédric. "You're not serious?"

The dean replied, "Dr. Hendriksen insisted. He doesn't want to expose any of his students to a radiation hazard."

Cédric shot back, "From a hundred and fifty grams of uranium? Are you kidding me? And you call this a research university?" If Cédric had had a hand grenade, he would have pulled the pin and tossed it on the table. Turning, he stormed out of the boardroom.

Cédric stood at the very same spot on the terrasse of his father's apartment overlooking the Seine, where he had been the week before. A hydrogen-supply barge was passing below him, heading upriver to refuel the water taxis and dinner boats of central Paris. The air was pristine, and the Eiffel Tower dominated the cityscape spectacularly to the northeast. He heard his father's footsteps behind him. He dared not turn around, waiting for the last moment before engaging the fiery darts he expected to be coming from his stern eyes. His father stood and said nothing, and when Cédric did finally turn around, the expression was unexpectedly gentle and sympathetic.

Cédric said, "I suppose you heard—they kicked me out of the university. I guess I really made a mess of things."

"That was rather reckless," his father said. "Come sit. There are some things I want to tell you." Mr. Rothschild dismissed the gardener, and the father and son sat across from each other on the lounge chairs.

After an awkward silence, Cédric said, "I am finished as a scientist, you know."

His father replied, "I doubt that very much, and you are certainly not finished as a man. After our acrimonious encounter last week, I did some soul searching," he continued. "For one thing, I tried to read your manuscript on dark matter and the variable speed of light. I am sorry to say I hadn't looked at it before."

"I wrote it when I was just nineteen after an introductory astrophysics class," said Cédric. "I have revised and improved it considerably since."

His father continued, "To say I understood very much of it would be an overstatement, but it gave me a glimpse into your soul. I could never figure out why you wanted to be a scientist, and I have no clue why you even care what the speed of light is in a distant galaxy." His father's voice broke, and tears formed in his eyes. "Your brother Antoine was pursuing the path I would have chosen for you as well. When he was killed during his second year of law school, my dreams were shattered. I had it all worked out that he would take over the family office when I retired. Then, when you chose science over law or business, I was devastated." He picked up his glass of water and took a sip. "I am really sorry, Cédric," he blurted out, barely controlling his emotions.

Cédric was stunned and speechless.

His father continued pouring out his heart. "I fear I heaped all my own failings and inadequacies on you, perhaps hoping that one day you would compensate for them the way I had expected Antoine to have done. I never gave you a chance. I am so sorry."

The two sat quietly contemplating the newfound honesty. Cédric did not know how to respond.

Finally, his father continued, "I suspect that you would have prevailed over this Dr. Hendriksen fellow in due course. The problem is that you backed the university into a corner and gave them no way to save face. I think you need a change of scenery. I deposited fifty thousand euros in your account this morning and instructed Nicolas at our château in Val d'Isère to get it ready for you. Perhaps you will consider setting up a laboratory in the workshop." He paused to take another drink of water and then said, "I know I never told you this before, but I am incredibly proud of you, and I think writing that exposé was the bravest thing I have ever heard of."

They both stood up and embraced for the very first time. His father said, "You might be interested to know that I told the chancellor that the next installment for the Rothschild Library may be delayed." This caused them both to laugh.

"Can I have Antoine's motorcycle when I get to Val d'Isère?" asked Cédric.

"Do you even know how to ride a motorcycle?" his father asked.

"No, but it's time I learned, don't you think?" This brought more laughter.

"Geraldine is out, and I am dining alone tonight. Would you care to join me for dinner?" his father asked. They walked together back into the grand salon.

Chapter 4: Val d'Isère

Cédric packed up the last of the shipping boxes containing his things—mostly books—and stacked them in the kitchen by the front door. He heard the hydraulic tailgate of the moving van drop down and peeked out the window to be sure they were not just delivering kegs of beer to the pub. Shortly, there was a wrap at his door, and a burly man with a clipboard was standing outside when Cédric opened it. A second man was standing behind him with a hand truck.

"Cédric Rothschild?" he asked.

"Yes. That's me," Cédric said. "Come in. Everything is stacked here in the kitchen."

"Just sign here," the man said, handing him the clipboard and a pen. "Please confirm the delivery address as 1 Champs d'Isère, Val d'Isère, France, by initialing the box there at the bottom of the page," he said, pointing to the place.

Cédric did so and handed back the clipboard. "Everything going is packed up into these boxes. Don't load the electric scooter and backpack though. I will be taking them with me," he said, pointing out those items. The second man already had his first load and was heading down the stairs to the moving van. All it took was three trips. Cédric hadn't accumulated very much of his own stuff in the three years he had spent in the apartment, which was furnished by the landlord.

Once the moving van was loaded and had departed, Cédric went down to the pub to say goodbye to the proprietor and give him two hundred pounds for cleaning and repairing any damage. Back in the apartment, he looked around for any items he might have overlooked. Everything seemed in order. The waterlogged book he had thrown in the wastebasket was now mostly dry and swollen. He picked it up and put it in his backpack, if for no other reason than it seemed a shame to discard it without at least taking a peek inside at some point. He strapped on his backpack and hopped on his trottinette to go to the university for the last time.

"I'm Cédric Rothschild, here to see Dean Hogbottle," Cédric said to the secretary of the Science and Engineering College.

"Yes, he is expecting you. Go right in," she said.

Dean Hogbottle stood when he entered and extended his hand, greeting him warmly. "Come sit down," the dean said. "What can I do for you?"

Cédric said, "I came to pick up my lasers and laboratory notebooks. I was told the decontamination of my laboratory is complete and it is open once again."

"Yes, about the lasers," Dean Hogbottle said. "Even though you apparently designed and constructed them at your own expense, the work was carried out in the university's facilities. The school has a strict policy that any work carried out in our facilities becomes the property of the school, so I am sorry to tell you that you cannot have them."

Cédric took a deep breath and shook his head from side to side. "Why does that not come as a surprise," he said. "Then just give me my laboratory notebook."

Dean Hogbottle acted startled and replied apologetically, "No notebook was ever found in your lab. Perhaps it was discarded during the decontamination," he said.

"Hendriksen!" Cédric said, grinding his teeth.

"Will that be all then?" Hogbottle said, standing up to indicate that the meeting was over, and he had more important things to tend to.

"Tell me something, Dean Hogbottle. What will happen to Dr. Hendriksen when it is discovered that his dark matter particle doesn't really exist?"

The dean sat back down and said, "I will let you in on a little secret, my dear Mr. Rothschild." Then he came closer and said in a whisper, "It doesn't matter. It doesn't matter in the least. Hendriksen has secured millions in research grants for the school that will keep the school flush with cash for years and years, churning out happy little graduate students and paying lavish salaries to the professors. By the time anyone determines whether or not this mysterious dark matter particle exists, we will all be enjoying our retirement pensions on the Côte d'Azur."

The top speed of eighteen kilometers per hour of Cédric's electric trottinette was not nearly fast enough to get him to the train station so he could escape the sour stench of Candlebridge

University. The bottom had just fallen out of his life. He had always believed that science involved the dogged pursuit of truth. He had just encountered something completely unexpected: a technocracy of science only for science's sake. So-called scientists who were only in it for the money. The outcome was irrelevant as long as someone was willing to pay for it. This sickened Cédric. He had been such an idealist and did not realize what was going on around him. Perhaps no one actually did care what the speed of light might be in a distant galaxy. He had been focused on his experiment for years and had finally succeeded in getting it to work. He had proven beyond a shadow of a doubt that mass altered the local speed of light. But who cared if you couldn't turn the discovery into hard cash? Cédric sank deeper and deeper into despair with every passing minute on his way back to London. His world had been turned completely upside down. Perhaps he should have accepted Dr. Hendriksen's offer to join his team and dutifully work with his other colleagues calibrating beam energies in the collider and constructing particle detectors that would never detect anything. At least that way he would have earned his PhD and have some published scientific papers for his curriculum vitae. Now he had nothing at all—no publications, no laboratory notebook, no lasers, no PhD.

He caught a plane from London to Lyon, where he took a taxi to the quiet village of Villefontaine to visit his mother. It was too late to go to the nursing home where she was staying, so he checked into a hotel nearby to spend the night.

The following morning was overcast with fast-moving clouds that threatened showers common to the Rhône valley at that time of year. He inquired at the front desk where he might find Madame Rothschild. The receptionist replied, "She is not taking any visitors today. Is she expecting you?"

"No," said Cédric. "It's a surprise. I am her son."

The receptionist asked for a photo identification and then called for an escort to lead him to the solarium. The sight of his mother was shocking. She sat in a wheelchair, head slumped forward, and eyes closed. A drip of drool hung from her lower lip that seemed to be trying to articulate speech.

"Hello, Mother," Cédric said tenderly. "I brought you a bouquet of your favorite red roses, like the ones you used to grow on the terrasse." He placed the vase of flowers on the table next to her.

"Oh, Antoine," she mumbled without looking up. "I was just thinking about you."

Cédric glanced up at the nurse in shock. It had been two years since his last visit, and he had been unaware of the extent to which her mental state had deteriorated since the Alzheimer's diagnosis.

"No, Mother. It's Cédric," he corrected her gently.

She squeezed her eyes tightly as if trying to recall that name.

"It's your second son, Cédric. I brought you red roses. I'm on my way to Val d'Isère, and I stopped by to say hello."

She raised her head and opened her eyes slightly. "Oh, Cédric. How nice. Just set them over there by the bed." Then her head slumped back down to the previous pose, and she continued muttering unintelligible sounds.

He looked up at the nurse pathetically. The nurse said, "I'm so sorry. Some days are better than others."

Cédric kissed his mother gently on forehead and briskly walked out of the nursing home. He hurriedly checked out of his hotel room and raced to the train station on his trottinette to catch the TGV maglev to Grenoble and then the regional train to Val d'Isère. He wished he had Antoine's Harley at that moment, thinking that if he could just go fast enough, he might be able to outrun the sorrow that was doggedly pursuing him. His father had wisely asked Nicolas, the caretaker, to give Cédric some lessons before wrapping the motorcycle around a tree. Cédric had subsequently advised him that his arrival would be delayed by a day. Nicolas was waiting for him when his train pulled into the station. It had been eight years since the last time Cédric had been in the sprawling ski resort in the Alps on the border between France and Italy. Nico had not changed in appearance one bit. They recognized each other immediately, and Nico gave him a big hug and kissed Cédric on both cheeks.

"I wasn't expecting you to meet me at the station," Cédric said. "I was planning to take a cab."

"Nonsense," said Nico. "Ever since your father said you would be coming, I have been overrun by anticipation. But I was expecting you yesterday."

"I decided to stop by Villefontaine on the way to see my mother," Cédric said. "I wasn't prepared for what I encountered."

"I understand," said Nico sympathetically. "You have been through a lot recently. Your father filled me in. Some hikes in the fresh alpine air, and you will be as good as new in no time. Val d'Isère is pretty deserted this time of year. Even the squirrels pack up and go on vacation."

Cédric put his things in the back of Nico's beat-up, four-wheel drive utility truck, and the two headed out of town along the river d'Isère to the Rothschild estate, a vast compound on the west bank of Lac du Chevril, about four kilometers north of the train station. As they headed up the tree-lined driveway to the main house, Cédric was flooded by happy memories of the place from his youth.

"You are the first person to visit here in eight years," commented Nico as they pulled into the driveway past the *grande maison* and stopped in front of a separate building in back. "You can stay in the big house if you want, but I took the liberty of getting the guest apartment set up for you above the work shed. It's cozier, and I think you will find it more to your liking."

At that moment, Annie burst out of the side door of the big house, arms flailing, and wrapped them around Cédric in a huge embrace. "You've come back. You've come back! Hallelujah."

Annie had been his nanny from as far back as he could remember. He had not seen her since Antoine was killed in the avalanche, and this reunion was sweeter than Cédric could have imagined. He couldn't control the tears that now flowed freely. She held him at arm's length. "Cédric, you look awful. You are as pale as bone china. Don't they have sunshine in England? And you are as skinny as a sapling. My oh my, do I have my work cut out to nurse you back to health. When you get settled, come into the kitchen, and I will see what I can do," she said, turning to go back indoors as it started to sprinkle.

Nico and Cédric headed toward the workshop. Nico swung open the double doors and said, "Without the tractor and haymaking equipment, there is now plenty of room for your laboratory." He led the way, switching on the overhead lights. The space was filled with some work benches. A collection of hand tools hung on pegboard on the walls, and there were toolboxes, a band saw, a drill press, and a metal-working lathe. "Your Harley is parked over there in the corner. I couldn't get it to fire up, so I took the liberty of disassembling the carburetor. It seems that the eight-year-old gasoline left in the tank gummed it up. I have it sitting in a tub of solvent over there on the workbench." Nico turned to observe Cédric, who had heard nothing he had said; he was still outside, looking up at the sign over the door.

"*Chandellepont*?" Cédric said. "Candlebridge in French. What's that all about?"

“I put that sign up over your new laboratory when I heard you were coming,” Nico said.

Cédric continued to look puzzled.

“What?” said Nico. “Did you honestly think you would graduate from that hoity-toity British university and just waltz into Stockholm to collect your Nobel Prize in Physics? No. You must earn it in the school of hard knocks. *Chandellepont* is your school of hard knocks. Your machinist apprenticeship begins tomorrow.”

“What do you mean by that?” asked Cédric.

Nico answered, “I have collected a good assortment of machine tools. I'm going to teach you to build all kinds of things with your own hands, if you are willing.”

“Oh,” replied Cédric with a sigh. “I think I am done with all of that.”

“Done?” replied Nico. “You haven't even started! I thought we would start out by building a steam engine.”

Chapter 5: The Harley

The unmistakable, deep-throated thrum of a Harley-Davidson motorcycle in the courtyard woke Cédric the next morning. He went to the widow in time to see Nico seated on the motorcycle. He had the born-to-ride look about him as he slumped in the seat and revved the engine several times before peeling down the long driveway toward the main road. Cédric was outside by the time Nico returned, flashing a delighted grin from the thrill he had just experienced.

"She's running a bit rough," he said, pulling the bike into the workshop and turning off the engine.

"Where did you learn to ride a motorcycle like that?" Cédric asked.

"Annie is making crêpes. Let's go have breakfast, and I will tell you about my wilder side."

Nico and Cédric sat down at a small, round table in the breakfast nook of the big house. Annie handed them both mugs of coffee and began serving crêpes with all the trimmings—whipped cream, strawberry preserves, maple syrup—and a bowl of scrambled eggs.

"So how was your first night in the guest apartment above the workshop?" she asked.

"Nico was right," Cédric replied. "That is a better place for me than here in the big house. I am haunted by way too many bad memories. After you quit being my nanny, I was no longer the center of attention, and my life went downhill. There was a string of country day schools and then boarding schools from the time I was nine. My parents were too busy for me, and I often wished you had been able to come back to rescue me. As you know, I never liked to ski, and I didn't like coming here, except that it always gave me a chance to see you, Annie."

Annie said, "This time you stayed away too long, and we are not going to let you leave again without a fight."

The three sat quietly eating and contemplating the renewal of their friendship. Cédric finally said, "I'm sure glad you still know how to make killer crêpes, Annie, but I'm waiting for Nico to tell me about his wilder side."

"Oh, my," she said. "Let me refresh your coffee then. This could take a while."

"I will tell you my story if you care to hear it," Nico said. "You know your mother never liked me very much, so she kept me away from you kids as much as possible. It's not too surprising that you haven't heard this before. My parents had moved to Val d'Isère for the Winter Olympics of 1992 when I was just a toddler. My dad started working for one of the ski areas as a lift operator and eventually ended up managing the whole area by the time I was a teenager. I was quite a skier. As you can imagine, I spent a lot of time on the slopes and aspired to race competitively. In fact, I was a good enough skier by the time I had finished high school that I got offered a scholarship to attend a university in the United States, in Colorado. I wasn't a bad student. I pursued engineering as my chosen major and was pretty good at it, but my passion was ski racing—fast ski racing. I was becoming a champion downhill racer on the university ski team. I was in the process of qualifying for the Olympics when I took a very bad fall and compound-fractured my leg."

Annie piled more scrambled eggs on Cédric's plate and refilled his coffee mug.

Nico went on. "Serious injuries to competitive ski racers are not uncommon, and the ones with strong characters and determination pull out of it and recover by sheer grit so they can begin competing again. I was not one of those. I descended into a spiral of depression and despair that ended for me in the bottle. I stopped going to class and started hanging out at a biker bar in a town in Colorado called Golden. It is ironic that the only thing in my life at that time that was golden was the color of the beer that I was consuming in ever increasing quantities. The owner of the biker bar I frequented was sympathetic but helpless to prevent my self-destruction."

Nico took a long swig of coffee. "It turned out that the owner of that bar had a teenage daughter. I had seen her several times helping on weekends and after school. She was the cutest thing I had ever laid my eyes on. She had strawberry-blond hair in braids on each side. She had a way of looking at me as if she was peering right into my heart. Occasionally, she would sit with me when she wasn't busy, and we would chat. She was intrigued by my French accent and longed to travel the world. Before long, I was visiting the bar just to see her. Her father sensed that things were getting a bit too serious and reminded me that she was sixteen and that if I didn't disappear, they would one day dig up my remains in a shallow grave in the desert.

"That's when I started riding motorcycles. There was a guy that frequented the bar who was trying to sell his Harley. I bought it and immediately rediscovered my need for speed. I traveled around the country with a biker gang, but drunk or sober, all I wanted was to pull into the parking lot of that bar in Golden and sit with the girl that had stollen my heart. We were secretly planning to elope to Las Vegas to get married when an immigration officer tracked me down and informed me that my student visa had expired. I was deported back to France—without Annie," he said, looking across the table and grabbing her hand.

"So, there you have it," said Nico, "my life on the wild side."

"Good grief," exclaimed Cédric. "Don't stop there. What happened next?"

"Annie, you carry on while I eat," suggested Nico.

"Well," said Annie. "Nico ended up getting a job in the service department at the Harley-Davidson dealership in Paris. We Facetimed every day for two years while he tried to figure out a way to get back to America or get me to France with my parents' blessing. Then he saw your mother's advertisement for a nanny, and he convinced me to apply. The problem was that the applicant needed to be fluent in both English and French. Since I didn't speak a word of French, that was not going to work, but Nico wrote my application in French and convinced your mom that I had written it myself. He wasn't the only one of us living on the wild side by the time I turned eighteen. Somehow, the fact that I did not speak French didn't show up on any of the character references, and the next thing I remember is arriving in Paris at your apartment door with my suitcase. You were just two, and we bonded immediately. Once your mother got over the shock of learning that I spoke no French, I started fitting right in. Cédric, you and I got to learn French together. Antoine was five then, and he and I never got close, but you and I were inseparable from the start."

"I so fondly remember you teaching me English and reading me to sleep with Bible stories," said Cédric. "But what about Nico? Where did he fit in?"

Annie looked over at her husband with a loving smile. "Your mom and dad were very protective of me. They wouldn't let me go out. This was not helped by Nico's drinking problem. Your father did not like him and would not let him come in, so our storybook romance was short-lived. We had a big fight and broke up. I told him I didn't want to see him again until he stopped drinking. And that was that. The end."

"The end?" exclaimed Cédric.

"Well, obviously not," replied Annie. "We did not contact one another for a couple of years. By that time, he had become the service manager for the Harley dealership. He came by your apartment one evening with a bouquet of flowers for me. I met him at the door, but he requested to talk to your father. 'Mr. Rothschild,' he said, 'I know you don't like me, and for very good reasons, but I just want you to know that I have been sober now for eighteen months. I just couldn't go on living without Annie and will do whatever it takes to win her back. Please forgive me and give me a second chance.'"

"Thereafter, Annie and I began to date," added Nico. "I must have won your father over because he asked me to become the caretaker of Château d'Isère. He hosted a lavish wedding for us in Val d'Isère and arranged to have Annie's parents fly over for the event. And we have been here ever since."

Annie added, "By then, you were six and in school. Your mom didn't need a nanny any longer. The four years I spent with you were truly wonderful. But, Cédric, I must say that you were the most precocious child I have ever encountered. It's no mystery why your mom didn't decide to look for another nanny. You were in your terrible twos when I showed up, and she was desperate. A French-speaking nanny was the last thing in the world she needed right then. What she really needed was someone who could keep up with you."

They all laughed. Cédric felt like he had come home at last.

Nico asked as they were finishing breakfast, "Are you ready for your first lesson in motorcycle riding?"

"I don't know," replied Cédric. "It seems a bit intimidating."

"You know how to ride a horse, don't you?" asked Nico.

"Of course," replied Cédric. "As Annie knows, I have been riding ever since I was a little boy. I was on the polo team at Candlebridge."

"Well, then," replied Nico, "you ride a motorcycle the same way. You treat it as a living thing. You listen to it and learn its secret idiosyncrasies, just like with a horse. If you forget this and abuse it like an inanimate object, it will turn and bite you one day with unpleasant consequences." Nico looked intently across the table at Cédric and said, "May I be blunt? Your brother never understood this. He never learned to master that motorcycle. He let it master him. Frankly, I thought that was how he was going to die young. It surprised me when the avalanche got to him first. Antoine was reckless to the core. Snowboarding out of bounds in a known avalanche area to impress his friends was just one of many examples. He did everything fast and furiously without regard for consequences to himself or others."

"I didn't really know him very well," replied Cédric sadly. "We were never close. I envied him because he always seemed to do things that made our father proud. He was outgoing and bigger than life, and I could never measure up. I tried to follow in his footsteps by going to Candlebridge, but he was killed during my first year, and that was that. As you both know, Mother never recovered from the loss, and my father subsequently got entangled in the affair with his gold-digging Parisian socialite mistress."

"Well," said Annie. "That's water under the bridge—under the Candlebridge, I should say. It's time for you to start afresh."

Nico and Cédric stood up and headed together across the courtyard to the work shed. Nico handed him a helmet and said, "This thing may keep you from splitting your head open, but I warn you, if you run into anything immovable at more than twenty kilometers per hour and survive the crash, you can expect to spend time in the hospital. The helmet won't prevent spinal injuries." Nico backed the Harley out and said, "Hop on. I will show you a few simple things, and I suggest you start out by going slowly up and down the driveway."

It wasn't long before Cédric got the hang of shifting gears and easing the throttle. Nico watched him carefully to be sure he didn't pick up any bad habits early on as he rode to the end of the driveway and back several times. On one occasion, Cédric encountered the moving van with his stuff at the end of the driveway, looking for the address. He proudly led the way back up and skillfully parked the Harley in the work shed. He directed the movers to the staircase leading up to his apartment, then went over to Nico to give him a hug without saying another word. Cédric was hooked.

Chapter 6: The Steam Engine

Cédric probably would have worked through the night if Nico had not come to call him to dinner at eight o'clock. He switched off the light over the engine lathe that held his in-process workpiece in a three-jaw chuck and went up to his apartment to wash up and change out of his shirt spattered with cutting oil.

In the big house, Nico asked him, "How is it coming with the boiler?"

Annie poured him a glass of wine as he was sitting down at the table. "I'm sorry I'm late," he said. "I completely lost track of time. Building a working steam engine from scratch has completely captivated me. The plans are detailed, and I am able to follow them for the most part. But it's not clear to me why I need to bore the boiler from a solid billet of stainless steel."

Nico replied, "There are easier and cheaper ways to build the boiler but not without considerably more risk of blowing things up. Your one-piece stainless boiler should handle fifty atmospheres or so of steam pressure. In the end, you will be better off with a higher-performance boiler without corrosion or leaky joints."

"I have finished boring the internal diameter and the O-ring groove for the head gasket. Tomorrow, I plan to drill and tap the bolt holes for the cylinder head," Cédric explained.

"Nico tells me you are rather handy with machine tools," commented Annie.

Cédric said, "I took a summer field session as an undergraduate and got some rudimentary instruction. I built a little glass-blowing swivel and a precision vise for the final project, but this is the first time I have ever done any serious machine work. Building this steam engine is going to take weeks if not months."

In between bites of tomato and mozzarella salad, Cédric said, "I'm all moved into the apartment now. I folded the boxes and stored them in the loft. I can tell that you added extra bookcases for me. Someone must have tipped you off that I collect books like some people collect art. There is a curious thing though; I have numerous books that I have purchased over the years and placed on the shelf, thinking that one day I might read them. But there is this little paperback that my astrophysics professor at Candlebridge gave me. It got soaked in a downpour, and now the pages are crinkled and fanned out. I couldn't find a place for it in the bookcases. Otherwise, it would have probably remained unopened like many of the others that I never got around to. I was planning to throw it out, but then I made the mistake of opening it. Have you ever heard of a guy named C. S. Lewis? He was an Oxford University intellectual who gave a series of radio talks to the British during the darkest days of the Second World War. It's quite remarkable and nothing like I expected. I don't know where he dug up the title *Mere Christianity*. I'm a third of the way into the book, and there is nothing so far about the Christian religion. You know, Lewis started out as an atheist and developed a comprehensive philosophy he called *natural law* based entirely on logical deduction. I am rather taken in by it." Cédric observed Annie and Nico exchange a pleased look as he dug into his meatloaf and potatoes au gratin.

Cédric continued, "Lewis makes a compelling case for good and evil, which is helping me understand the grave injustice I experienced at Candlebridge."

Nico said, "Annie gave me that same book when my life was in shambles. I will tell you a little story. She is the only one who knows this, and I have never shared it with anyone else. The broken leg from my fall during the Olympic trials was not an accident. Someone tightened the binding so my ski would not release. I was always diligent to check the setting before I raced, but on that occasion, for some reason I got distracted and failed to do so. I was always pretty sure I knew who did it. There was a skier on the team who wanted to knock me out of the running so he could go on. My anger and bitterness toward him nearly drove me to murder. I became obsessed with doing him harm. Annie told me once that unforgiveness is like drinking poison and waiting for the other guy to die. My poison was alcohol. Cédric, you were treated very unjustly at Candlebridge. There is no excuse for that. The guy who messed with my binding didn't even finish in the top twenty in the Olympics, and now he is long forgotten. The same will happen to the professor at Candlebridge who sabotaged your experiment. Working through bitterness when you have been wronged is no easy feat, but you need to do it. That book saved my life, and I suspect it will save yours as well, if you let it."

"Getting cheated out of an Olympic medal is hardly commensurate with a Nobel Prize," responded Cédric, then paused. "Oh my, I'm sorry. That came out wrong."

"Cédric, dear," said Annie, "it's no easier to forgive someone for messing with your ski binding than for wrecking your experiment. Injustice is injustice. The extent of the injury is incidental."

"It is asking a lot to forgive Hendriksen," said Cédric. "I don't think I will ever be capable of that."

During the days that followed, Cédric began to settle into a sort of routine. Nico helped him with the steam engine project. He rode the Harley each morning for coffee and croissants at the café in town and then spent a few hours in the workshop before lunch. He began taking daily afternoon walks in the mountains and generally worked until after midnight, writing in his journal and developing his variable light speed theories. About once a week, he borrowed Nico's truck to drive to Grenoble to purchase valves and fittings for his steam engine, which was progressing nicely. He had completed the boiler and pressure-tested it on the stove in Annie's kitchen. The steam piston was turning out to be more challenging, however. It was a simple bump valve design, but getting the valves to seat properly on the outgoing steam stroke was anything but simple. Nonetheless, the steam engine was starting to take shape by the beginning of September. He had fabricated a dynamo that was operated off the drive shaft by a belt, having concluded that a steam engine would be rather worthless if the power output could not be measured. With the dynamo, he would be able to measure the watt-hours going through a load and compare it to the amount of kerosene consumed by the burner to determine the Carnot cycle efficiency of the engine. Converting heat into work at the maximum possible efficiency had preoccupied scientists for centuries.

By the beginning of September, Cédric had become sufficiently accomplished on the Harley to begin making the trip to Grenoble on it. The journey between Val d'Isère and Grenoble had become almost routine, and he looked forward to it, whether or not he actually needed something in Grenoble. There was a café about halfway between the Val d'Isère and Grenoble that he frequented for lunch in the mountain town of Saint-Michel-de-Maurienne. The café was just off the autoroute but sufficiently off the beaten path so as not to attract the hordes of tourists at the nearby rest stop. The proprietor became familiar with the sound of Cédric's motorcycle when it pulled up and often came out to greet him. The café was frequented mostly by locals who came for the familiar settings and reliably good food and service. Sometimes there was a gentleman sitting alone at one of the tables in the back, drinking coffee and working on his computer, engaged in some project that appeared to be quite involved and complex. On a couple of occasions, Cédric considered introducing himself to the man, but that particular day, he was pressed for time and wanted to get on to Grenoble. The days were getting shorter, and he wanted to be able to return to Val d'Isère before dark. He took his sandwich and iced tea out to the deck, where the view of the surrounding mountains was stunning and the air was fresh. He finished his lunch quickly and headed back to the autoroute, passing a nondescript warehouse on the right with a curious sign over the door that read "NaPiles."

In Grenoble, Cédric picked up the ball valve he had ordered from the machinery supply store and decided to ride back through town rather than go directly to the autoroute. He noticed a bookstore and decided to stop in. He was searching for another book for his collection dealing with neutron stars. He couldn't find anything he didn't already own. After leaving the science section empty-handed, he passed what was designated as the religious section. Generally, like the gardening section or the murder mystery section, the religious section was of no interest to him, except this time his eyes fell on a hardbound multivolume set of the works of C. S. Lewis, which included the book *Mere Christianity* he had received from Dr. Edwards at Candlebridge. He thought maybe it was time to replace the rain-damaged copy with a new one that would look nicer on his bookshelf. Also, Lewis had tweaked his curiosity, and the other books in the set had intriguing titles like *The Great Divorce* and *The Screwtape Letters*, which he removed and began thumbing through. He observed that it was dedicated to J. R. R. Tolkien, one of his very favorite authors, and that was all the motivation he needed to purchase the set. At the checkout, he grabbed that day's copy of the local newspaper, *Le Grenoble Matin*.

He hopped back on his motorcycle, and by the time he had passed by Montmélian and headed up into the foothills on his return to Val d'Isère, a light drizzle had begun. Cédric could feel that the pavement was getting slippery, and his traction was not great, so he slowed down and took suitable precautions on the road. The same could not be said for the driver of the tourist bus that fishtailed into him on a hairpin curve and knocked him into the guardrail and up over the embankment.

Annie and Nicolas were at his bedside at the hospital in Montmélian when he regained consciousness the following day.

"Where am I?" asked Cédric. "How did I get here?"

Annie replied, "You are in the hospital. An ambulance brought you yesterday."

"I don't remember a thing," said Cédric as he began to be aware that there was something attached to his aching head.

"It's a good thing," said Nico. "Your accident is not something you want to remember."

"Is the Harley okay?" asked Cédric.

"That's pretty unlikely," replied Nico. "It's at the bottom of a two-hundred-meter-deep ravine, which is where you would be if they hadn't found you clutching the signpost by the side of the road saying, 'Slippery when wet.'"

"How badly was I injured?" asked Cédric. "I don't feel a thing."

Nico replied, "Don't worry. You will be in plenty of pain before too long. You hit your head pretty hard, but I suspect your helmet saved your life. You broke several ribs and punctured a lung. Other than this, you ruptured your spleen. Miraculously, you didn't break any other bones except your left pinky. Your father is on the way and should arrive any minute."

"The Harley is at the bottom of a ravine?" repeated Cédric.

Annie held up the saddlebag that had been behind the seat. "This got knocked off the bike in the wreck and was lying by the side of the road."

Cédric struggled to remember what was inside. Annie opened it and showed him the new ball valve for his steam engine, the five-volume set of C. S. Lewis books, and yesterday's copy of *Le Grenoble Matin.* A nurse entered the emergency room and held his wrist to take a pulse and check the monitors for his other vital signs. She checked the intravenous supply and made notes on the clipboard at the foot of the bed.

A second nurse entered a few moments later and said, "Good. He's conscious and alert." She picked up the clipboard and reviewed the details about the patient. "What is your full name?" she said, glancing at Cédric.

"John Cédric Rothschild," he replied.

"Date of birth?" she asked.

"Bastille Day. July fourteenth, twenty-ten."

"The nurse looked over at Annie and Nico. "Are you his relatives?"

"No, just friends," said Annie.

"Who will be signing the insurance waiver for the surgery then?" asked the nurse without emotion.

"Cédric's father is on the way and should be here any minute," replied Nico.

"Surgery? What surgery?" asked Cédric.

The nurse responded, "To repair your spleen. You are bleeding internally. The operation has been scheduled for 13h00." She glanced at the clock on the wall and said to Nico, "We will be transferring him to the operating theatre in about thirty minutes." She flipped over the top page of the clipboard and studied the form that followed, saying, "Dr. Rochambeau will be the surgeon. He is quite capable." Then she turned and departed the emergency room.

"Will you be here when I come out of surgery?" Cédric asked Annie and Nico. His voice betrayed the sudden onset of fear.

"We will be in the recovery room," said Annie lovingly. "And hopefully by then your father will be here."

Cédric said, "I picked up the ball valve in Grenoble. As soon as I install it, we should be able to fire up the steam engine."

Standing up and walking over to his bed, Annie stroked his forehead gently. His right eye was black and blue and swollen shut. “There’s no rush, dear. You need to take time to recover.”

Chapter 7: The Abbey

After a week in the hospital, Cédric was becoming restless and discouraged by the slow pace of his recovery. The pain medications were making him drowsy and leaving him with a sense of diminished mental capacity, so he began cutting back to the point where the pain was just barely tolerable. He had turned on all the charm he could muster to convince the attending nurse to let him climb into a wheelchair to be pushed out onto the veranda for some morning sunshine. The hospital was located on the bank of the Isère. The distant drone of the traffic on the autoroute on the other side of the river disturbed what would have otherwise been a completely tranquil setting. The veranda was a popular place for visitors to meet with convalescing patients. The orderly pushed Cédric out to a quiet place near the outer railing so he could read without distraction. There was a wide path beyond the railing that followed the river in both directions for as far as anyone would care to go. It was filled with a selection of pedestrians passing by—some appearing to be going nowhere in particular and others with a purpose, joggers, recreational bicycles and trottinettes and skateboards, and the ever-present serious cyclists in groups with fancy bikes and matching team uniforms. The scene provided endless entertainment for any spectator needing to pass time. The week-old copy of *Grenoble Matin* was next to him in the wheelchair, and one of the books from the C. S. Lewis anthology called *The Problem of Pain* lay in his lap.

His father had yet to visit him as he had hoped. Nico had explained that his father had planned to fly to Grenoble, but Geraldine had insisted that they drive from Paris, stopping by the hospital before heading on to Château d'Isère for a holiday. The delay had been the result of the ensuing confusion over getting everything ready for the unscheduled trip, but Cédric took this lack of empathy from his future stepmother personally.

The bell in the steeple of the nearby abbey chimed eight times. He opened the newspaper for the first time since the accident. There was an article that immediately caught his attention.

Local entrepreneur Charles Gilbert announced this week the official opening of a research and development company in the mountain community of Saint Michel-de-Maurienne. According to Mr. Gilbert, the company will be developing a revolutionary new type of storage battery based on sodium rather than lithium. The company is aptly named *NaPiles*, which stands for sodium batteries. Gilbert claims that world supplies of lithium are dwindling, and that sodium is plentiful and distributed almost everywhere on the planet. He claims to have developed a way to replace lithium with sodium to make batteries that are not only less expensive but more powerful than their lithium counterparts. Mr. Gilbert has an immediate opening for a qualified machinist with a firm grasp of physics and electrochemistry, and experience designing and building complex machinery.

Cédric tore the article from the paper and placed it in his book while he finished the newspaper. The warm sunshine and cool mountain breeze combined to clear the fog in his brain resulting from the strong medications. Two surgeries and a host of complications had left him helpless to resist the medications that at least made his slow recovery bearable. He felt like he had been replumbed with spare parts. He had thought that perhaps there might be some answers in *The Problem of Pain*. The book turned out to be nothing like he expected. Lewis said, “Lay down this book and reflect for five minutes on the fact that all the great religions were first preached, and long practiced, in a world without chloroform.” This insightful comment in the introduction confirmed that his decision to read the book had been a good one.

He had become completely engrossed in the book, which addressed a great deal more than just the physical pain caused by his motorcycle accident and began chipping away at his emotional pains caused by a life of rejection and ill-treatment. The bell in the abbey steeple chimed eleven times before Cédric was even aware of the passage of the hours. He looked up from his book to see a gentleman standing on the other side of the railing, staring at him.

“I see that you are reading one of my favorite books,” the man said. “May I join you?” He walked up the stairs to the veranda and slid a chair up next to Cédric. Extending his hand, he said, “Hi. My name is Brother Andrew. I live at the abbey next door.”

“Are you a monk?” inquired Cédric, unable to collect his wits sufficiently to know what else to say.

"No. Just a brother. All monks are brothers, but not all brothers are monks. What is your name?" he asked.

"Cédric. Cédric Rothschild," he responded.

"You look to be in very bad shape," commented Brother Andrew. "Are you going to be okay?"

Cédric replied, "I had a very serious motorcycle crash a few days ago. They are still trying to put me back together."

Brother Andrew inquired, "Are you the guy that got knocked off the road by the tour bus? I was told it was a complete miracle that you survived at all. I saw the photos of your bike at the bottom of the ravine."

"Apparently, I grabbed onto a road sign, but I have no recollection of the accident," replied Cédric. "I woke up here at the hospital the next day."

"It sounds to me like an angel was dispatched on your behalf," said Brother Andrew.

"I don't know anything about angels," replied Cédric, "but based on the agony I have been experiencing this week, I wish the angel had let me go to the bottom of the ravine with my Harley. Say, I think I have had a bit too much sun. Would you mind wheeling me over to one of those tables under the awning? I was thinking of having something to eat. Would you care to join me?"

Brother Andrew released the brakes on the wheelchair and positioned him at one of the tables. "What can I get you?"

Cédric replied, "I really want a cheeseburger, fries, and a bottle of rosé, but about all I am able to keep down is chicken broth and ice water."

"Okay. I will be right back," said Brother Andrew

"Charge it to room twenty-three," instructed Cédric.

"No. I've got this," replied Brother Andrew as he headed inside to the cafeteria. He returned with a bowl of chicken broth for Cédric and a tuna salad sandwich for himself.

"Tell me, Brother Andrew. What do you do at the monastery?" asked Cédric.

Brother Andrew replied, "There are fifteen brothers right now in the order who have taken a vow of poverty and chastity. We serve our Lord Jesus and are devoted to prayer and meditating on scripture. It's not nearly as restrictive as it sounds. We are free to come and go. Although there are only fifteen of us brothers in the monastery, there is a vibrant community of more than one thousand believers in the area associated with us who participate in worship services and various community relief projects. We have a robust outreach to Eastern European refugees."

Cédric made no response. Such charitable activities had never interested him very much.

After a brief awkward silence, Brother Andrew added, "Otherwise, I write science fiction books in my spare time. That's kind of a newly discovered talent for me. I was trained as a materials scientist and spent eight years at CERN in Geneva, constructing superconducting magnets for the Large Hadron Collider before I burned out from the stress."

Cédric placed his soup spoon next to the plate and sat upright in his wheelchair. "CERN? Large Hadron Collider? Dark matter?"

"Yes," replied Brother Andrew, "but I never actually visited the collider. That was in another facility clear across town. CERN is an enormous operation with thousands of scientists spread out all over the place. That was the problem and why I finally left. Everyone was working on their own little piece of the project, but no one ever got to view the big picture. But what is your interest in dark matter?"

Cédric answered, "I think it is a fantasy. It doesn't exist. It is an artifact of galaxy formation. I was nearing completion of my PhD at Candlebridge University in Great Britain before I was kicked out of the school for spouting these controversial views."

"Wait a minute!" exclaimed Brother Andrew. "You aren't by any chance that guy who wrote the scathing diatribe against Professor Hendriksen that showed up in the London paper are you?"

"Guilty as charged," replied Cédric, grinning.

"That exposé went viral, you know," Brother Andrew replied. "Hendriksen is infamous in the dark matter community. He is well known as a prig. We all cheered when that 'disgruntled graduate student' let him have it. It is, indeed, an honor to meet you," he said, bowing his head to Cédric respectfully.

Cédric said, "I would be pleased to tell the whole inside story, but I am feeling rather fatigued now and think it's time to head back to my room. Is there any chance we could reconvene tomorrow?"

"Of course," said Brother Andrew. "I will return tomorrow at eleven o'clock sharp. Permit me go to the front desk now to tell them you are ready to go back to your room."

The following day, Cédric decided to dispense with the wheelchair and make the difficult trip to the veranda using just a walker. Brother Andrew was waiting for him as scheduled.

"You seem to be doing much better today," he said.

Cédric grimaced as he transferred from the walker to a chair and said, "I can't exactly say that I am in less pain today than yesterday, but I can say that today I am possessed with a greater will to overcome it. I just read in *The Problem of Pain* where Lewis says, 'God whispers to us in our pleasure, speaks in our conscience, but shouts in our pain: it is His megaphone to rouse a deaf world.' If that's the case, then God has the volume turned all the way up for me."

Brother Andrew said, "I see God's hand mightily upon you, Cédric. It is no coincidence that you are in this hospital and we met yesterday. I searched everywhere on the internet to find out more about you. I was surprised to discover very little except your diatribe against the university and an anonymous rebuttal saying your variable light speed theories are nonsense, but I could not find anything that actually says what those theories are."

"That's because they are unpublished," replied Cédric. "I never found a journal that would accept my manuscript. I can send you a copy if you like."

"Why don't you explain it now," said Brother Andrew. "I used to sit in on lectures at CERN from time to time by the theorists and particle physics guys. Most of it was over my head, but I got the gist of it. I have a pretty good grasp of cosmology and the theory of dark matter."

"My theories are not all that complex," replied Cédric. "Some high school physics is all you need. When I was little, I had a poster on the wall of my bedroom of a spiral galaxy that mesmerized me growing up. My birthday is on Bastille Day, and besides fantasizing that the fireworks were on my behalf, from a young age, I was struck by the similarity between the evolving forms of the pyrotechnic stars and the galaxy on my wall. I would stare at the static image of the galaxy and play in my mind a video in fast motion of its birth, from its origin to its present state, just like the exploding fireworks in real time."

Cédric paused to take a sip of coffee and judge Brother Andrew's level of interest. He reached for a paper napkin from the center of the table. "Do you have a pen?" he asked. He made a single dot on the napkin and said, "Imagine this dot representing a black hole. The possibility that all the matter and energy contained in the galaxy on my wall originated from a black hole the size of the dot on that napkin always intrigued me. During a high school physics class one day, we were learning about black holes. I was told that they are so massive that the gravitational field prevented even light from escaping. I casually asked my teacher what the speed of light inside the black hole was. He glared at me and didn't answer. Everyone knows that the speed of light is constant everywhere in the universe. But this question stuck with me. The images coming from the space-based telescopes at the far reaches of the universe looked a lot more to me like the night sky over the Eiffel Tour on Bastille Day than anything I would have expected from the big bang. The idea occurred to me that perhaps the speed of light—just like the speed of the pyrotechnic fragments of the fireworks—was zero, or close to zero at the instant of the explosion. I read all kinds of books on cosmology to try to reconcile the apparent discrepancy between conventional theory and what my eyes were telling me. I finally arrived at the startling conclusion that the speed of light had to be almost zero within a black hole."

Brother Andrew let out a whistle. "Why is that even controversial?"

Cédric replied, "Because Lorentz and Einstein postulated that the speed of light is constant, and scientists ever since have interpreted this to mean that the speed of light must be a universal constant, even inside a black hole. But this was only a postulate. It cannot be proven."

"What about the Michaelson and Morley experiment?" asked Brother Andrew.

Cédric answered, "That experiment did not prove that the speed of light is constant. All it proved was that the speed of light does not depend on velocity—the velocity of the earth through the galaxy in that case. You will always measure the same speed of light at the same time and place. What I hypothesized in my dark matter paper is that the speed of light starts out at zero in a black hole when a galaxy is born and increases as the galaxy expands."

"Is that even possible?" asked Brother Andrew.

"Einstein's greatest contribution to science was demonstrating that energy is equal to mass times the speed of light squared. I am confident that energy is conserved in any closed system, whether it is a galaxy or the black hole from which it came into being. The speed of light inside a black hole cannot be exactly zero, but it could approach zero in the limit of infinite mass. Troubling mathematical singularities aside, for energy to be conserved, the enormous mass of a galaxy confined to a black hole, like the dot on that napkin, must be compensated for by a correspondingly small speed of light to make mc^2 constant. All I did was postulate this possibility, and propose a velocity profile for galaxy expansion that involved a time-dependent relationship between mass and velocity that preserved constant energy. This, of course, also required the speed of light to be time-dependent."

“That seems reasonable,” said Brother Andrew. “Unorthodox, perhaps, but hardly grounds for getting expelled from Candlebridge.”

Cédric continued, “It is impossible to detect variations in the speed of light because the way it is measured depends on the assumption that it is constant. In my dark matter treatise, I proposed that there is a difference in the speed of light between the inertial mass of stars in galaxies, as observed by their motions, and the apparent mass of the stars based on their luminosity. This is because the speed of light was much slower, and the mass much greater, in the early stages of galaxy formation. I believe the discrepancy accounts for the so-called dark matter. This is what got me into trouble at Candlebridge, because I was claiming that dark matter was simply an artifact of galaxy formation. This did not sit well with Hendriksen, who was shoveling piles of cash into the university coffers in pursuit of his Hendri particle. This is what my experiment at Candlebridge demonstrated so compellingly—that the speed of light, as determined by the transit time of a light pulse, can be slowed down in the presence of a dense object. Brother Andrew, I slowed a light pulse by two nanoseconds when I passed it through a ten-centimeter-long hole through a tube of uranium. It takes one-third of a nanosecond for light to travel ten centimeters in free space. My light beam took two and one-third nanoseconds to travel through the uranium tube. That means the speed of light in the tube was about forty-three million meters per second.

That's one-seventh the free space value for the speed of light in vacuum. From the standpoint of the light pulse, the tube seemed to be seventy centimeters long, not just ten." By that time, Cédric was very energized and excited. It was the first time in months that he had had the opportunity to explain his theories to anyone. He suddenly felt an overwhelming urgency to recover and get back to work with Nico in his shop at Château d'Isère.

Chapter 8: The Big House

Cédric had just dozed off for his afternoon nap when he was awakened by a gentle rap at his door. "Come in, Father. It's good to see you."

"I hope I didn't wake you," his father said.

"Not at all. I was just taking a boredom nap. I am starting to get stir crazy, and napping is about the only thing I have for passing time."

"Nicolas tells me you are doing pretty well and should be released from the hospital in a couple of days."

"I think they need the bed," Cédric said. "I am far from recovered. I will need some weeks of physical therapy."

His father walked over to the bed and took his hands. "You had us so worried. The reason it took so long to get here is that when we heard about the accident, I started immediately for the airport to catch a flight to Grenoble. But Geraldine insisted on coming along. Then she suggested we drive because the five hours it would take to drive would be nearly as fast as flying. Then she suggested that we stay in Val d'Isère for a couple of months while you recover. Anyway, we finally made it. She is at Château d'Isère now with Nicolas, lining up contractors for the remodeling the big house. She wanted your room to be perfect."

"But I like my apartment above the workshop," said Cédric. "I don't want to stay in the big house."

"Okay then," said his father. "We will figure it out. Anyway, Geraldine will be too busy interviewing cooks to care."

"Cooks?" exclaimed Cédric. "What's wrong with Annie?"

"No," responded his father. "Geraldine wants a real French cook."

Cédric released his father's hands and pulled up the covers.

"You don't care much for Geraldine, do you," his father said. Cédric made no response. "There is another matter that I needed to discuss with you in private. The divorce is now finalized. You need to know that I did not divorce your mother because I no longer care for her. There is the delicate matter of my personal holdings in the family office, the value of which is substantial. If I were to predecease your mother while still legally married to her, it would trigger a very complex financial event since she is no longer mentally competent."

"So, you are leaving everything to Geraldine then," Cédric said.

His father seated himself and said, "No, Cédric. I am leaving everything to you." He allowed a long pause while this unexpected news sank in and then said, "I had my lawyer draft a prenuptial agreement. I haven't shown it to Geraldine yet. She will end up with plenty, and I also set up a generous trust that will cover all your mother's needs for as long as she lives, but the bulk of my estate will go to you. I estimate it to be worth about sixty-five million euros."

Cédric was in shock, trying to figure out if this was good news or bad. Then his father continued, "At some point, we can determine what you need to live on, but my lawyer told me yesterday that the company operating the tour bus that caused your accident has offered an out-of-court settlement of three million euros. My lawyer recommends that you accept it. I imagine you can live on that for a while."

"Then are you planning to marry Geraldine?" asked Cédric.

"Yes," his father replied, "as soon as she signs the prenup."

"That's nice. I wish you the best," Cédric said sadly without conviction.

"Well, then," his father said, standing to go. "I should be heading back to Château d'Isère before it gets dark. Is there anything you need?"

Cédric shook his head and waved goodbye.

Nico raced past the reception desk after midnight.

"Sir! It is after visiting hours!" the duty nurse said, picking up the phone to call hospital security.

Nico bolted up the two flights of stairs to Cédric's floor and burst into his room. "Cédric, Cédric! The most horrific thing just happened. You father is dead. Geraldine shot him. Right in the chest with the twelve-gauge shotgun next to the fireplace. It's awful! There are police everywhere." Nico was still panting when the night duty hospital security officer arrived to ask him to leave.

Cédric's only thought was that he must have shown her the prenup.

The memorial was a somber affair with little emotion. People from all over the world attended the service held in the main hall of the Panthéon in Paris. The murder had rocked the city to its core. Cédric was surprised by the number of people in attendance. He had not realized how prominent and influential his father had been. It was clear that his father had been respected by all, venerated by a many, but adored by none. The adoration had all gone to Geraldine. The quiet sobs that echoed above the hushed whispers were only for her, from people unable to imagine how their beloved friend could carry out such a heinous act. They would have to wait for the trial for any insights.

His father had been an only child, and there were no close relatives, except Cédric, who sat in the front row between Nico and Annie. A priest had been conscripted to conduct the ceremony. He babbled on with fanciful notions of the afterlife and some vague assurances that his father was now in a better place. Cédric had read enough C. S. Lewis by that time to know that those remarks were rubbish. He allowed himself to become districted by the newly refurbished Foucault pendulum hanging from the central dome, marking the relentless passage of time as entropy increased irreversibly as the universe expands. He reflected on Léon Foucault's more important contribution to society: the first reliable measurement of the speed of light.

Statues of famous dead Frenchmen surrounded him, many of whose works he had carefully studied. Their lifeless replicas paid tribute "to the great men from a grateful nation," according to the motto over the door. Their ashes were now interred in the crypts of the mausoleum down below. All Cédric wanted at that moment was to return to the guest room in the dormitory at l'Abbey de Montmélian that Brother Andrew had arranged for him when he had been released from the hospital.

After the ceremony, a man approached Cédric and handed him a business card. "Permit me to introduce myself. My name is Henri Soufflot. I am your father's personal attorney. This is a sad day for all of us. I know how hard this must be for you. I will be handling the settlement of his estate, and I will be getting in touch with you in a few days." Cédric nodded and placed the card in his pocket. Then he walked away.

Chapter 9: Montmélian

It was after ten in the morning when Cédric awoke. He was in a small room in the dormitory-style building adjacent to l'Abbey de Montmélian. Heading out of his room to the common bathroom, he saw a note that had been slipped under his door.

It read: "If you are up to it, will you join me for a promenade and a picnic lunch along the river? You have yet to convince me that dark matter is a fantasy." It was signed *Brother Andrew.*

Cédric instinctively felt his ribs for lingering tenderness. His abdominal pain had mostly subsided, and although still weak, he decided that this would be a good day for some serious exercise. Grabbing his towel and shaving kit, he headed for the shower down the hall.

He waited in the common room for Brother Andrew to come in from the vegetable garden bearing two beautiful tomatoes. Holding them up, he said, beaming, "Vine ripened for our sandwiches. Let me grab a knife and my backpack, and we can be off."

The two walked out to the bike path and a kilometer down the river to a park where Brother Andrew spotted a vacant picnic table in the shade of a magnificent weeping willow. He spread a red checkered tablecloth over it and began unpacking the lunch supplies. "I hope egg salad is okay for you. I made it myself with the help of Henrietta, our most productive hen." He proceeded to slice the tomatoes, the block of cheese, and two fresh baguettes from the abbey bakery. "It must have been a rough week for you in Paris," he said. "Help yourself to a bottle of water. I packed a bottle of rosé. I will open it if you like."

"Yes, please. I would love some wine," Cédric said. "The memorial was surreal. Those were all people I had no connection with. I had this odd sense that they were there to see if there was some financial benefit to be gained by my father's death. At least my childhood nanny and her husband were with me. From the time my parents shipped me off to boarding school in Switzerland, I never felt at home in Paris. My father was imperious, and he could be very demanding at times. He was always busy and had no time for me. All his attention was focused on my older brother, who always seemed to do things right. Something interesting happened, though, the day my father was murdered. He had stopped by to visit me in the hospital, and there was a side of him I had not seen before. It was as if he was trying to get his life in order."

"Was your brother at the memorial service?" asked Brother Andrew.

"No. He died several years ago in an avalanche. I am my father's only surviving heir. I never gave much thought to what comes next—I mean when we die. I always figured everything just fades to black. It's interesting that I vividly remember the tour bus coming toward me, but I don't recall anything else until I woke up in the hospital. If I had gone to the bottom with my Harley, would I have woken up in heaven instead, or maybe hell?"

Cédric finished preparing his sandwich and took a seat on the bench to enjoy it. “So, you said in your note that you wanted me to convince you that dark matter is a fantasy. But first, I want to hear about your science fiction novels. Tell me what you think the future looks like.”

“Novel,” corrected Brother Andrew. “I have only written one so far. It’s not really science fiction though. I write in a style I call science fantasy. Most science fiction tends to be dark and dystopian with evil creatures invading earth and dining on humans before they move on to the next planet. Frankly, I don’t think the future will be anything like that. God created the earth to be good. It is good now, and I have every expectation that it will be good in the future because that is God’s nature. At times, we may feel like we have been abandoned, but even in the midst of pain and suffering, God is still good. If mankind encounters alien beings in the future, I expect them to be created by the same God that created us, except they may be more technologically advanced and have mastered things like antigravity. This is the kind of thing I like writing about.”

“Antigravity?” Cédric replied. “I don’t think antigravity is all that far-fetched—that is, once we learn how to master the speed of light. Science fiction writers love to imagine traversing the galaxy faster than the speed of light, but that’s impossible. What they haven’t considered, though, is slowing light down. You remember my experiment at Candlebridge. I slowed light down by almost an order of magnitude. The effect is not huge but certainly measurable. Imagine how significant the effect would be around really dense objects like neutron stars and black holes. I have some theories about how gravity works, but they are radical, and I haven't worked out the details yet. I am working on an idea that has eluded theoretical physicists for a long time that links gravitational fields to the speed of light."

Cédric held up a plastic wine glass for Brother Andrew to fill. Off in the distance, a maglev train was heading east. Cédric pointed it out to Brother Andrew. "How fast do you think that train is going?"

"Three hundred kilometers per hour, perhaps," Brother Andrew replied.

"Do you suppose it has been going that speed for a long time?" Cédric asked.

"I suspect, not," replied Brother Andrew. "It just left the Montmélian Station a couple of minutes ago."

"Precisely!" answered Cédric. "The Maglev TGV was stopped at the station and must have accelerated to its current speed according to some velocity profile. You probably wonder what this has to do with light. That is at the heart of the question. If the speed of light is constant like everyone presumes, then claiming it can have zero velocity—or more correctly can approach zero velocity—is troubling. But this is what must be the case inside a black hole. A black hole is simply a train station for light if you will. The light photons are frozen in stationary quantum states. I can argue this on theoretical grounds. But bear with me and accept the premise for now. If light started out with zero velocity, its velocity must have increased somehow. Was the increase sudden or gradual? The answer to this question leads to speculations about dark matter. Back to our train stopped at the station. If you knew its velocity profile between the time it left the station and reached the speed you see now, you could calculate the distance it traveled. The engineer must reduce the acceleration to reach the terminal velocity following some sort of velocity profile. The limits of that profile require that the velocity is zero at the start and approaches a terminal velocity after some length of time. Such a profile could be described by any number of mathematical functions, but I chose the simplest one to describe the propagation of light from an expanding black hole at the center of a galaxy to the edge of the fully formed galaxy. I chose a simple exponential function that has the property that it goes to zero in the limit as time goes to zero and goes to some terminal velocity in the limit as time goes to infinity. This kind of function shows up all the time in physics. The function I chose satisfies the requirements in the limits and is elegant in its simplicity. Theorists have all kinds of ideas about how light behaves in a black hole, but they have a dilemma. If the speed of light is constant, then either it has the same value inside the black hole that it has outside, or else it switches on instantaneously the moment the black hole stops being a black hole. My model allows the speed of light to increase smoothly and monotonically with the expansion of a black hole. Take that train, for example. We, the observers, clock the speed at three hundred kilometers per hour, but we have no way of knowing how fast it will be going ten minutes from now. We have the same problem with the speed of light. We can measure it very precisely, but we cannot tell if it is changing with time because the very means we use to determine its value—namely the wavelength of a particular light—also changes commensurately with time in the measurement frame. We have no way to tell if the speed of light is changing. That is, unless this information is contained somewhere else, for example in the discrepancy between the apparent or gravitational mass of a distant galaxy and the effective mass of that galaxy based on the total luminosity of the stars it contains. This discrepancy is what people attribute to dark matter. It doesn't exist. It is an artifact of increasing light speed."

"You can prove this?" asked Brother Andrew.

"No," replied Cédric. "It is only a hypothesis but a good one. Acceptance of it would require a leap of faith and revision of all the cosmological models. This is why everyone is so determined to discover the dark matter particle. If this particle exists, then all the constant light speed models hold up, and no one will have to revise their textbooks. It's just like with Copernicus's proposition that the earth revolves around the sun. Nothing could have been more disruptive in his day. I am probably in no danger of being burned at the stake, but my claim that dark matter is an artifact of increasing light speed had everyone at Candlebridge in an uproar. Hendriksen has nothing to gain and everything to lose if I were to be right. So, he sabotaged my experiment and ruined my life."

Brother Andrew nodded his head and responded, "What you have been describing is remarkable. It seems so reasonable to me, and it is hard to imagine why you haven't received a proper forum for vetting your theories."

Cédric replied, "Oh, I will get my chance. And the day will come when they lead Hendriksen off in handcuffs and disgrace for fraud and abuse, not to mention fooling around with the coeds."

Brother Andrew said, "Cédric. I fear you are consumed by bitterness. You will need to forgive him at some point, you know."

"Oh," replied Cédric. "That will never happen."

"Didn't you read the chapter on forgiveness in *Mere Christianity*?" asked Brother Andrew.

"No," replied Cédric. "That's when Mr. Lewis and I parted company, and I set the book aside."

"What are your plans now that you are mostly recovered?" asked Brother Andrew. "Will you be going back to Val d'Isère?"

Cédric stared out across the valley to reflect on the question without responding. Finally, Brother Andrew broke the silence, looking squarely at Cédric, and said, "Cédric, why don't you just concentrate on perfecting your light speed experiments and postpone the crusade against dark matter for another day?"

Cédric knew in his heart that this was sound advice, but his pride would not allow him to follow it. "I don't see how I can return to Val d'Isère after what happened. I have been enjoying my time here at the abbey. The fellowship with you and the brothers and the others in the community has led me to consider buying a place nearby."

"You can stay at the guesthouse as long as you like," said Brother Andrew.

"Thank you very much for the offer, but I was thinking of something more permanent," Cédric replied. "I just received a settlement check from the tour bus operator that should cover the cost of the kind of place I have in mind. I will need a big enough garage to house my experiments."

"I might have some ideas," said Brother Andrew. "If you are up to it, we can explore the community after lunch. I know a wonderful realtor in the fellowship."

"This is perfect," Cédric said to the realtor as he stood on the south-facing balcony of the second-floor master bedroom. The ancient farmhouse was perched on the hillside overlooking Montmélian. The snowcapped peaks in the distance framed the horizon. The bell tower of the abbey, about two kilometers away, poked through the trees, and the train station was just below him. "It's quite a bit bigger than I had in mind. You said eight hundred and ninety-five thousand euros?"

"Yes," replied the realtor. "With the property in bank foreclosure, the transaction may be complicated. The previous owner had ambitious remodeling plans before running out of money."

"This place will require a great deal of work," Cédric said, looking around as they went back out into the courtyard. "I presume you will be able to transfer all the building permits over to me so I can finish the remodeling. And I will need to have an assessment of the utilities to be sure the barn has enough power for my needs."

The work on the main house was mostly completed, but only the slate roofs of the other buildings had been replaced so far. The ancient limestone stonework was magnificent, requiring only minor repairs. The house plus adjoining buildings was 200 square meters in size. The U-shaped courtyard looked out over the rows of grape vines gracing the hillside to the east. Altogether, the property was six hectares in size. "You said the vineyard is included?" Cédric asked.

"Yes," replied the realtor, "but the grapes and harvesting are handled by an annual contract with the winery. As you can see, this year's crop has already been gathered in. The property also comes with a spring and associated water rights that feeds the cistern for the house."

"I'm ready to sign a contract at the full asking price," said Cédric, turning to the realtor.

"That's good," replied the realtor. "There are three other interested parties, so I will need to draw up the contract immediately. The bank is going to want to see some credit references."

Cédric replied, "Just tell them this will be an all-cash transaction. I can put as much money down in advance as they require."

He walked into the barn for a second time, looking it over carefully to assess how much effort would be required to get it ready for his experiments. He made a mental note that the dirt floor would not suffice. A concrete floor had to be poured before he could install his equipment.

Chapter 10: Villa Chandellepont

Cédric pulled up to the main gate at Château d'Isère and got out of his car to unlock the padlock. The For Sale sign wobbled in the wind. Fingers of ice extended into the lake from the perimeter, and it would be only a matter of days before Lac du Chevril would be frozen clear across. This was the first time he had returned to the property since his father had been murdered there. Brother Andrew had volunteered to accompany him, but this was something he wanted to do on his own. The trees lining the driveway were bare and lifeless. Splotches of snow covered the hayfields on either side, and a dozen cows huddled together, munching stubble and oblivious to Cédric's interruption. Round bales of hay were neatly wrapped in plastic and stacked at the far side. The surrounding mountains were obscured by low clouds. He left the gate open for the moving vans, which he expected to arrive at any minute.

Nico and Annie had departed for the United States after the memorial and had not returned to Val d'Isère. Whether or not they would ever come back to France was in doubt. The big house had been ransacked and nearly everything of value removed by vandals. The property, which had been worth ten million euros six months earlier, was now listed for two point eight million, and not a single interested buyer had come forward even at that price. But this was Henri Soufflot's problem now. The property was part of his father's estate, which would be contested in the courts for years, and the army of lawyers his father had employed would be all too happy to drag the settlement out as long as possible.

Cédric was saddened to see that the doors to his workshop had been wrenched off their hinges. A quick look around revealed that, although some hand tools appeared to be missing, the workshop was still pretty much intact. Most importantly, his steam engine was still there on the workbench. He loaded it into the trunk of his car and headed upstairs to his apartment to check the damage. A few things were missing, including his computer, but the vandals apparently had no interest in his library of physics books. Most important of all, his journals remained on the bookshelf untouched. He retrieved the cardboard boxes from the loft and began packing up what remained of his things.

The moving van pulled into the driveway and honked the horn to get Cédric's attention. A second flatbed truck for moving the heavy machine tools followed behind, which dispatched a forklift from its hydraulic tailgate. Everything from the workshop was removed. The machines were secured on the flatbed, and everything else went inside the moving van. Cédric piled as many of the boxes from his apartment into his car as he could fit, and the movers took the rest. The work was completed in under two hours, and the loaded trucks headed back down the driveway, taking the right turn on the highway toward Montmélian. Cédric took one last look around and noticed the sign that Nico had made still over the door: *Chandellepont*. He removed it and placed it in the passenger seat, then headed down the driveway, locking the gate behind him. He caught up with the movers to lead them to his farmhouse in Montmélian.

Brother Andrew, Brother Sylvestre, and Brother Benedict waited at the front door of Cédric's main house after pressing the doorbell. Cédric emerged from the barn on the other side of the courtyard. "Over here," he said. "Come. There's something I want to show you. You are just in time see me fire up my steam engine."

The three brothers looked on with interest at the gleaming stainless steel and brass contraption that Cédric had been working on for months. Steam was venting from the overpressure relief valve on top of the boiler with a hiss.

Cédric explained, "The original design called for a kerosene heater, but I decided to replace it with an electric cartridge heater. This way, I can accurately measure the power consumed for making steam. Now watch!" he said as he opened the ball valve on the high-pressure steam line connecting the boiler to the steam piston. The brothers looked on in wonder as the engine came to life. The steam piston started moving in and out, with a puff of steam being ejected at the end of each stroke. A centrifugal governor controlled the speed of the drive shaft, which turned a wheel attached to the dynamo by a belt. Cédric squirted oil onto the bronze bearings and looked up at his friends with a satisfied smile. He pointed to the wattmeter attached to the dynamo. "One hundred and eight point six watts," he said. Then he checked the wattmeter attached to the cartridge heater and said, "Five hundred and thirty-eight watts." He entered the values into his calculator and announced, "The conversion efficiency is 20.2 percent. Not bad! It may seem strange that I am using electricity to make electricity, but this is the best way to measure the efficiency. The steam engine is arguably the most important invention since the wheel. Prior to batteries and fuel cells, virtually every machine for doing work operated on the principle of heat engines." Cédric turned off the power to the heater, and the steam engine began slowing down.

"Come over here," he said, motioning for them to follow. "There is something else I wanted to show you." Spread out on a workbench were several shiny metal washers. He picked one up and handed it to Brother Andrew.

"It's unusually heavy for a metal. What is it?" he asked.

"Processed uranium. It's the uranium isotope left behind when the radioactive isotope is removed," replied Cédric, picking up several of the washers and stacking them on top of one another. "It's not radioactive. I can make cylinders of arbitrary length by just stacking up these washers. You recall my mishap with the administration at Candlebridge. If I had thought of this then, I could have avoided my encounter with the police. I needed a ten-centimeter-long tube with a one-millimeter-diameter hole running down the middle, and I only thought of getting it made from a single piece of metal. I tried everything I could think of to find a vendor of such a tube from processed uranium. Dr. Hendriksen also knew this. Although I knew he was threatened by my experiment, I had no reason to suspect that he actually wanted to sabotage me. He knew of a device called a Fergusson transmutation tube. I think he had made an investment in the start-up company. The idea behind it was that a gas of some material, like sodium, would be passed through the hole in the tube, and alpha particles from the decay of U-235 would bombard the stable sodium-23 isotope, transmuting it into magnesium-23, which has a short half-life. When it decays, it becomes sodium-22, which has a half-life of a couple of years. Sodium-22 is valuable and has some interesting medical applications. The idea never worked, however, and I'm pretty sure I now know why, but that is a discussion for another day. Anyway, Fergusson went out of business, and apparently Hendriksen lost money from his investment in the company. He knew the tube supplier in Sheffield and sent me to them, knowing full well that I would try to smuggle the radioactive tube into the lab, and he could entrap me in an illegal activity. At the time, I didn't realize that processed uranium was available in sheets, and all I needed to do was to laser-cut discs from the sheets and then drill the one-millimeter holes. Oh, well. Now I know. Anyway, the fabrication of my light speed experiment is progressing nicely. I am just waiting for some parts to arrive for the pulsed laser, and I should be able to start testing in a month or two."

Brother Andrew said, "I'm not sure you were aware that Brother Sylvestre used to teach mathematics at the University of Grenoble."

Brother Sylvestre added, "We have been going over your light speed manuscript and have some questions about the fitting parameter, alpha."

"I'm not surprised," replied Cédric. "I have been meaning to revise the manuscript to clear this up." Looking at Brother Benedict, he asked, "Are you also a scientist?"

"No," Brother Benedict said. "I never finished high school. I manage the abbey winery. That's actually why we came." He reached in his bag and retrieved a couple of bottles of white wine. Handing them to Cédric, he said, "This is a housewarming present."

Cédric observed the label, "*Vignoble de l'Abbeye de Montmélian—Vin de Savoie*. What is this?" he asked.

Brother Benedict replied, "Most of the *jacquère* grapes in this valley get squeezed, and the juice is sold to several local wineries like our abbey. We ferment it and age it in our own oak barrels. Then we bottle it and sell it under our own private label to raise money for the abbey."

Cédric said joyfully, "Then let's go into the house and enjoy it while we discuss the fine points of the dark matter fantasy."

Cédric opened one of the bottles and poured glasses for his three friends and himself. He set out crackers and Camembert and green grapes. It was the first time he had entertained guests in this house, or anywhere else, for that matter. Brother Andrew offered a toast to the new home and the success of the light speed experiments.

"Okay, Cédric," said Brother Sylvestre. "I am well acquainted with your exponential function, but I can't figure out how this applies to dark matter."

"I realize in hindsight that I should have clarified this," said Cédric. "I sidestepped the potential objections that would arise if I talked about the time rate of change of velocity, which would imply acceleration. Since light cannot possibly experience acceleration in the classical sense, I glossed over the issue. But this does not mean the exponential function does not have a time-derivative, dv/dt. In fact, it is important that this derivative exist. Otherwise, serious mathematical complications would arise. The derivative is just the speed of light, c^*, in the long time limit, times [α Exp$(-\alpha\ t)$]. Alpha has units of reciprocal time, so you will notice off the bat that this function has units of distance per time squared, or meters per second squared, if you like. The same units as ordinary acceleration. However, this function has the unusual property that at time, $t = 0$, the function evaluates to $c^*\alpha$, and as time goes to infinity, it goes to 0. Alpha describes how fast the speed of light increases as the black hole expands during the birth of a galaxy."

"How sure can you be that galaxies originate at black holes?" asked Brother Andrew.

"That is such a good question," replied Cédric, "and cuts to the crux of the issue. For a long time, I accepted the traditional notion that the universe came into being all at once at the Big Bang. I could just never get the mathematics of increasing light speed to work out. It wasn't until I decoupled galaxy formation from the troubling aspects of the singularity introduced by the Big Bang that I started making serious progress. I guess you must take it on faith that galaxies are born from black holes, but once you make the leap, the mathematics work out in a most beautiful and elegant way. Each galaxy has its own clock, so we can affix time at $t = 0$ with certainty, without worrying about the clocks in other galaxies. As far as anyone knows, dark matter only exists within galaxies. If it exists in the regions between galaxies at all, there is no possible way to observe it. Dark matter within galaxies, on the other hand, is manifested as the discrepancy between the gravitational mass of the stars, which determines the angular momentum of the rotating galaxy and the apparent mass based on the star luminosities. This effect is completely explained by the increasing light speed hypothesis."

"I think this is consistent with the biblical view if you restrict creation to our own Milky Way galaxy," commented Brother Andrew.

Cédric said, "There is something else. That pesky fitting parameter, alpha, holds the key to the size and age of our own galaxy. We assume the age of the universe at some billions of years, based on the accepted constant speed of light, but alpha can be chosen to make the universe as young or as old, or as small or as big as you like. We are taught in school that the star Alpha Centauri is some four light-years away. That's based on the accepted constant speed of light, but I can adjust alpha so that Alpha Centauri is one hundred light-seconds away if I like."

"Okay, Cédric," said Brother Sylvestre. "Now you are testing the limits of credulity."

Cédric replied, "And that's not even the strangest part. Not only are distances shortened by increasing light speed; time itself is modified by the effect I call lensing. Astronomers tell us that the center of our Milky Way galaxy is twenty-seven thousand light-years away, and they tell us there is a supermassive black hole at the center. Consider that for a minute. Do you think another galaxy is about to be born at the center of this one? What lensing does for time is similar to how the Doppler effect shifts the frequency of light. Slow light from earlier times arrives much later than faster light from more recent times. When we look in the direction of the center of the galaxy, we are actually looking back in time. The black hole that scientists claim to be there doesn't actually exist. It is the very black hole that gave birth to our galaxy. Incidentally," continued Cédric, "I should point out that the speed of light can speed up with time, but it can't slow down. This would cause time to pile up like some kind of cosmic sonic boom because the past would be arriving before the present."

"That's too much to take in," objected Brother Sylvestre. "Now you are talking science fiction."

"Go spend some time with that function," said Cédric. "You will see how all this works."

"More wine?" asked Brother Benedict to lighten the mood.

"Yes, please," said Cédric, holding up his empty wine glass. "That's terrific wine. How much do you produce?"

"Only about one hundred cases is all," replied Brother Benedict, "but we have won some prestigious awards, and this brings in quite a few visitors to our gift shop."

"Everyone, help yourself to cheese and crackers," said Cédric, picking up the plate from the coffee table and passing it. "Brother Sylvestre, no one appreciates how disruptive these ideas are more than me. I would say they are controversial, but I have yet to even reach the point of controversy. My ideas were so vigorously opposed at Candlebridge that I never got a chance to discuss them publicly with fellow scientists—really until just now. If you can accept the hypothesis that galaxies are born from black holes and that the speed of light inside a black hole approaches zero, then the rest is just mathematics. The galaxy will expand at the increasing speed of light until matter begins to condense out, at which point gravity takes over to keep the galaxy from expanding without limit. If you integrate the velocity function that I proposed in equation Eq.2 in my manuscript, you get equation Eq.3, which gives the functional form for the distance from the center to the edge of the galaxy. It is not quite so easy to see by simple inspection, but if you simulate it on your computer, you will appreciate what I am talking about by changing the value of the parameter, alpha. It's a hypothesis. No more and no less. The problem is that if my hypothesis turns out to be correct, it will put a whole lot of scientists and their research facilities out of business."

Chapter 11: Slow Light and Cream Cheese

Cédric had finished constructing his apparatus by the spring and was starting to accumulate data from hours of successful tests. One significant modification he had made was that the uranium tubes, made from stacked washers, were mounted into a fixture that could be swiveled in and out of the beam path. This way, he could calibrate the two beams with identical path lengths in vacuum and then move the uranium tube into position with one of the beams passing through it, without having to open the vacuum chamber and pumping back down—a procedure that, otherwise, took about an hour. He had confirmed his previous results at Candlebridge, plus a lot more data using tubes of various lengths. By May, he had finished his manuscript describing the details of his experiment and the results and sent it off to the leading physics journal for publication.

Having done as much as he could at that point, he decided to take a break from the work and go to Paris to meet with Henri Soufflot, who had some matters that needed to be settled regarding his father's estate. He fished out the card that he had been given at the memorial and called the number.

"Soufflot," said the voice on the other end.

"Yes, my name is Cédric Rothschild. I would like to speak with a Mr. Henri Soufflot."

"Cédric! This is Henri Soufflot. It's good to hear from you."

Cédric paused to ponder how the most influential layer in all of Paris might answer his own phone. "I guess I was expecting a receptionist to answer," he said.

Henri replied, "The number I gave you is my private number. What can I do for you?"

Cédric replied, "You have been sending me messages about settling my father's estate. I have been too busy to reply, but now I am thinking of coming to Paris. I don't know where your office is, and I don't really know Paris all that well. I was wondering if you might be able to recommend a hotel."

"Hotel?" Henri replied. "Why don't you just stay at your own apartment?"

"You mean my father's apartment?" Cédric asked.

"Cédric," he said, "that apartment is yours now."

"I would have thought it had been sold," Cédric commented.

"Sold?" Soufflot replied. "It's sitting idle. I can't do anything with it unless you direct me to do so. No one has entered it since before the memorial."

Cédric remained quiet, trying to process the news. He had given no thought to his father's estate up to that point, and the shock of the sudden realization that he had new responsibilities caught him by surprise.

"Cédric," Henri finally said, "we have a lot to discuss. If you tell me when you will be arriving, I will have housekeeping get the apartment ready. Would you like me to arrange for a maid?"

The mention of servants caused Cédric some confusion. "I can't afford a maid," he said.

"Cédric," Henri responded, "I have been waiting for you to provide your banking information. There are ten million euros sitting in the bank waiting to be transferred to your account. This is money your father designated for Geraldine. She won't be needing it where she will be spending the next couple of decades," he said with a chuckle.

This was more news that Cédric didn't know how to process.

"Look," said Henri. "I will get your apartment ready, and we can discuss all of this when you get to Paris. Just let me know when you are thinking of coming. I will dispatch a private jet to pick you up in Lyon."

"Okay," Cédric said weakly. Prior to that moment, he had never realized that he was now a very wealthy man. His father's activities had always been hidden from him, and it had been clear to him that there was no room for a physicist at the family office.

Over the following days, Cédric's reluctance to enter his father's world slowly transformed into eagerness. He began imagining himself slipping into Parisian society, basking in the fame of his remarkable discovery, and being the one to topple the towers of scientific orthodoxy surrounding constant light speed theory. He imagined that as soon as his paper was published, he would approach the University of Paris to complete his PhD. Then he would accept a prestigious professorship while he waited for his Nobel Prize.

He had stopped by to visit his mother on his way to Lyon. Her decline in recent months had been rapid, and she was now in a vegetative state. Cédric had kissed her on the forehead as if saying goodbye to a corpse. Then he had gone to the Lyon airport to meet the private jet that waited on the tarmac for him. The limo from Orly dropped him off at the front door of his apartment.

The doorman at the apartment building greeted him warmly. "Bonjour, Monsieur Rothschild. It is very good to see you again."

"Please just call me Cédric," he said, shivering inside at the formality he was not accustomed to. The last time he had been addressed as Mr. Rothschild was by the chancellor at Candlebridge, and the sound of that booming voice was something he would never forget.

"Of course," said the doorman. "I will call for the elevator. Do you remember the code? I will have your things sent up."

"No need," said Cédric, indicating that everything he had brought with him was in his backpack.

The apartment was strangely vacant and sterile. Everything was just as he remembered, except there was no sign that anyone he had known had ever lived there. Henri Soufflot had arranged for a thorough cleaning, and the scent of disinfectant and air fresheners was strong. He opened the sliding doors to the terrasse and walked out into the lovely June dusk. The lights of Paris sparkled, and the dance of the light show on the Eiffel Tower gave the city a particular liveliness. The planters along the railing that had held his mother's prize red roses were empty and now filled with fresh mulch.

He walked into his father's bedroom for the very first time. It had always been off-limits when he was growing up. There was a portrait of his grandfather on the wall that he had never seen. Otherwise, there were no clothes or personal effects of any kind in the bedroom suite. He considered moving in but decided to stay in his own room for the time-being while he got accustomed to being alone in the apartment. He was flooded with childhood memories as he walked around. The refrigerator was stocked with things to eat, and a sheet with restaurant recommendations was on the countertop. The past was slowly being eclipsed by the present and would soon be forgotten in the future.

Cédric's headache the following morning reminded him that he would need to exercise more moderation in his consumption of alcohol. He had failed to set the timer on his coffee maker, and although he was accustomed to making his own breakfast, he decided to go out and explore Paris. He checked his emails. There was one from the brothers at Abbey de Montmélian wishing him safe travels and saying he was in their prayers. The second email was the one he had been anticipating eagerly. It was from the physics journal editorial office informing him that his manuscript had been entered into their system and that it had been correctly formatted and deemed appropriate in length and style. It had been distributed to the reviewers for comment, and a decision for publication should be available within four weeks. Cédric rejoiced at the news and headed out the door to celebrate. His meeting with Henri Soufflot was not until the afternoon, so his first item of business was to go to the university to inquire about enrolling as a graduate student in astrophysics.

When he asked in the administration building where to go for graduate admissions, the desk clerk pointed to an adjacent waiting room where a dozen or so other people were in the queue for the next available admissions officer. Cédric waited an hour. The thought occurred to him that he would be treated with more respect if they only knew what it would mean to have such a wealthy and distinguished Nobel Laureate among their alumni.

"What can I do for you?" the admissions officer asked at last.

"My name is Cédric Rothschild. I would like to transfer to the astrophysics college as a graduate student."

"Where will you be transferring from?" she asked.

"Candlebridge University in England," he responded.

"You are seeking a postdoctoral position then?" she inquired. "You need to go to the Astrophysics and Astronomy College dean for that."

"No," replied Cédric. "I have completed all of my qualifying exams, but I have not completed my dissertation."

"You want to transfer? Why aren't you finishing at Candlebridge?" she asked.

This was the very question he had dreaded. "I got kicked out of the school," he said.

She studied him carefully. "This is rather unusual," she said. "Did you bring your transcripts?"

"No," Cédric replied. "I only have a copy. You would need to request that Candlebridge provide you with my official transcripts."

The admissions officer let out a deep sigh and handed him a graduate admissions application form. "Fill this out as best as you can and bring it back. Ask for me. My name is Emily. I presume that you are a French citizen, correct?"

"Yes. Thank you." Cédric took the form and placed it in his backpack.

His next course of action was to get a real haircut and shave, followed by purchasing a wardrobe. His customary casual style of dress was not suitable for the meeting with Henri Soufflot at his office on the Champs-Élysées. The salespersons at the upscale men's clothing store were more than attentive once they realized that their client had no spending limit. Cédric arranged for all the shopping bags to be delivered to his apartment along with his backpack, for which he had no further use. He walked out of the store sporting a fashionable, light beige summer suit with white shirt and open collar.

He dropped into a restaurant along the Champs-Élysées for a late lunch before his meeting with Henri. From the way he was treated by the host, he realized that the transformation of his appearance must have been working. He was now a beautiful person fitting right in with the other beautiful people of Parisian society.

"I have an appointment with Mr. Soufflot at three," Cédric said to the attractive young receptionist at the law offices of Soufflot & Soufflot. She looked at him admiringly. The feeling of being part of the French aristocracy was a new experience for him, and he was beginning to like it.

She stood and said, "Follow me. He is waiting for you. I will show you to his office." Cédric was quite taken by her beauty as she led the way. It was the first stirring he had had in years to be attracted to a young woman.

"Cédric! Welcome!" Henri Soufflot said, standing from his seat at a conference table at which a half a dozen people were seated. "Let me introduce you to your legal team."

Cédric had not realized how complicated his father's home office had been, with extensive holdings around the world. No amount of integral calculus had prepared him for the world of high finance. One by one, the people at the table showed slides on the screen of the vast network of enterprises and investments that were held by his father's holding companies. It was overwhelming, and after about two hours of balance sheets and profit-and-loss statements, Cédric began daydreaming about variable gravitational effects resulting from the increasing speed of light. A new question had been percolating in his head that if the speed of light was not a universal constant, why shouldn't "Big G," the gravitational constant, also be variable? The contortions that theorists were going through to explain the motion of galaxies reminded him of the complex mathematical models that were developed to explain the orbits of planets in the Aristotelian, earth-centered solar system. Cédric politely nodded his head during the briefings as if he understood what they were explaining. In the end, he hoped these people really knew what they were talking about and would be able to run his father's financial empire without input from him. As he was leaving the office for the day, he asked the pretty receptionist if she would care to have dinner.

"Sorry," she said with a smile, flashing an enormous diamond ring on her finger. "I'm engaged."

"Lucky fellow," Cédric said as he got on the elevator.

During the week, he was in and out of the Soufflot offices, signing trust documents, powers of attorney, authorizing asset transfers, and the like. He was hoping that his growing disinterest in financial matters was not too obvious. In any event, they surely knew by the end of the week that he would sign anything they presented to him.

He had been exploring the various Paris neighborhoods at night. He had found that his quiet apartment on the Seine might have been a good place to raise a family, but it really did not suit him. He had been looking for an apartment closer to the university where the intellectual climate was more stimulating. He had informed Henri that he would be putting the apartment up for sale as soon as he found another one. He had wanted to explore the neighborhoods around the Pompidou Center, so on Saturday he walked all around the third arrondissement, taking photos of apartment buildings and units with "*a vendre*" signs hanging from the balconies. He stopped in at several real estate agencies to see what kinds of places were available, but nothing really grabbed him, and by evening, he was exhausted. He decided to walk south past the Hotel de Ville, across the Pont d'Arcole and on to the Rive Gauche and Latin Quarter, where he planned to have dinner at a restaurant that he had begun to frequent along Rue Saint-Jacques on the way up to the university.

He passed in front of the Notre Dame Cathedral and joined the line of enthusiastic tourists on an impulse. He had gone by it many times but had never actually gone in. From the moment he entered, he was impressed with a sense of awe. The quiet reverence of the visitors was overwhelming. He took a seat to rest and take in the magnificence. They were tuning the pipe organ for the concert that evening. Each solo tone of a pipe resonated as the frequency was adjusted minutely up and down until sonority was achieved with the echo of the massive cathedral. Then a chord was played to confirm the pitch before moving up the chromatic scale one pipe at a time. Cédric was mesmerized. He felt as if God Himself were speaking to him from the heavens—not in melodies but in distinct tones with ever so slight variations in pitch. His mind searched hard for an interpretation of the significance. After a long while, one of the ushers asked him to leave so they could get ready for the concert.

The following morning, he made his own breakfast. He had arranged with a realtor to visit an apartment near the Musée Pierre-et-Marie Curie that had caught his attention. He finished breakfast and called down to the doorman to call for a taxi. He checked his emails one last time and noticed a new one from the physics journal with the heading, "A decision has been reached." Cédric found this odd, as he was not expecting a response for at least a couple more weeks. "Dear Mr. Rothschild, based on the recommendations of three reviewers, the editors have decided that your submission is not suitable for publication." Cédric was in total shock as he opened the website to see the actual reviews. Reviewer 1 rejected the manuscript without comment. Reviewer 2 recommended major revision, but his comments seemed to be directed at someone else's paper. The comments from Reviewer 3 hurt the most. "This manuscript presents some interesting experimental results purporting to show that the transit time for a light pulse through a block of dense metal is longer than expected, but the author's speculations on the nature of dark matter are total rubbish. He might as well be proposing that the moon is made of cream cheese."

Chapter 12: The Crossing

Cédric sat at the pool bar at the rear of the cruise ship, sipping his second rum punch before lunch. He watched the faint brown trail of smoke drift off behind them to the east, with hardly any breeze to disturb it. There were no clouds in the brilliant blue July sky one week before his thirtieth birthday. The North Atlantic Ocean was as flat as a mill pond. For Cédric, the rejection had been the last straw. He was beyond rage, and depression had not yet overtaken him. He was mostly just numb and needed a change of scenery. The travel agent in the Paris office of the French-Canadian Lines had told him that the cruise ship departing the following day for Montreal was fully booked but indicated that if he showed up at the departure terminal in Le Havre, there was a pretty good chance that there would be a last-minute cancellation if he wanted to take his chances. He had packed some clothes into his valise and caught the TGV to Le Havre. The travel agent had been right; there was an executive suite available for 12,000 euros. This had seemed like a lot of money, but since it was his first cruise, he had no sense for how much it should cost.

"What are you drinking?" asked the man sitting next to him at the pool bar.

"Rum punch," said Cédric.

"Nice," the man said. "I prefer Manhattans myself."

"I'm not a very experienced drinker," Cédric replied. "I will try one of those next."

The man responded, "You will be a pro by the time we get to Montreal. The drink package will ensure that."

"Drink package?" asked Cédric. "What is that?"

"You didn't purchase the drink package?" that man asked, looking shocked. "For just five hundred euros, you can drink as much as you want for the duration of the voyage."

Cédric gave this some consideration and then replied, "Five hundred euros seems like a lot of alcohol to me."

"Knocking down those rum punches at twenty euros a pop, and you will run up one heck of a bar bill," the man said, hopping up to get out of the pool. "See you later. I'm going to grab that cabana over there before someone snatches it."

"Another round?" asked the bartender.

"No thanks," responded Cédric, holding out the pass on the lanyard around his neck for the bartender to scan. "You can close out my tab. I have had too much sun, and I need to find some shade." He climbed out of the pool and into a hot tub under a canopy. The morning aerobics class was just starting on the fantail. The instructor started bouncing up and down to loud hip-hop music, inviting people to join in. Two very pale and overweight women and a boy showed up first.

"Come on, everybody," the instructor barked over the loudspeaker. "Get out of those lounge chairs and start your blood circulating. You," he said, pointing in Cédric's direction. Cédric looked around to see who he was pointing at. "No, you. The guy in the hot tub. This isn't a spectator sport. Get your butt down here."

Cédric was feeling pretty good from the rum punches and a bit adventuresome, so he accepted the challenge. He had done practically nothing athletic since his motorcycle accident. Aerobic exercise was totally new to him, but before long, he was on the dance floor with the others, following the commands of the instructor. After thirty minutes, the alcohol had worn off, and he was tired and hungry. For the moment, he had avoided any further descent into depression. Thereafter, he stayed away from the bars and showed up faithfully every morning at eleven o'clock for the aerobics class.

By the third day, he was pretty much over the cream cheese comment and began thinking about his next project. After lunch, he went to the library on the top deck to do some research. The ship's Wi-Fi was slow, but the library maintained a hard drive with almost everything ever written. His light speed experiments had kindled a curiosity into why the Ferguson transmutation device had never worked. He had a theory, but he wanted to investigate it in the literature to see what scientific papers he could find. To his amazement, it turned out that one of the inventors was none other than Professor Hendriksen. Candlebridge had sold the patent to Ferguson, and Hendriksen had made a sizeable personal investment in the company. Cédric downloaded the patent and all the papers he could find on the topic onto his tablet computer and returned to his stateroom to do some study. However, before he could accomplish this, he would have to freshen up on his understanding of nuclear physics because it had been a couple of years since he had seriously studied the subject. He became immediately ensconced in the pursuit of relearning this subject. He had forgotten the personal satisfaction that he got from learning new things.

He was also glad to have a chance to revisit the subject of deuteron-deuteron fusion. It had been a while since he published his one and only paper during his early years as a graduate student. He had been studying the claims of several credible investigators that helium gas was generated when deuterium was introduced into palladium metal. Helium was the hallmark of deuteron fusion, and the levels detected were well above what was expected in the background. The idea of spontaneous fusion had captured the imagination of many scientists as an almost limitless source of energy, but no one could figure out how to increase the rate of reaction to generate enough heat to be useful. Cédric had calculated the probability of deuteron-deuteron interaction sufficient to tunnel through the coulombic repulsion and concluded that the interaction time would need to be increased by some twelve orders of magnitude to have a reasonable probability for the reaction to occur. This was when he had begun thinking that the speed of light could be slowed down in the vicinity of a heavy mass, and by slowing down the local speed of light, more time would be available for the reaction to occur. He had performed some preliminary experiments as first-year graduate student at Candlebridge with uranium deuteride and found an anomalous increase in the helium yield over what was observed with the less dense metal, palladium. He described these experiments and submitted a manuscript to a journal well known for publishing papers without excessive scrutiny in the review process. He had planned to continue this experiment for his PhD, but he had decided instead to focus his attention on the more compelling experiment to measure the speed of light through a hole in a block of uranium.

Cédric had lost track of time and was late for dinner. One of the perks that came with his executive suite was that he got to sit at the captain's table. It had turned out that the captain was quite knowledgeable about marine systems engineering, and the two had begun a serious dialogue about the need to replace the diesel engines that were consuming more than five tons of biodiesel per hour. The captain had become intrigued by Cédric's optimism that compact fusion reactors—what he called microfusion—for making steam might be possible and had promised to give him a VIP tour of the engine room after dinner.

Cédric had settled into a comfortable routine: up at dawn, twenty laps of the quarter-mile jogging track, light breakfast, reflections and journaling until the aerobics class at eleven, light lunch followed by serious study and a nap before dinner at the captain's table, then hard work until the wee hours of the night. He had become as productive as at any time in his life. His intellectual pursuits were split between microfusion and trying to understand the Ferguson device. The latter made no sense at all. The claim of the patent was that alpha particles from the decay of uranium were captured by a gas of the stable isotope of sodium and transmuted into an isotope of magnesium before decaying to the radioactive isotope, sodium-22. Cédric had realized that this was total nonsense. Magnesium would decay to a stable isotope of aluminum. The only way to make sodium-22 would be to bombard magnesium with deuterium, giving up a tritium nucleus, itself a radioactive and very dangerous hydrogen isotope. Hendrickson was shrewd and duplicitous, fully capable of defrauding the university and Ferguson's other investors, but he was not stupid. He would never have invested his own money in a scheme he knew would never work. There had to be another angle. Cédric worked doggedly to figure it out. But by the time his cruise ship entered the St. Laurence Waterway, he still had no credible resolution. He did have a new *raison d'être*, however—to expose Professor Hendriksen's fraud.

The lights of Canada twinkled on the horizon. Cédric could detect the pungent odor of seaweed that signaled the approaching shoreline as he sat on his balcony with growing anticipation. This was his first trip to America. At 42,000 gross tons, his cruise ship was not huge, but what it lacked in size was made up for with luxury for the eighteen hundred pampered passengers. The one thousand doting crew members ensured this. The sun was just breaking the eastern horizon as the ship inched into the cruise ship pier at Quebec City. A flurry of activity below his starboard-side balcony ensued, with numerous waiting dockworkers grabbing lines and securing the ship to the stanchions. This was the ship's first and only port call since leaving Le Havre. It was scheduled to depart at eight o'clock that evening for Montreal, its destination. The ship would then head back out the St. Laurence River and head south for a port call in New York City before returning to France.

Tour busses began arriving to take passengers on shore excursions. Cédric had surveyed the various itineraries and found nothing that captured his interests, so he decided to spend the day exploring Quebec City by himself on foot. It was hard to imagine that in just four months the weather would be unbearably cold, and the St. Laurence Waterway would turn to ice, only to be kept navigable with great difficulty using icebreakers. By December, his luxury cruise liner would be stopping at all the magical places in the Caribbean for the Christmas holidays. Cédric had inquired about the possibility of extending his cruise but was told that it was already overbooked. Instead, he arranged for a hotel for three nights in downtown Montreal with the help of the concierge while he figured out where to go next. While growing up, his life had been carefully managed by his father, who always planned family vacations around his own convenience and tastes. His father had hated the United States and cared only slightly more for Canada. These were merely business venues for him, requiring short trips, which were never considered to be vacation destinations. This was the first time in his life that Cédric had the means and freedom to choose wherever he wanted to go.

It was overcast and chilly by the time he had finished breakfast on the ship. The weather forecast called for light showers in the afternoon. His plan was to explore the historic Citadelle de Québec that in times past provided a commanding fortification against British invasion. He headed back to his stateroom to get a jacket. Out on his balcony, he observed that the internet on his computer was strong from the shore-based broadband signal. He did a quick search on "Hendriksen" and got several new results that did not turn up in the ship's library system. In particular, one of these caught his eye. The patent he had been trying to make sense of for the past five days had been revised recently with several new claims, one of which had to do with using the transmutation tube for promoting deuteron fusion. Cédric quickly scanned the revised sections to discover language that seemed to be lifted directly from the draft of an unpublished paper he had been working on at Candlebridge. The only other person to have seen the draft was his adviser, Dr. Cecil Edwards, who had asked permission to show it to Dr. Hendriksen for clarification on some aspects of the nuclear physics, a topic about which he lacked expertise. Cédric stared at the plagiarized text. He checked the date of the published revision on the patent to confirm that it was written after he had shown the document to his adviser. He was beyond rage. All the pieces began to fall into place. Hendriksen had known all along that slowing down the speed of light inside the tube was a necessary condition for fusion. This had already been disclosed in Cédric's earlier published paper, but it was the matter of activating sodium gas with deuterons to produce tritium that made fusion feasible. This was the basis of the manuscript that he had shown Dr. Edwards, who had come back with the response from Hendriksen that the idea was not feasible.

Cédric immediately called Paris.

"Soufflot," came the reply.

"Henri, this is Cédric Rothschild." He immediately regretted that he had addressed his father's lawyer by his first name, but his excitement had gotten the better of him.

"Cédric! Where the heck are you?"

"I'm in Canada. I will be in Montreal tonight," Cédric replied. "Do you know a good intellectual property law firm with offices in Paris and Montreal?"

"What's this all about?" asked Soufflot.

"It's complicated," replied Cédric. "I need a patent lawyer, a really good patent lawyer."

Soufflot took a long breath and exhaled slowly. "I will see what I can do, but, Cédric, there's some paperwork I need you to sign. You have a purchase offer for Château d'Isère."

"That's good news," replied Cédric. "I don't know when I will be back in Paris. Can you take care of it?"

"What? You expect me to just forge your signature?" replied Soufflot.

"Okay," said Cédric. "Find me a law firm in Montreal that you trust, with a strong patent division, and I will sign over a power of attorney to you from there."

"But, Cédric," he replied, "you have responsibilities. You can't just disappear and go off around the world."

"Henri," responded Cédric, "the Rothschild family office is in good hands with you. I trust you. My father trusted you. I will be back in France in a couple of months to sort things out. In the meantime, please arrange for the sale of the Paris apartment. It is too big, and it doesn't suit my needs."

Henri Soufflot let out a sigh of resignation. "All right, then. It is too late in the day for me to find a law firm I can recommend, and anyway, all of France is on vacation, but I will see what I can do in the morning. Let me know where I can reach you in Montreal and stay in touch."

"And Henri. Do you by any chance have a forwarding address for Annie and Nicolas Delquoi?" asked Cédric.

"I only have a post office box in a place called Palisade, Colorado. I sent their last severance check there, but I don't think they want to be found. They were both eyewitnesses to your father's murder, and the French police have been trying in vain to depose them for the trial."

This comment caused Cédric to smile. The court had wanted to send Geraldine away for life, but without Annie's or

Nico's testimonies, she only got sentenced to nine years. He knew that nine years in a French maximum-security prison was probably a life sentence, but in the event that she was to be released, being penniless and friendless in Paris was plenty of punishment.

"*Bonne soirée.* I will contact you tomorrow," Cédric said, and hung up. He sat back in his lounge chair to reflect on the ramifications of what he was uncovering about Hendriksen. It seemed that Hendriksen was even more evil than he had imagined. He had not only set out to ruin his work at Candlebridge from a desire to protect his own professional integrity or that of the university. He probably did not give a rip about dark matter and perhaps even knew all along that no dark matter particle would ever be found. Hendriksen had probably suspected that his light speed experiment would succeed, and he was motivated by personal greed to cash in on Cédric's fusion discovery.

Chapter 13: Palisade

Cédric surveyed the directory for the offices of La Forêt and Associates in the lobby of the office building in downtown Montreal adjacent to McGill University. He took the elevator to the fourteenth floor and entered a plush waiting area for what was clearly a very affluent legal practice. He was fifteen minutes early. "Hello. My name is Cédric Rothschild. I have an appointment at ten with a Mr. Slogane," he said to the receptionist.

"Oh, yes," she replied. "He is expecting you, but he is with a client at the moment."

"No problem," replied Cédric. "I'm early."

"Here are some documents we have prepared for your signature," she said, handing him an envelope with his name neatly typed on the tab. "On top is an engagement letter for the firm's services, and the second document is an assignment of power of attorney to a Mr. Henri Soufflot in Paris. Your signature on that one will need to be notarized. If I can have your passport, I would like to make a copy for our records. May I bring you a cup of coffee while you wait?"

"Yes please, black," Cédric replied. He appreciated the red-carpet treatment and was pleased to discover that Henri had such prominent international connections. He stood at the picture window in the waiting area that looked out over the campus of McGill University. He was planning to visit it next to see if it might be somewhere he would consider carrying on his research. He knew that without a PhD after his name, he would not be able to have the kind of impact his discoveries warranted. He was thinking that Canada was far enough away from Europe to be free of the disgrace of being kicked out of Candlebridge. Perhaps the Canadians would be more open-minded to his radical theories.

"Good morning, Mr. Rothschild. Francis Slogane," said a man, extending a welcoming hand. "I'm sorry to make you wait. Here, I reserved a conference room for us." He said pointed to a glass-enclosed room off the lobby.

They were seated, and Cédric opened the envelope. "I didn't have time to read these," he said.

"No problem," replied Slogane. "It's just a lot of drab legal stuff. When you are ready, I will call in a notary for assigning the power of attorney to your lawyer in Paris. We do, however, have a problem with the engagement letter. It turns out that one of our clients is the plaintiff in a patent infringement case with your company. This firm cannot ethically represent you without a conflict of interest."

"I have no knowledge of such matters," replied Cédric, regretting for the first time not having paid attention to the briefings in Paris about the activities of his father's family office.

Slogane said, "Why don't you describe for me your issue, and then we can consider your options. Perhaps we can refer you to another firm."

Cédric began, "I have been studying a patent application filed by a professor at Candlebridge University in the United Kingdom that plagiarized some of my own work."

"That's a very serious allegation," said Slogane, pulling a lever under the conference table that caused a computer keyboard to pop up. "What is the name on the patent application?"

"Hendriksen," replied Cédric.

Slogane typed it in, and the entire patent dossier came up on the flat panel screen in the front of the room. He studied it and scrolled down to the bottom to get a sense of the status. "It looks like the original disclosure was revised just a little over a year ago."

"Yes," replied Cédric. "The plagiarism is in the revision. Hendriksen copied the idea for a revised set of claims from a manuscript I had written. Then he set me up for expulsion from the school."

"Very interesting," replied the lawyer. "Can you provide me with the link to your manuscript? Was it published under your own name?"

"That's just the problem," replied Cédric. "It was never published."

"Then how do you know your work was plagiarized?" asked Slogane.

Cédric reached in his pocket and pulled out a memory stick. "My manuscript is on this."

"You wrote this while you were a graduate student at Candlebridge then?" asked the lawyer.

Cédric nodded.

The lawyer leaned back in his chair for a moment to contemplate the situation. "If what you say is true, then it might be possible to seek an injunction. Let's start by you describing how much the invention will be worth once it is commercialized."

"That will never happen," replied Cédric. "The invention won't work as described in the patent claims. Uranium is one of the densest things on earth. The effect of enhanced fusion can be seen in it, but it would need to be about five orders of magnitude denser to manifest a high enough fusion flux to be commercially viable. No such material exists—in neutron stars perhaps, but not on the earth."

"Then what sort of damage award are you seeking?" asked the lawyer.

"Hendriksen ruined my life," replied Cédric. "I just want him to pay. I just want vindication and due credit for my invention."

"And reinstatement to the university?" asked the lawyer.

"I would never go back to Candlebridge," replied Cédric. "Anyway, they kicked me out for criminal charges."

"Criminal charges?" asked Slogane.

"Well," responded Cédric, "trumped-up charges that were dropped. I smuggled contraband uranium into the lab."

The lawyer swiveled his chair to look out the window before turning back around. "Cédric," he said, "intellectual property theft is not a capital offense. It seems to me that you are seeking far more that financial damages."

"I would settle for getting Hendriksen fired and disgraced," replied Cédric.

Slogane asked, "Will the university back up your story?"

"Not a chance," replied Cédric. "They are all in this together. Hendriksen is a valuable rainmaker. Without the millions in research grants he brings to the school each year, their research program would be in trouble."

Francis Slogane stood up and went to the door to hail the receptionist. "Will you ask the notary to step in here?" Then sitting back down, he said, "Cédric, I'm sorry to tell you this, but neither this firm nor, I suspect, any other firm would take your case. I am afraid that there is just no legal path for settling vendettas."

"But I have been grievously injured!" exclaimed Cédric.

The notary entered at that moment, and Slogane slipped the power of attorney letter across the table to Cédric for him to sign. Smiling, he said, "With your net worth, Cédric, I doubt that anyone would show much sympathy for your injustice."

Cédric was crushed. He bowed his head in final defeat and sadly said, "What good is money if I have no way to ever realize my dreams?"

Time seemed to come to a complete stop as Cédric exited the office building and wandered aimlessly around the McGill University campus. Even walking through the library—a safe place that had always inspired him—failed to break through the daze. He finally drifted back to his hotel in the late afternoon. There was a mob scene in the lobby with countless sports fanatics crowding in, waiting for the arrival of some sort of ice hockey celebrity. He went into the lounge to observe the commotion and took an empty seat at the bar.

"What can I get for you?" the bartender asked him.

Cédric replied, "Manhattan. On the rocks, please," figuring he was expected to purchase a drink and feigning the air of a sophisticated drinker. "What's all the fuss about?" he asked.

"I gather you're not a hockey fan," replied the bartender. "Jacques Terrenoire is expected to make a big announcement."

"I have never heard of him," said Cédric.

The surprised bartender replied, "He is probably the most famous hockey player of all time. He scored the winning goal in this year's Stanley Cup finals. It is rumored that he plans to retire. I guess at the ripe old age of twenty-eight, he has decided to call it quits while he is still on top."

This comment caused Cédric to reflect on the fact that the career for this hockey player, who was about his same age, might already be over. Cédric and Jacques Terrenoire were now facing the same challenge of what to do with the rest of their lives.

Cédric drifted west to Toronto, across Lake Ontario to Niagara Falls and through the border crossing into the United States, where they did not even ask to see his passport. He finally ended up in Buffalo, New York, in a hotel on the waterfront with an old US Navy battleship outside his window. His plan was to fly to Denver as soon as he was able to secure a plane ticket, but everything was booked, as people were busy getting their vacations in during the last week of August. He had begun thinking about driving to Colorado and found that no rental cars were available anywhere. There was, however, a Ford dealership near his hotel, and he stopped in to consider the option of purchasing a car for the cross-country trek. There was a black pickup truck in the showroom that he couldn't take his eyes off. He was experienced at purchasing lasers and turbomolecular pumps, but he was completely out of his element purchasing an automobile.

A salesperson stood by while he walked around the truck. "Do you have any questions I can answer?" she asked.

"It says 'all electric.' Is that correct?" Cédric asked.

"Yes," the salesperson responded. "It comes standard with lithium-ion batteries with a range of two hundred and fifty miles."

"That's not very much," replied Cédric, trying to appear knowledgeable about electric vehicles.

"There is a range extender battery pack that fits in the king cab behind the driver's seat that increases the range by one hundred miles, if you are interested," said the salesperson.

"Four-wheel drive?" questioned Cédric.

"Actually, sir," she replied, "this model just came out this year with all-wheel drive. Each wheel is independently powered by its own electric motor. This truck will climb walls."

"I'll take it," said Cédric. "How much?"

This caught the salesperson completely off guard. "You want to purchase one of these trucks?"

"No," said Cédric, opening the driver's door and hopping behind the steering wheel. "I want to purchase this truck. Now."

"This truck's not for sale. It is the floor model," she protested.

Cédric got out and headed for the front door.

"Wait!" she said. "Let me get the sales manager." She came back momentarily with a man whose expression indicated that he had better things to do than entertain the dreams of some drifter thinking he could afford to buy a $170,000 automobile.

"Helen says you may be interested in a truck," he said.

"Yes," replied Cédric, "but only if I can get it with the hundred mile range extender."

The sales manager rolled his eyes, looked over at Helen, and said, "Sit him down and get a credit check started." Then looking a Cédric, he asked, "Do you even have the seventeen-thousand-dollar down payment? From your French accent, I am going to guess you are Canadian. It will be a challenge to finance the balance."

"No. I'm French," replied Cédric.

"French Canadian then," said the sales manager.

"No," replied Cédric, becoming increasingly irritated. "French-French, from Paris! And I want to buy this truck for cash, no credit terms, just cash. With the range extender."

The sales manager and Helen stared at each other in disbelief. "You have that much cash?" he finally asked.

"You tell me the final amount, and I will be back in two hours with a cashier's check to drive my new truck out of the showroom."

The sales manager remained skeptical until Cédric showed up later with a cashier's check for $178,369.23, including dealer discount and sales tax. "We don't have the range extender in stock, but it is being shipped overnight from the factory in Detroit," he said.

Cédric responded, "Then I will be back tomorrow after you have installed the range extender."

The following day, the paperwork was executed. The dealership needed a US mailing address for where to send the title, and Cédric gave them Annie's and Nico's post office box in Colorado that Henri had given him. He had no idea if the address was still active, but he would be able to sort that out once he got to Palisade. The dealership had their cash and wasn't worried about ever having to get their truck back. Helen gave him a final briefing on all the features before opening the double doors as the stunned sales manager watched the brand-new black electric pickup truck with Cédric behind the wheel drive out of the showroom.

"*Bonne journée*," Cédric said, waving. "Now I want to see what this baby can do." All four tires squealed as he departed the parking lot.

Cédric did not begin to fully appreciate the features of his new truck until he was past Cleveland, heading west on Interstate 80. The truck came with climate control, leather seats with integrated heating and cooling and built-in massage, satellite downlink, and autopilot. Also, the dealership had thrown in a camper shell for free. A stop at a camping supply store near Toledo, and he had everything he would need to set up his new home in the back. With the range extender installed, he only needed to recharge the batteries at night at a truck stop.

The drive to Palisade along the interstate was uneventful except for his run-in with the state patrol outside of Omaha. He had been clocked going 95 miles per hour, which Cédric tried to explain by saying that he was confused between miles per hour and kilometers per hour. The officer shook his head as he wrote out the ticket and court summons. It took another hour for them to confirm that the truck had not been stollen. Cédric paid the fine in cash, and the officer waived the court appearance with a stern warning that this was not France, and everyone needed to obey US laws.

Some days later, with the help of the built-in navigation system, Cédric pulled into the parking lot of the post office in

Palisade, Colorado, and went inside. He showed the woman at the window a photo he had on his cellular phone of Annie and Nico and said, "I am trying to track down these friends. All I have is their post office box number at this location."

The woman stared intently at the photo for a moment and then, smiling broadly, said, "Of course. That's Annie and Nick Smith. They operate a bed-and-breakfast just south of town."

"I am trying to get in touch with them," said Cédric. "Do you happen to have a phone number or email address?"

"No," she replied. "They are living totally off the grid."

"Can you give me directions to their house then?" he asked.

She looked at him suspiciously. "I'm pretty sure they wouldn't want me to give that information out," she replied, "but Nick stops in for coffee every morning about this time at Jimbo's. You will know when he arrives by the sound of his motorcycle. I think he has customized it for maximum noise. It is totally obnoxious, and you can hear him coming for miles," she said with a grin.

Chapter 14: Peach-Eze

Nico's arrival at Jimbo's Café was announced by the ear-shattering roar of his Harley-Davidson motorcycle. He walked up to the counter and said to the proprietor, "Just coffee this morning, Bill. Annie needs me back for the peach picking."

Bill replied in a low voice, "There is a guy at that table in the corner that has been asking for you."

"French accent?" asked Nico.

"Yes," replied Bill.

"Uh-oh," said Nico. "French policeman?"

"He doesn't look like a cop," replied Bill. "Do you want me to distract him while you go out the back door?"

Nico turned his head slightly to catch a glimpse. "Cédric? What the heck?"

Cédric acknowledged with a broad grin. "You sure aren't a very easy person to track down."

Nico grabbed his coffee and headed to the table where Cédric was sitting. They embraced. "How did you know to come to Jimbo's?"

"The woman at the post office told me you would likely show up around this time," said Cédric.

"That's Mabel. She's a dear. Everybody in town is trying to hide us from the French police," said Nico. "Annie and I failed to answer the summons for Geraldine's trial, and France has been trying to extradite us. It seems that Geraldine's lawyer has been trying to implicate us somehow in the murder and has filed an appeal. They have our sworn testimony, and Geraldine was convicted, but the French courts won't let it drop. Anyway, what the heck are you doing here?"

"My father's lawyer gave me a forwarding address for you at a post office box in Palisade. I was passing through Colorado on my way to California, so I thought I might be able to track you down."

"Oh, Cédric. I am just blown away. Annie will be apoplectic to see you. Come stay with us. We operate a bed-and-breakfast on the outskirts of town with a small peach orchard.

Cédric trailed Nico out of town past neat rows of trees loaded with peaches and baskets of freshly picked peaches on the ground. They turned onto a dirt side road at the sign that read, "Peach-Eze Bed-and-Breakfast, No TV, No Internet, No Distractions."

Nico came to a screeching stop at the house with a cloud of dust and ran inside. "Annie, look who came by to see us!" he said excitedly.

Annie followed him out of the house, expecting to see a contingent of French police. "Cédric? No way," she said, running to embrace him as he was getting out of his truck. "Wow! What a surprise. I can't believe you are here." She took notice of Cédric's black pickup. "I love your vehicle. Is it a rental?"

"No. It's mine," said Cédric. "I bought it in Buffalo."

Nico added, “He was passing through on his way to California. No one is scheduled for the guest apartment. Perhaps we can convince him to spend some time with us.”

“Did you come all this way to help us pick peaches?” Annie asked jokingly. “Come inside. I just took a peach cobbler out of the oven I made for the church bake sale, but I’m sure they won’t miss it.”

“So, what’s up with this Nick and Annie Smith thing?” Cédric asked as they entered the kitchen

“Smith is my maiden name,” Annie replied. “My mom and dad had this place up for sale when we fled from France, and they sold it to us so they could retire to Arizona.”

Nico added, “Annie is still a US citizen, so I am here more or less legally, but Nick is my cover. I don’t think anyone knows we exist other than as the Smiths, and the locals seem willing to protect our anonymity.”

“We are completely off the grid,” said Annie. “We don’t use cell phones. The only connection with the outside world is an old-fashioned telephone landline. That’s the only way people interested in booking the apartment can contact us.”

“We generate all of our electricity from solar panels and a wind turbine,” added Nico.

Annie prepared three portions of hot peach cobbler with a scoop of vanilla ice cream and joined Cédric and Nico at the table. “What were you doing in New York?” Nico asked.

“Running away,” replied Cédric nonchalantly.

"From what?" asked Annie.

"Oh, that would take me back into a dark place," replied Cédric. "Do we really need to go into it?"

"Only if you want," Nico replied. "We are simply eager to catch up with what has been going on in your life."

"No, it's okay," said Cédric. "I will explain. I guess I was just running away from everything—from Paris, from France, from life. I was just trying to stay one step ahead of the depression that was beginning to overwhelm me. After I reproduced my light speed results in my laboratory in Montmélian, I shared my dark matter ideas with some friends at the abbey there. I had finally gotten up the courage to revise my manuscript on dark matter along with my newest test data and submit it to a leading physics journal. The guys at the abbey liked my ideas and encouraged me to do it. I don't know what I was thinking. I had such high expectations, but the paper was rejected. One of the reviewers even suggested that I would have more success if I had proposed that the moon was made of cream cheese. I was devastated, and I needed to get out of France. I needed to go somewhere—anywhere. I caught a cruise ship from Le Havre to Montreal, thinking this would give me a chance to get my head back on straight. I should have let the matter drop and simply enjoy the cruise, which was fantastic, by the way." He took a bite of the cobbler. "Annie, you are such an incredible cook."

"Stick around," Annie said, "and I will fatten you up in no time."

"But I couldn't let it drop," continued Cédric. "The anger and sadness over Candlebridge, my father's murder, and the manuscript rejection stalked me. I couldn't escape it, and I entered a death spiral of despair and depression. I started spending time in the only safe place I have ever known, the library. There was a good one on the cruise ship that I had pretty much to myself. I think all the other passengers were in the casino. I began researching some aspects of light speed and dark matter when I came across a patent by none other than the notorious Professor Hendriksen, the very man who destroyed my life."

Annie and Nico sat quietly while Cédric finished his cobbler and stood up to put his plate in the sink. "More cobbler, dear?" asked Annie.

"No thanks," replied Cédric, sitting back down. "I guess you might like to know what I found in that patent application. Hendriksen had plagiarized one of my unpublished manuscripts and filed the patent using some of my very own ideas. That's when I tripped out of sync. I went to the pool bar and began downing rum punches until I was nearly unconscious. It didn't help. When I got sober, I was still angry and depressed, compounded by a pounding headache. I was in such a rage that I had my father's lawyer in Paris arrange for a consult with an intellectual property firm in Montreal, where I was basically told I had no case and that I should just go live large on my inherited wealth. I ended up in Buffalo, New York, bought that cool black truck out front, and decided to follow that lawyer's advice. I had no plans, no place I had to be, and no spending limit. All I had was a post office box number in Palisade, Colorado. So, here I am."

"We are sure glad you are here," said Annie tenderly, "and perhaps you will stay with us for a while."

"I want to tell you about an interesting encounter I had while I was in Montreal," said Cédric. "Have either of you ever heard of a professional hockey player named Jacques Terrenoire?"

"You mean from the Montreal Canadiens?" asked Nico. "Of course. He scored a hat trick in the Stanley Cup finals. I heard he was just traded to the Colorado Avalanche with the largest signing bonus of all time."

Cédric said, "It turns out that he was staying in the same hotel as me in Montreal. There was a big celebration for him. I got a glimpse of him addressing the throngs of cheering fans. I got to see firsthand, and with considerable envy, what it looks like to be famous and adored. The next day, I spotted him sitting alone in the hotel lounge. I asked him where all his fans had gone. He told me that after he had announced that he was leaving Montreal for another team, they felt betrayed, and all moved on to adore the next sports superstar. I have to say I never thought it was possible for fame to be so fickle. We started talking. I invited him to dinner, and he accepted. We slipped out of the hotel undetected and found a quiet, out-of-the-way French restaurant nearby. I think it meant something to him that I had never heard of him. He said it was the first time in years that he was able to be someone other than a sports celebrity. Here we were, two guys barely thirty years old, with more money than either of us knew what to do with, sharing fine cuisine and a bottle of fine French Bordeaux wine, telling life stories, and making small talk. He told me that, at best, he might have five to ten more years as a hockey player, and he had no idea what he would do after that. Both of us faced uncertain futures, and for that moment, it didn't matter. It was as if the past and the future just got swallowed up by the present."

Annie got up from the table to put the dishes in the dishwasher. "Are you going to stay in touch with him?" she asked.

"Probably not," replied Cédric. "I think our encounter was simply a signpost for both of us."

"So, how was my peach cobbler?" she asked.

"Fabulous," replied Cédric and Nico at the same time.

"Good. I have a special treat to wash it down," Annie said, placing three shot glasses on the table and filling them with an orange-colored liquid. "You are my guinea pigs. I have been experimenting with a new recipe for peach cordial. I call it Peach-Eze Delight."

"I think you got it right this time," said Nico after the first taste. "I think the vermouth makes all the difference in the world."

"What's in it?" asked Cédric.

Annie replied, "Fresh peaches from the juicer, heaps of raw cane sugar, vodka from the liquor store, and, as Nico mentioned, some vermouth."

"Why don't you make your own alcohol from fermented peaches?" asked Cédric.

Nico replied, "This is our first year with the orchard, and we are considering test-marketing the cordial to have something to sell throughout the year. There is a microbrewery in town that has gone out of business, and their equipment is to be auctioned off. I am considering making a bid for one of the five-hundred-gallon fermenters, but I have no experience with this kind of thing, and Annie thinks the project is too ambitious."

"Perhaps I can help," replied Cédric.

Nico stood up from the table and said, "Well, the time has come to go pick some peaches."

"That's backbreaking work, Nico," Annie said with a giggle. "Cédric just got here, and he's not used to such hard labor."

"Don't worry, Annie. I will break him in gradually," Nico said as he went out the door with Cédric following. "You will earn twenty-five dollars per bushel."

"I will get Cédric's room ready," said Annie. "And the hot tub. He will need it."

Nico turned to Cédric as they walked together past the first row of trees and asked, "Do you know what ripe peaches smell like?"

"You mean the ones when you bite into them, the juice runs down your forearm?" replied Cédric.

"Well, yes," said Nico. "That's ripe all right, but if you wait until they are that ripe before picking, they will be rotten by the time they get to market. Picking at the right time is a skill that takes years to acquire."

"So, tell me, Nico, how did you learn so quickly how to grow peaches?"

Nico didn't answer right away. The trees in the orchard were full of the bright orange fruit. He turned and headed up one of the paths between the rows of evenly spaced trees in the orchard and stopped at a machine with a robotic arm that was busily carrying out some tasks. Nico turned around to face Cédric and said, "People don't pick peaches anymore. Robots do it. Watch the arm. At the end is an optical sensor that spots a peach and measures its size and looks it over for defects. If it seems to be a good candidate, it approaches it and samples the smell. A perfect peach gives off a characteristic odor. If the computer determines that the peach is already ripe, it is placed in one crate for immediate sale. If it is just right, it goes into another crate, and if it isn't ripe enough, the robot records its exact location and leaves it alone."

"So, I guess you won't be paying me twenty-five dollars per bushel to pick them then," Cédric said with a laugh.

"Sorry, Cédric. The robots work around the clock, and the crates are loaded onto autonomous collection wagons that take the fruit to the barn. Neither of us is needed anymore. We are superfluous." Nico tested the firmness of several of the larger peaches on a low branch and selected one, handing it to Cédric. "But you can't beat a handpicked peach for pure eating pleasure," he said. "Enjoying the taste of a fresh peach is something a robot will never be able to do."

The challenge of building a still had captured Cédric's imagination. He and Nico visited the defunct microbrewery in town to assess the scope of the task. Then they went to the hardware and lumber supply store to get some idea of tools and fittings they could obtain locally. The cellular telephone coverage at Peach-Eze was poor, but Cédric had figured out that if he parked his truck close to the side of the guesthouse, he could access the internet from his computer in the bedroom through the satellite downlink in the truck. Thus began his quest to learn everything he could about biochemistry and fermentation. He had always admired the great inventors like Leonardo DaVinci who could broaden their intellectual pursuits without limits. All the modern scientists that Cédric knew had become so specialized that they knew almost everything about an ever-narrowing field and practically nothing about things outside their field of expertise. He was not afraid to roll up his sleeves and learn new things. This was one of the only positive consequences of his research at Candlebridge. Since he had received no support whatsoever from the university, it had forced him to learn to do a lot of things himself and explore new fields that other graduate students never got the opportunity to pursue.

One of the immediate challenges of distilling ethanol from a broth of fermented peaches was that it required a lot of heat. Traditionally, this heat would have been provided by burning wood, but Nico insisted on using an electric heater. The problem was that the electric power required would exceed the supply of available electricity from the solar panels and wind turbine during the winter months. Either Nico needed to install more panels or Cédric needed to come up with a way to do the job with less heat. He initially considered vacuum distillation, but the technique was deemed too costly and too complex for a simple barn operation. Cédric was wandering up and down the aisles of the hardware and appliance store, looking for ideas, when his eyes fell upon a device for heating water instantly right at the kitchen sink. The thought had occurred to him in a flash of insight that it was only necessary to boil a small stream of the fermented liquid and not the entire vat all at once. He purchased the unit and set up a small laboratory in the barn to see if the idea was feasible. He modified the thermostat on the water heater to make steam, and for the test feedstock, he just used beer. The cleverest innovation of all was that he forced the steam jet consisting of water and alcohol through a venturi to bring it to supersonic velocity at the outlet. He reasoned that ethanol, being heavier, would drop down into the condenser, while the water would continue by inertia into a collection tank and heat exchanger. The idea was a triumph. Cédric was able to double the volume fraction of alcohol in water with each pass of the liquid through the heater, using far less electric power than used by a traditional still. By the end of November, he had scaled the system to the five-hundred-gallon fermenter purchased from the microbrewery and was making eighty–proof vodka from all the reject peaches that previously had gone into the compost pile. Annie's Peach-Eze Delight, made with their own peach vodka, was an overnight sensation. Orders started coming into the liquor store in town that handled the distribution, and production of the magnificent cordial could not keep up with the demand.

From constructing the steam engine at his Chandellepont machine shop in Val d'Isère, Cédric had gained valuable experience in handling steam at high pressure. He continued making steady refinements to the vodka still with plumbing supplies available from the local hardware store, but it had become evident that he had reached the limit of pressure that the common household fittings he was using could handle. He had contracted for some custom fitting to be fabricated at a machine shop in Grand Junction. One Friday afternoon, he went to check up on the progress of his parts. The shop had closed early. It was hunting season, and businesses often closed without warning in that part of the country. He decided to drop in at Tipsy's Tavern for a beer on his way back to his guest apartment at Peach-Eze. One beer led to two. And then a cheeseburger and fries and a third beer and a fourth. That's when a fantastic country western band from Texas took the stage, and a cowgirl grabbed his hand and started teaching him how to line dance. It was more fun than Cédric had had, maybe in his entire life.

It was after midnight when the squad car pulled into the driveway of Nico's and Annie's place. The officer rang the doorbell. The porch light came on, and Annie stood at the open door in her bathrobe.

"What's up, Arny?" she asked.

"Sorry to bother you at this hour, Annie," he said. "There is a guy in the back of my cruiser that says he is staying here."

"Oh, no. Cédric!" she exclaimed. "What did he do?"

The officer went back to the car to let Cédric stumble out. "It seems he was trying to drive here from Tipsy's. I found him stuck in a ditch, slumped over the wheel, and passed out."

Annie ran to Cédric to help him into the house. "He is very drunk," said the officer. "He seems like a nice guy. There's no point in having him spend the night in a jail cell. I will release him into your custody if you promise to bring him into the station on Monday for his arrest summons."

"Of course," said Annie. Nico had appeared by that time to help get Cédric up the stairs to his bedroom.

"Will you be bringing one of your famous peach cobblers to the bake sale at church tomorrow?" the officer asked. "I need to know how early to show up to be first in line."

Annie ran into the house and came out with a pie pan covered in aluminum foil. Handing it to him, she said, “Thanks, Arny, for bringing Cédric home. We probably won’t make it to church tomorrow but enjoy the cobbler.”

Chapter 15: Going Home

Annie and Cédric sat next to each other quietly at the table in the interrogation room at the police station in Grand Junction. The inspector entered and sat down across from them. Without looking up, placing a file on the table in front of him, he said, "Mr. Rothschild, may I see your driver's license and passport, please?"

"I only had a few beers," Cédric said defensively. Annie patted his hand on the table to indicate for him to be silent.

The inspector removed a sheet of paper from the file and looked up at Cédric. Passing the paper over to him across the table, he said, "This is the bar tab that you apparently forgot to pay before leaving Tipsy's Tavern. It says you owe them for nine draft beers and four Manhattans." He paused to let the news sink in, then said, "That's not exactly what I would call a few beers."

"Some of those were for the cowgirl I met," Cédric replied.

Annie said, "Hi. I'm Annie Smith. We operate the Peach-Eze bed-and-breakfast in Palisade, and Cédric is staying with us. I have known him practically his whole life."

The inspector thumbed through the pages in the file and studied Cédric's driver's license and passport. "There is no stamp indicating when you entered the United States," he said.

"No one asked for my passport when I crossed the border into the US," replied Cédric. "But it was just a couple of days after I entered Canada. There should be a stamp when I disembarked from the cruise ship in Montreal."

The investigator slowly flipped through the mostly blank pages of the passport. "So, this is your first time in the United States?"

"Yes, sir," replied Cédric.

The investigator was jotting down some notes. "I see that you entered Canada on August 12 then. Is that correct?"

"That sounds about right," replied Cédric.

The inspector asked, "Are you aware that you have exceeded the time permitted in the country on a tourist visa?"

Cédric made no reply as the investigator continued to dig into his file.

"It looks like you got a speeding ticket in Nebraska for going twenty-five miles an hour over the speed limit," the investigator said, not expecting any response. "On top of that violation, you now have earned a citation for driving while impaired. Combined, I would need to revoke your driving privileges. Do you understand this?"

"Yes, sir," replied Cédric.

The inspector continued, "Are you aware that the temporary tags on your vehicle have expired?"

"I have the title," replied Cédric.

"That's good to know," responded the investigator. "At least I won't need to add vehicle theft to the list of offenses. Did you know you needed to register the vehicle in the state of Colorado?"

"No, sir," replied Cédric.

"And apparently you didn't bother to insure the vehicle," added the investigator. "Your truck has been towed to the impound lot. You will need to remedy these matters before you can retrieve it."

"Yes, sir," replied Cédric.

The inspector looked at Annie and said, "Mrs. Smith, Mr. Rothschild cannot legally drive in this state. I would revoke his license if I had any clue how to process a French driver's license. Anyway, Mr. Rothschild is in the country illegally. He needs to return home to France before he is deported. I suggest that he assign responsibility for the vehicle to you, and then we could release it into your care. Otherwise, the truck becomes the property of the state and will go up for auction."

Cédric let out a long exhale, then looked over at Annie in panic for advice.

The inspector leaned back in his chair and looked intently at Cédric, saying, "I am going to recommend a sixteen-hundred-dollar fine, and given that no one was injured and that this is your first offense, if you promise to leave the United States within one week, I will waive the court summons. The only outcome would be expulsion anyway. We can't really incarcerate a foreign national for misdemeanors. Stay here while I have them draft the paperwork for your signature." The investigator stood to depart. He stopped in the doorway and turned around. "Don't forget to settle your bill with Tipsy's."

Nico and Annie were seated at the kitchen table when Cédric entered. "I booked my return trip to France," he said. "How can I print out the itinerary to show to the police?"

Nico replied, "You should be able to airdrop the document onto my office computer. It should show up on your portable as 'Peach-Eze-One'"

"It is beyond me how in the world you get by without Wi-Fi," commented Cédric.

"It is challenging," said Nico. "As soon as the heat dies down from the French court, we will probably cave in and install internet."

"How will I be able to stay in touch with you when I get back to France?" asked Cédric.

Nico and Annie exchanged a puzzled look. "Call us on the landline," replied Nico, "but just don't ask for Nicolas or Annie Delquoi. There's no one here by that name. Remember, it's Nick and Annie Smith."

Cédric poured himself a cup of coffee and sat down at the table. Clearing his throat, he said, "Annie. Do you think I have a drinking problem?"

"Well, I am concerned about your binge drinking," she replied.

"That last one was pretty bad, wasn't it?" Cédric paused, then said, "I have been reflecting a lot about my life these past months. You allowed me to be withdrawn and didn't push too hard to draw me out. I have enjoyed attending church with you, and it has had a bigger effect on me than you are probably aware." He drank his coffee slowly while Nico and Annie sat quietly. "It's just that my bitterness toward Hendriksen stalks me relentlessly and sometimes overwhelms me. When I drink, it subsides, and after a few beers, it goes away completely. This last time at Tipsy's and the trouble it caused brought me to a point where I know I need to get control of my anger or it will kill me. Annie, you said once that harboring bitterness is like drinking poison and waiting for the other person to die. You remember the book *Mere Christianity* that you recommended? I read it carefully as far as chapter seven. You might even say that I studied it carefully. C. S. Lewis has a way of speaking directly into my heart. The problem was that when I got to chapter seven on forgiveness, I couldn't go on. Forgiving Hendriksen was simply something I was unwilling to do. Since my episode at Tipsy's last Friday night, I picked up the book again and continued reading, beginning at chapter seven. It's hard to explain, but his words ground me up into fine powder and left me powerless to demand self-justification. I guess I finally reached the bottom, and the time has come to get over it. In time, I may be able to forgive Hendriksen, but that will be in God's time, not my own."

The three sat quietly sipping coffee. Then Cédric said, "I think I am now ready to return home. I am done running away." Annie smiled in such a way that he knew she was in agreement and that it was the right decision. "I had some ideas from constructing the ethanol still that I am eager to work on in my shop in Montmélian." Cédric turned to Nico and asked, "Do you have the title to my truck handy?"

"It's in my office," Nico replied. "I needed it to get your truck out of impound. Wait here. I will go get it."

"You know, Annie," Cédric said while Nico was out of the kitchen, "you always reminded me that I was impetuous and impossible to control."

Annie said, "That's true. The moment our eyes met when you were just two years old, you had a scowl that said, 'Good luck keeping me in line.' But I sense you have changed."

Nico came back into the kitchen and handed the title to Cédric, who grabbed a pen from the counter and signed his signature in the seller's block.

"What are you doing?" asked Nico.

"I am signing the truck over to you," he replied. "I don't need it anymore. It's almost winter, and you and Annie need a reliable vehicle beyond your Harley. Anyway, your car is older than me, and I would prefer that you take me to the airport tomorrow morning in the truck."

Cédric stopped in to see his mom on the way home. He bought a dozen red roses and approached the reception desk at the nursing home in the outskirts of Lyon.

"Hello. I am Cédric. I am here to see my mother, Madame Rothschild."

The receptionist quickly disappeared and returned shortly with a nurse. “Hello, Mr. Rothschild. We have been trying to contact you for quite some time. I am sorry to tell you that your mother passed away about a month ago.”

The news did not come to him as a shock. He responded, “I have been out of the country for several months, and I haven’t been very diligent about checking my messages. Will you please give these roses to someone who might appreciate them?” He turned and walked out of the nursing home, dazed. He had anticipated the inevitable news, which did not make him sad. A season of his life had finally come to an end, and a new one was about to begin. Perhaps the sadness of becoming an orphan would come later.

Chapter 16: Houseguests

Cédric took a taxi from the train station in Montmélian to his villa. Even though it was a short walk up the hill, he had several bags, and there was the potential for some light drizzle. He was hoping that the key to the front door was still in the secret place where he had left it for Brother Andrew to check up on the property from time to time while he was away. As the taxi entered the courtyard, chickens and goats scattered in all directions. A group of children were playing football. Cédric hopped out of the cab and shouted in loud French, "*Qu'est ce qu'il se passe ici?*"

The startled children stopped in their tracks and turned. One of them ran into the workshop where the double doors were wide open and came back out holding the hand of a man wearing a work apron and pushing safety goggles up onto his forehead.

"What's going on here?" Cédric repeated in English.

The man approached him and extended his hand with a warm greeting. "Welcome! You must be Cédric. I'm Oskar. We were not expecting you so soon. Brother Andrew said you were in America and did not know when you would return."

Cédric looked around the courtyard in astonishment while the taxi driver placed his bags next to the front door and stood waiting to receive his fare and tip. "What is this all about?" Cédric asked.

"Didn't Brother Andrew explain this in his messages?" Oskar replied. "We are refugees from Armenia. Brother Andrew was gracious enough to put us up here." Seeing Cédric's bewildered expression, he said, "Surely you knew this?"

Cédric continued to look around the courtyard of his villa in puzzled astonishment at the unexpected scene teaming with the exuberant children and farm animals. "Actually, I have not checked my emails for several weeks. You say Brother Andrew put you up here?"

"Yes," replied Oskar. "The tall boy over there is my son. Some of the others belong to my sister and niece. Come inside. I want you to meet my wife."

A woman appeared at the side door to see what all the excitement was about. "Miriam, this is Cédric!" Oskar said.

"Cédric? Oh my," she exclaimed, running over to wrap her arms around his waist. "Thank you! Thank you! Thank you!" she repeated, beginning to sob.

Cédric reached in his pocket and handed Oskar a twenty-euro bill. "Would you mind giving this to the cab driver?" His bags had already disappeared into the house.

Oskar returned and signaled for the children to get on with their game in a language Cédric did not recognize. Oskar said to Cédric, "Most of them speak some English but practically no French. My niece, Noni, has placed your bags upstairs in your bedroom suite, along with the boxes that arrived from Paris. She will make up your bed with fresh linens if that's okay with you."

"What were you doing in the workshop?" Cédric asked.

"Come see," replied Oskar, turning to lead the way.

"Dinner will be served in ten minutes," said Miriam, releasing Cédric from her embrace.

As they entered the workshop, it seemed much brighter than Cédric had remembered. The air was pungent with the smell of sawdust. Piles of unfinished wood planks were on drying racks in the back. A young man operating a table saw switched it off. "That's my eldest son, Johann," Oskar said proudly.

"What's going on here?" Cédric asked, looking around the spacious workshop and noticing several pieces of woodworking equipment, his light speed experiment carefully wrapped in plastic and stored near the back.

"We are making furniture," Oskar replied. "This is what we did in Armenia before we were forced to flee. I owned a small furniture-manufacturing company there. I hope you don't mind that we took over your workshop. We were very careful not to disturb any of your things. As you see, we wrapped your instruments in plastic."

Looking around in astonishment, Cédric said, "Don't worry about my light speed experiment. That work is obsolete now. You say you are making furniture?"

"And other things," replied Oskar. "We turned your garage into a bunkroom. I hope that's okay. Brother Andrew said you don't own a car."

"But there is no plumbing or electricity in there," Cédric commented.

"We took care of that," said Oskar with a smile. "Would you like to see?"

Cédric and Oskar walked into the adjacent building. Bunkbeds in two rows stacked three high could sleep six boys. A second room for girls was similarly equipped. A large, brightly lit bathroom was filled with children from the football game cleaning up for dinner.

"Who are all these kids?" asked Cédric.

Oskar replied, "Family and children of friends. Some were orphaned when their parents were murdered by the Islamist militants that swept into our city." Oskar pointed out a little girl barely able to reach the sink. "That's Julia. Her father and mother were missionaries. She is the only survivor from her family. My niece, Noni, brought her out. Noni's father is back in the country rescuing as many of the surviving children as possible, but we have not heard from him in a couple of weeks, and now we fear the worst." He let out a sigh of deep sadness, then said, "No one thought it was possible that the genocide that took place in Armenia over a hundred years ago could ever happen again. The Christian community in our country goes back to the first century, and animosity has been directed at our people ever since. The entire world sat by and just let it happen again." He turned to walk out, heading across the courtyard to dinner.

Cédric followed. "What do you mean, 'They just did nothing'? The UN Security Council in Geneva is discussing what action to take right now."

Oskar stopped and turned around to stare at Cédric. He cocked his head sideways and rolled his eyes. Then he turned and headed back toward the house without further comment.

Twenty minutes earlier, Cédric had arrived at his villa expecting it to be dark and lonely. He had thought he would spend some days or weeks trying to figure out what he was going to do with the rest of his life, only to discover that his friends at l'Abbaye Montmélian had turned his home into a shelter for Christian refugees. After he got over the initial shock, it began to sink in that this was the new beginning he had been longing for all along, and now he knew for certain why he had purchased the estate that was ten times too big for him.

Two large, round tables filled the grand salon, with a dozen hungry children piled into the surrounding chairs. A turntable filled with bowls of food in the middle of each table swiveled back and forth in a tug-of-war as each child tried to position their favorite dish in front of them so they could serve themselves. The bowls were emptied as quickly as new ones were brought out of the kitchen.

The minute Oskar entered the room, the chatter ceased, and everyone joined hands for the dinner blessing. Oskar bowed his head and spoke reverently in their native tongue, and then the enthusiastic banter resumed immediately.

Cédric looked around mesmerized at the grand salon that had been transformed into a mess hall. Noni came up to him and invited him to sit at the table with the adults. Another woman approached him and said, “Hi. I am Oskar’s sister, Naomi. If you are wondering what happened to all your furniture, it is safely stored away. And don’t worry. No one is allowed upstairs, and you will find your bedroom just as you left it. Come have some dinner.”

“More coffee?” Naomi asked Cédric as Noni cleared the dinner plates.

“No thank you,” he replied. “It has been a long day, and I am still pretty jet lagged. I think I will turn in.”

“See you in the morning then,” said Oskar. “I want to show you the new cistern we are building to hold water from the spring to augment the supply. It seems the children are enjoying long, hot showers a bit too much.”

Cédric was awakened the following morning by the blast of the horn coming from a truck entering the courtyard. He peeked out of the bedroom window to see Brother Andrew and Brother Sylvestre greeting the children who were swarming around the truck. He looked at his watch to see that it was already nine. He had slept for nearly twelve hours.

It was a beautiful, sunny morning, and the air was crisp when Cédric exited the house. The brothers and Oskar were busy unloading crates of produce and supplies from the truck. Brother Sylvestre handed Oskar a wad of cash and said, “The Fontaines love the coffee table. Here is the six hundred and fifty euros they owe you for it.”

"But the price was only four hundred seventy-five," responded Oskar.

Brother Sylvestre just shrugged his shoulders and continued with the unloading. Then he said to Oskar in a low voice, "I heard this morning that they blew up the Sevan Monastery."

"No!" gasped Oskar, nearly collapsing. "That monastery goes back to the ninth century."

"Apparently they are levelling the site to build a mosque," Brother Sylvestre added in disgust.

Upon seeing Cédric emerge from the house, Brother Andrew said, "Cédric! You're back." The two greeted with a hug. "The last message I got from you was that you planned to drive the Transamerica Highway all the way to the southern tip of South America."

"I only made it as far as Colorado," said Cédric.

"Oskar says you never saw my messages to you that we had turned your place into a halfway house," said Brother Andrew.

Cédric replied, "Frankly, until about a week ago, I wasn't planning to come back to France anytime soon, so I quit reading my messages."

"So, what made you change your mind?" asked Brother Andrew.

"The United States Immigration Service," Cédric replied. "They kicked me out of the country.

“Well, it must have come as quite a shock to come home to this,” said Brother Andrew. “I’m sorry.”

“You mean you are sorry that you turned my place into a refugee camp while I was gone?” said Cédric jokingly.

Brother Andrew replied, “Don’t worry. We are working on procuring another facility in Montmélian for the flood of refugees. But we were desperate, and this was the only place we could come up with at the time.”

“No. They all must stay. There is no need to evict any of them,” said Cédric. “Once I got over the surprise, I realized that there is no better place on earth than Villa Chandellepont for such a mission. I’m all in.”

Brother Andrew reached behind the driver’s seat of the truck and retrieved a soft carrying case. “I brought you a present,” he said, handing it to Cédric. There was a faint, pathetic meow coming from inside.

Cédric pulled back the cover to see a light tan kitten.

“She’s just a couple of months old,” said Brother Andrew.

“I don’t know anything about cats,” protested Cédric. “What’s its name?” he asked.

“Her name,” corrected Brother Andrew. “And how should I know? Naming the kitten is your job.” He went to the back of the truck and pulled out a bag of kitty litter and some cans of food. “Come. We can set up her new home in your closet upstairs. She will adjust in no time.” Brother Andrew was through the front door before Cédric realized he was supposed to follow.

The little blonde girl named Julia who Oskar had pointed out the day before had been watching intently. “Mr. Cédric,” she said, “may I come see your new kitten?”

“Certainly,” he replied. “Come with me.” He took her by the hand and led her into the house. “Where did you learn to speak such good English?” he asked.

“Oh, I am an American,” she replied. “My parents were Christian missionaries. We came from Boston. I used to have a kitten named Sally, but we had to take her to the animal shelter before we came over to Armenia.”

Chapter 17: Julia

Cédric had settled into a comfortable routine by the end of the year, which consisted of teaching the children French in the morning and studying by himself in the afternoon. The household was maintained by Miriam, with help from Noni so that he did not need to do any cooking or cleaning—things he detested anyway. Miriam's sister, Naomi, had returned to Armenia to join her husband. It had turned out that he was alive and well, working underground with a covert paramilitary group that was arranging safe passage out of the country for the countless at-risk Armenians left behind. A heavy snowfall the week before Christmas had nearly paralyzed the region, but the brothers managed to deliver plenty of food and supplies of warm winter clothing to Villa Chandellepont that had been donated by the Montmélian community eager to help in any way they could. On one occasion, they dropped off several sleds, which the children put to good use on the surrounding hillsides. As quickly as children could be placed in homes and orphanages around Western Europe, new ones would arrive from the regions of Central Asia overrun by the spreading Islamic insurgency that the West seemed powerless to stop.

Cédric's cat was no longer a kitten, and she roamed freely throughout the compound, generally with Julia in close pursuit. It had seemed odd to Cédric that other than Oskar's two sons, Julia was the only child left from the original group who had not yet been resettled. One morning at breakfast when he was sitting alone with Oskar, he asked, "What is Julia's story? Why is she still here?"

Oskar placed his elbows on the table and folded his hands in front of his face. Letting out a long sigh, he replied, "I'm afraid Julia is a very difficult case. She's an American, you know. We have been trying to get the embassy to issue her a passport, but she has no documentation proving her identity. Both of her parents are dead, and apparently her closest living relative is a paternal grandfather who denies her existence."

"That's absurd!" exclaimed Cédric. "How can that be?"

Oskar continued, "Julia's father, Walter, was an American, but her mother was Armenian. She had been attending university in the Boston area when she became pregnant with Julia. No one knows who her biological father is. Presumably Julia got her blonde hair and blue eyes from him. Walter was working at a crisis pregnancy center in Boston when he met Julia's mother. As the story goes, he talked her out of getting an abortion and then married her. I guess Walter's father was some sort of bigwig in Boston, and the marriage created quite a scandal. The estrangement from his father was not helped by their announcement that he would be going to Armenia as a Christian missionary."

"Why didn't they flee when the insurgency began?" asked Cédric.

"Of course, that's what we did," replied Oskar. "Miriam and I grabbed the boys, hopped in the car, and headed west while the roads were still open. We tried to convince Walter to do the same, but he was not about to abandon his friends who had no means of escape. He piled as many of them as possible into his own van and sent them off."

"And Julia?" asked Cédric.

Oskar replied, "After her parents were carted off, Noni snuck into the house and found her hiding in a closet."

"She must have been completely traumatized," said Cédric.

"You would think so," replied Oskar, "but God in his great mercy seems to have wiped clean any memories of the event. Perhaps the memories will come back one day, but she is as carefree as any seven-year-old could possibly be—as if none of this ever happened."

"Does she know her parents are dead?" asked Cédric.

"I don't know," answered Oskar. "Miriam and I don't bring it up."

At that moment, the cat bounded through the kitchen. Julia, out of breath, was calling after her. "Sassy, it's time for breakfast."

Julia stopped in front of the breakfast table and put her hands on her hips with a look of irritation. Huffing, she said, "Sassy just won't listen to me this morning."

Cédric's eyes puddled with tears. "So you call her Sassy?" he asked.

“Well,” Julia replied authoritatively, “that’s her nickname. Sassafras just takes too long to say. Then she went along in search of her cat.

When she was gone, Cédric asked, “What will happen to her now?”

“She’s an orphan,” Oskar replied. “She is such a special child. Miriam and I can’t bear the thought of sending her off to an orphanage.” The two sat quietly at the breakfast table, sipping the last of their coffees. Finally, Oskar stood up and said, “We have a Christmas present for you. Come with me upstairs.”

Oskar asked Cédric to wait outside the door of the spare bedroom that Cédric had been using as a storeroom for all his stuff packed away in boxes that he had hoped to get around to unpacking one day. Oskar slipped inside to confirm that Johann had everything ready for the surprise. Then he signaled for Cédric to come in. Johann was grinning from ear to ear from behind a huge desk. “Voila! Solid walnut,” he said, waving his hand over the beautiful piece of furniture.

Oskar said, “Johann made this himself, and also that credenza.” He pointed to the matching piece behind it against the side wall. “He also made all those shelves for your new bookcase.”

“Bookcase?” Cédric said, barely able to get the word out. All his books had been neatly placed on the shelves of the bookcase built into the wall.

“Your new study!” exclaimed Oskar.

Cédric looked around the room in complete astonishment at every detail. Everything was perfect. A wood fire radiated warmth from a Franklin stove, with a recliner and reading lamp positioned in front of it. "How in the world did you do all this renovation without me ever finding out?" he asked.

"Believe me," said Oskar. "It wasn't easy. Merry Christmas."

By the spring, Oskar's furniture business had outgrown Cédric's workshop, and he had relocated it to a vacant warehouse in town, which was big enough to include a showroom. Oskar, Miriam, and their two sons moved out into an apartment close to their factory. With their departure from Chandellepont, their room was turned into a nursery. Naomi and her husband, David, had somehow managed to sneak out of Armenia with a busload of children—many of them infants. David had reported that the brutality of the insurgents was unimaginable. They would typically execute the adults and leave the children behind to starve to death. Their intention was to use the chaos of the humanitarian crisis as cover for their political activities. David had been traveling back and forth to Geneva to report to the United Nations on the conditions in his country.

Meanwhile, Cédric had rekindled his interest in nuclear reactions, and in particular, transmutations. He had theorized that the half-life of radioactive decay was proportional to the local speed of light. By slowing light down, this would give reactions more time to take place. This was also the premise of the idea that Hendriksen had stolen from him for his patent, but the sting of that injustice had faded away, and the writings of C. S. Lewis on forgiveness had been massaged into his soul. One piece of equipment he knew he would need to prove his hypothesis was a mass spectrometer so he could quantify the amount of the various isotopes in his specimen. After looking everywhere to purchase such an instrument, he finally reached the conclusion that one was not available to his specifications, and he would have to build his own from scratch. With the furniture manufacturing now gone, he was able to turn his workshop into a first-class machine shop and laboratory.

Julia would typically sit on a chair in the workshop with Sassy on her lap while Cédric was working, doing the French homework he had assigned to her or reading to him out loud from one of the French primers he had given her.

One morning in late April, Cédric heard a delivery truck enter the courtyard and sound its horn. He peaked out the door, assuming it was Brother Andrew, but it turned out to be a postal courier. Cédric walked out to meet the driver.

"I am looking for a Mr. Cédric Rothschild," he said.

"I am he," Cédric replied.

The driver said, "I have a package for you. I need you to sign for it. Can I please see some identification?"

Cédric showed him his driver's license and signed for the package. He opened it carefully, wondering what kind of trouble he might be in this time. Inside was Julia's new US passport. Henri Soufflot had come through again. Cédric had asked him to do whatever it took to expedite the replacement passport. There had been several inquiries of late by the French immigration service about Julia's residency status, and Cédric worried that they would be coming by any day to pick her up for deportation.

Cédric pulled the kitty carrier down from the top shelf of the storage cabinet in the workshop where he had put it in anticipation of just this occasion. He looked at Julia, who was still sitting in the workshop, and asked, "How much do you trust me?"

She had a puzzled look and did not know how to respond.

"Let's put Sassy in her carrier," he said, "and you go to your room to pack some things. We are going to Disneyland."

She let out a delighted whoop.

"But it's a secret," said Cédric, putting his index finger in front of his lips. "Don't tell a soul."

They walked down to the train station in Montmélian and headed to Lyon and then on to Charles de Gaulle Airport to catch the nonstop flight to Los Angeles. "Remember," said Cédric as they stood in line to purchase plane tickets, "if anyone asks, tell them I am your uncle, and we are heading to Disneyland."

"What about Sassy?" asked Julia.

"Oh, for sure she's coming with us," Cédric replied. "We will need to leave her in quarantine with a veterinarian in Los Angeles for a couple of days while we go to Disneyland. That's all."

At the rental car counter in Los Angeles, Cédric hoped and prayed that his driving record from the prior year had never made it to California. One day at Disneyland was enough, and Julia managed to convince Cédric to drive down the coast to Sea World. By the time they returned to Los Angeles, Sassy had been issued a clean bill of health, and the three headed northeast on the interstate.

The following day, Cédric crept up the driveway of the Peach-Eze Bed-and-Breakfast. Annie came out of the kitchen to greet the new customers and nearly collapsed for joy when she saw Cédric get out of the car.

They hugged for a long time. "Why didn't you tell us you were coming?" she asked through sobs.

Nico followed her out of the house. "Who do you have in the car with you?" he asked.

Cédric opened the passenger door, and Julia emerged with Sassy. "This is Julia," he said. "And, Julia," he said, taking her by the hand, "these are my dearest friends in all the earth, Nico, I mean Nick, and Annie Smith."

After exchanging greetings, Cédric asked Annie if she would take Julia inside while he talked privately with Nico. "I need a huge favor," Cédric said when he and Nico were alone. "I need you to take care of Julia for a while."

"You what?" asked Nico.

Cédric replied, "It's sort of complex. I kidnapped Julia in France because they were about to deport her to the United States and turn her over to Social Services and foster care. She is an orphan. Her parents were killed in Armenia. I need your help."

"Kidnapped? Cédric, have you lost your mind?"

"It's just for a little while," replied Cédric. "I promise, she will be no trouble. I just need you and Annie to take care of her until I arrange for the adoption."

"Adoption?" asked Nico. "Who is going to adopt her?"

"I am," replied Cédric.

Nico said, "Cédric, you aren't even married."

"I'm working on that," said Cédric. "I'm desperate, Nico, and you and Annie are the only ones I know to turn to. Julia is precious beyond measure. I love her more than you can fathom. Please help me."

Chapter 18: Sodium

Cédric was seated at the desk in his study at Villa Chandellepont late in the afternoon when he received a request on his computer for a video conference from a website in the United States he did not recognize. He opened it to see Nico's smiling face on the screen.

"Hey, Cédric," Nico began. "I took your advice and had internet installed at Peach-Eze. It seems that your hotshot lawyer in Paris got the French courts to give up the pursuit."

"Hi, Nico," replied Cédric. "That would be Henri Soufflot. He was my father's lawyer, but he seems to know how to do things."

Nico inquired, "How is the wife-hunting thing going?"

"Not so good," said Cédric with a sigh. "The matchmaking agency seems to have concluded that I am an odd fellow. It probably didn't help when I told them I would settle for a marriage of convenience with some cute Russian girl looking to get out of the country." They both chuckled.

"You know, Cédric, it might help your prospects if they had any idea of your net worth."

"I don't want a wife who loves me for my money," replied Cédric sarcastically. "I learned that lesson from Geraldine."

Annie showed up on the video screen at that moment and said, "There is someone here that wants to say hi."

"Hi, Uncle Cédric. I really love it here. Uncle Nick and Aunt Annie are *so* nice." Julia held Sassy up to the camera and waved a paw. "I'm going to start first grade next week."

"First grade!" exclaimed Cédric. "I sure hope you are easier on Annie than I was at your age."

"She's an angel compared to you, Cédric," injected Annie. "I told the elementary school in Palisade that Julia's parents were traveling in France and requested that we enroll her in school while they are gone. That's all it took. Is anyone still looking for her?"

Cédric replied, "The French immigration officials finally showed up to deport her, but Naomi, the woman here who is responsible for all the children, convinced them that Julia had been relocated outside of France. Apparently, this satisfied them, and they went away. The US State Department started making some inquiries, but after the American embassy in Yerevan was overrun and the ambassador and his family taken hostage, they had more urgent matters to attend to. Thankfully, it seems that Julia has dropped off everyone's radar screen."

By the end of that year, the surge of Armenian refugees had slowed to a trickle, and Villa Chandlepont was no longer needed as a halfway house. Once again, Cédric had the place to himself. His role had increasingly become providing financial support for resettlement of refugees. He walked into town almost every day to have fellowship with the brothers and attend evening services at the abbey. Otherwise, his focus had been mostly on his research. He had come to realize that although his light speed measurements were convincing—at least to him—they were still not compelling. He had begun exploring alternative ways to observe the effects of light slowing down in the vicinity of a heavy mass. This led him to a deeper study into the fields of astrophysics, cosmology, and nuclear physics. The latter led him to the hypothesis that radioactive decay rates might depend on the speed of light. If this were the case, then measuring the half-lives of radioactive decay might provide a more sensitive way to observe the slowing down of the speed of light, since the decay rate was determined by an exponential function with orders of magnitude more sensitivity than just trying to measure the transit time of a light pulse directly.

He had completed work on his homemade quadrupole mass spectrometer and directed his attention to constructing a proton beam accelerator. He had discovered early on that using proton beams to transmute isotopes was rather difficult. He had found a source of polyethylene with deuterium instead of ordinary hydrogen in the polyethylene molecules. He began using this material as a target in his reactor. By bombarding the target with his proton beam, he was able to knock out slow neutrons from the deuterium nuclei. By adjusting the proton beam energy, he found that he could produce neutrons with almost any desired energy, and with these neutrons, he could generate a wide range of nuclear isotopes of atoms in the beam path. He tested dozens of substances and finally settled on sodium because he could transmute the stable sodium isotope found in ordinary table salt to a radioactive isotope of magnesium with a half-life of about fifteen hours, which was just about perfect for his measurements. The key was to be able to carry out the experiments in real time. In this way, he could measure with considerable precision any changes in decay rate with, or without, the near proximity of a heavy mass. Whereas before he had used a block of uranium for light speed measurements, he soon discovered that ordinary lead was sufficiently dense for the decay rate experiments.

After several months of painstaking experimentation and repeated cycles of success and failure, Cédric had finally arrived at an experimental technique that could prove his hypothesis convincingly. The biggest challenge was to provide a precisely calibrated supply of gaseous sodium atoms inside the reaction tube within the vacuum chamber. This required several very clever innovations to maintain the exact temperature of the molten sodium crucible, from which the gaseous sodium evaporated. The rate of generation of sodium gas needed to be constant over long periods of time. By precisely measuring the average time required for sodium atoms to transit the reactor tube, he could establish the length of time a given isotope spent inside the reactor. A small amount of the gas from the far end of the reaction tube was continuously sampled and passed to the mass spectrometer, which could clearly differentiate these species from the ordinary sodium, and more importantly, the changes in the fractions of these isotopes could be measured with precision as a function of the residence time the isotope spent in the reactor. Cédric now had a tool for measuring the decay rates over the many hours required for an experimental run after switching off the neutron beam. When he subsequently inserted the reaction tube into a block of lead, he found that the half-life of the magnesium isotope had increased by nearly 10 percent, in approximate agreement with his earlier light speed measurement by time of flight. He knew that the only possible explanation was that the half-life for the decay had to be proportional to the speed of light and that the speed of light had been slowed down by the lead block. It was an exquisitely designed experiment of which Cédric was duly proud. His exuberance was inexpressible. He had finally proven beyond a shadow of

doubt the direct link between the speed of light and mass that he had hypothesized in his dark matter paper. In the ensuing weeks, he repeated the experiment numerous times to be sure the results were consistent within the statistical error of measurement. Then he invited Brother Andrew and Brother Sylvestre to Villa Chandellepont to show off his work.

"Cédric, this is just incredible!" exclaimed Brother Sylvestre when Cédric described the results. "What are you going to do now?" he asked.

Cédric paused for a moment while he contemplated his response and then quietly replied, "Nothing."

Brother Sylvestre exclaimed, “Nothing? What do you mean nothing? You can’t be serious. This is a huge scientific breakthrough. Let me contact some people I know at CERN. They would surely be interested in this.”

“No,” replied Cédric. “I only brought you here to share in my jubilation, not to promote my fame and fortune. I have no need of fortune, and well, fame?” Cédric smiled and said, “I used to be interested in fame. I used to dream of winning a Nobel Prize, but not any longer. My exuberance is not for fame or recognition by others. My joy comes from getting to peek into the inner workings of God’s universe. What does the psalmist say? ‘The heavens declare the glory of God, and the sky above proclaims His handiwork.’ When I look out at the night sky, I can imagine God speaking light into existence and giving birth to galaxies from black holes. Just knowing the Creator is all the glory I need. I don’t need to prove that dark matter is a fantasy. I will let the scientists figure that out when they get around to it. Anyway, what’s the use of theories about galaxy formation? It’s interesting to make speculations about cosmology, but I have the first chapter of the book of Genesis, and that’s all I really need to know.”

“Cédric, you’re not serious!” said Brother Andrew. “Does this mean you are finished with research and your experiments?”

“Oh, absolutely not,” replied Cédric. “Not in the least. This is just the beginning. But I have come to realize that just doing science for the sake of doing science—for fame and fortune, if you will—is not what I am called to do. There is a practical aspect to these discoveries that I intend to pursue, which will be to the betterment of all humankind."

"Are you going to give us a hint?" Brother Sylvestre asked.

Cédric flashed a mischievous grin and said before heading out of the lab, "First I must prove that the moon is not made of cream cheese." He laughed out loud, then said, "After that, I intend to unlock the mystery of deuteron fusion and build a practical microfusion reactor. I think I know how to do it now. All I need is a block of something ten orders of magnitude denser than lead—a cluster of neutrons, perhaps, like you might find at the center of a neutron star."

Cédric had been rearranging the books in his office one evening when the help-wanted ad from NaPiles, which he had used as a bookmark at the beginning of chapter 7 in *Mere Christianity*, fell out onto the floor. This triggered some interest in knowing what might have come of the company in the year since he had seen the ad in the *Grenoble Matin* newspaper. He perused the NaPiles website and searched for articles that might give him insight into the company's progress. There wasn't much except that the proprietor, a Mr. Charles Gilbert, had encountered some unforeseen technical difficulties with his sodium battery that had resulted in a substantial delay. Cédric was able to piece together the story from an issued patent and several referenced patents. The issued patent listed Charles Gilbert as the sole inventor, whereas the earlier patents had been assigned to the automobile battery manufacturer where Gilbert had previously been employed. The patents gave Cédric insight into how Charles's mind worked. The most important stuff in the patents was found not so much in what was said but in what was left unsaid. Cédric knew that good inventors never disclosed enough for someone else to practice the invention without help. It was the stuff between the lines where the trade secrets resided.

The Gilbert patent was quite innovative. Charles had designed his cells around a thin-walled, hollow sphere made of microporous ceramic. The interior was filled with molten sodium, and surface tension kept it from flowing out through the pores. The spheres were pressurized on the inside with argon and sealed with a nickel wire extending out of the side port serving as the positive terminal. The outsides of the spheres were then encapsulated with a coating of sodium ion-conducting polymer to serve as the electrolyte. Finally, the spheres were immersed in a bath of nickel-ionic liquid with a nickel mesh negative electrode. The battery had an open-circuit potential of about 3 volts and the highest energy density of any battery available on the market. The only problem was that it had to be maintained at a temperature of about 120°C to keep the liquid sodium from freezing. This was not an issue as long as the batteries were left on a recharging station because an electric heater was integral to the unit. But if the vehicle happened to be left out in the cold at night or during a car-camping expedition, the battery would be dead by morning.

It was a press interview that had really caught Cédric's attention, however. Mr. Gilbert had discussed the challenges he faced in depth, but he seemed anything but vanquished. He exuded a deep sense of optimism and expressed his view that the time had come for a radical new energy technology. He called it "a neutron star in a bottle." Cédric knew instantly that Charles Gilbert was someone he had to meet.

The following morning, Cédric went into his laboratory to start making the radioactive isotope of sodium, Na-22. He discovered right away that it had been a lot easier to insert a proton into the nucleus of ordinary sodium to make Mg-23 than it was to knock a neutron out to make Na-22. Before long, though, he had dialed in the correct proton beam energy required to knock a neutron out without getting captured itself. In no time, he was generating a few milligrams of the radioactive Na-22 isotope per day and had collected enough for a reasonable demonstration.

He caught the train to Saint-Michel-de-Maurienne to visit NaPiles and meet this curious dreamer who owned the company. He stopped in at the café he had frequented the prior year and spotted the man sitting at a table in the back just as before, poring over his computer and a jumble of papers. Cédric recognized him from the video interview and approached him. "Mr. Gilbert?" he asked.

Charles looked up and peered over his reading glasses at Cédric with some apparent annoyance at the interruption. "Yes," he said gruffly.

Cédric produced the help-wanted ad and passed it to Charles. "I was wondering if you ever filled this position."

"I placed that ad more than a year ago," said Charles. "Yes. I filled it—three times over, in fact. I just fired the last worthless technician a month ago. Nobody knows how to do anything but play video games these days."

Cédric asked, "May I sit?"

Charles pointed to the chair across from him and folded up his laptop. He picked up his cup of lukewarm coffee and stared at Cédric.

Cédric began, "I have been reading as much as I can about NaPiles. It seems that your batteries require some heat to keep the sodium electrode molten."

"Yes, go on," said Charles.

"So," said Cédric, "I guess that you have installed some sort of electric heater inside that is powered by the battery or the recharger. I presume that in cold weather, the batteries self-discharge prematurely, and the sodium freezes."

"You figured that out from my website?" replied Charles. "My bankers don't even know that."

"I just put two and two together to reach that conclusion," said Cédric. He paused and then said, "I think I know how to solve the problem."

"I would be quite interested to hear what you have to say, but I need a refill," Charles said, holding up his coffee mug.

“Let me get it,” Cédric said, hopping up and heading to the bar. “Two coffees please, for that table in the back.”

“Mr. Gilbert likes some cream,” said the barista. “How about you?”

“Black, please,” replied Cédric.

Sitting back down at the table, Cédric said excitedly “As you know, ordinary sodium melts at slightly above the boiling point of water. It has a high heat capacity, and a well-insulated reservoir of it should stay molten for quite some time. Your battery is quite revolutionary in this respect.”

Charles nodded at the compliment but made no reply.

“Some people have tried to use an alloy of sodium and magnesium to lower the melting point but, of course, at the expense of power density.”

“All this I know,” said Charles. “Where are you going with this?”

“Sodium has a radioactive isotope with one less neutron, Na-22, which has a half-life of two and a half years. It isn’t radioactive enough to be particularly dangerous. It decays into neon with a beta particle of intermediate energy that can be stopped with some shielding. The point is that the decay from a small fraction of Na-22 mixed in with the ordinary sodium would probably generate enough heat to keep the reservoir molten indefinitely. You wouldn’t even need the cartridge heater.”

“How in the world do you know all of this?” asked Charles.

"I tinker," replied Cédric, downplaying the implications of the question, and reaching into his coat pocket, he pulled out a metal canister and unscrewed the lid. A sealed vial of silvery molten metal was visible, encased in insulation.

Charles stared at the liquid in wonder as Cédric swirled it around before replacing the lid, saying, "It is a bit radioactive, so it's best not to leave it unshielded for too long. If you hire me, I think I can make this work in your sodium battery."

"What is your name?" Charles asked as the coffees arrived.

"Cédric, sir," he replied.

"Well, Cédric," said Charles, taking a sip of the hot coffee. "I couldn't hire you even I wanted to. I am nearly broke and one step ahead of bankruptcy."

"What if I were willing to work for deferred compensation?" replied Cédric.

"You mean for free?" asked Charles.

"Yes, with one stipulation," replied Cédric with a grin. "As soon as we get your sodium battery business back on track, we start building a neutron star in a bottle."

Charles replied with a smile, "In that case, perhaps you would like a tour of my shop just down the street."

Chapter 19: NaPiles

Charles punched in the code to unlock the front door and switched on the lights. It was hot and humid inside the facility. He turned to Cédric upon entering and said, "I apologize for conditions inside. I have turned off the air conditioning to save money. It will cool off once I open the dock door." He undid the padlock and raised the door. The weather in June was pleasant outside, and soon it was comfortable inside. "I will be right back," said Charles. "I just need to put my things in the office."

Cédric strolled around the factory floor, observing the variety of specialty equipment and in-process wares. "Did you build all of this yourself?" he asked when Charles returned.

"Heavens no," Charles replied. "Most of this equipment was designed and built by my partner, Hugo, and his team of engineers."

Cédric's attention was directed to a screened-in cage area filled with an assortment of machine tools sufficient to fabricate and build almost anything.

Charles said, "You can see that everything is shut down. I haven't been back on the production floor in a while. I come into the office a couple of times a week, but I mostly prefer to work at the café where there are other people around. Here, let's start at the beginning of the process." He moved to one end of the room and stood next to a series of workbenches. "This is where we fabricate the hollow ceramic spheres." He picked up a plaster of

Paris mold set. "We use a process called slip casting. It's basically the same process used to make a wide variety of porcelain products like figurines and garden trolls. We developed a proprietary ceramic formulation that, when partially sintered, gives just the right porosity to hold the molten sodium in the pores by surface tension like a sponge." Opening a lever to reveal the place where the plaster molds were held in place on a carousel, he said, "This is the slip casting machine. The ceramic slip is injected into the mold through this hole from that reservoir above, and the water in the slip gets wicked away into the porous plaster, causing the thin wall of the sphere to become firm enough to handle. After a couple of minutes, the mold is turned upside down, and a tube is inserted into the mold to blow air in and force the remaining slip to drain out. After drying overnight, the parts are removed from the molds and loaded onto refractory to be placed in that furnace over there."

Charles picked up one of the sintered bulbs from a tray on the table and handed it to Cédric. "The thickness of the wall is only about one millimeter. The spherical geometry gives it remarkable strength, just like you would find with a chicken egg."

Cédric admired the part that he estimated to be about three centimeters in diameter. "I assume the purpose of this port on the side is for filling it with sodium," he commented.

"Yes," replied Charles, "and for inserting the nickel wire for the positive electrode. Once the bulb is filled with sodium, the inside gets pressurized with nitrogen, and the port is sealed with silicone to make it gas tight. All the operations involving liquid sodium are carried out in these nitrogen-filled glove boxes to prevent the sodium from oxidizing," he said as they walked past the glass-fronted enclosures. The black rubber gloves designed for the operators to handle the parts inside lay limp, as the gas supply had been turned off and no work had been carried out for weeks.

"The rest is pretty simple," Charles said. "Once the filled bulbs get coated with a polymer that conducts sodium ions, they can be exposed to room air. The rest of the battery consists of a well-insulated enclosure filled with nickel wool immersed in an ionic liquid polymer."

"And a cartridge heater," Cédric said, pointing to the device inside one of the battery enclosures on the workbench that was partially assembled. "You said you have a partner?"

"Had a partner," replied Charles. "I ended up buying him out. Hugo was responsible for most of what you see. As I'm sure you can tell, he was a very capable fellow. Several years ago, we were working together in the research and development department of a large automobile battery manufacturer in Valence. Everything we were making was based on lithium-ion batteries. The company had been observing the steady rise in lithium prices while the prices of Chinese batteries were actually declining. They suspected that this was an attempt to drive us out of the market, so the management tasked us to come up with a battery based on sodium. Sodium is abundant and readily available almost anywhere in the world. Many companies were trying to develop sodium-based batteries at that time as a response to tightening lithium supplies. We were having only limited success trying to replace lithium with sodium directly before we began developing liquid sodium anodes. We saw this as a game changer for price and performance, but the company ultimately abandoned our project, saying it was too risky to introduce a new, unproven battery technology into a market where lithium-ion batteries had a long track record and worked well enough. To be honest, I think the company was only using our work as leverage against the Chinese manufacturers. In any event, Hugo and I started talking seriously about forming our own battery company with the technology we had developed. We proposed to license it from our employer, and they liked the idea because it gave them a way to recover some of their investment while transferring all the business risk to Hugo and me."

Charles shrugged his shoulders. "I would love to offer you a cup of coffee, but the coffee maker is broken. Anyway, it's past lunchtime, and I suggest we head back to the café and discuss the terms of your employment over sandwiches." He closed and locked the dock door and switched off the lights.

"Surely you had other employees?" queried Cédric as the two headed down the street. Thunderclouds were starting to billow up in the surrounding mountains, and it was threatening to rain.

"Most assuredly," replied Charles. "We had five engineers and technicians at one point. We had managed to win a government grant for three million euros. You can do a lot of serious science with that much money, and for a time, we were on top of the world. That was when I found out that Hugo had a drinking problem. He had hidden it from me for years, but I guess the stress of the job put him over the edge. His marriage failed, and I had to buy out his stake piece by piece just to keep him and the company afloat. One day he disappeared. A week later, they discovered his body with a self-inflicted gunshot to the head. Now I am the sole proprietor of a totally worthless enterprise."

The two walked along in silence. What Cédric had just heard was a lot to take in. He pondered that if the opportunity were to present itself, he might consider making a financial investment in NaPiles. He liked what he saw on the tour and was becoming fond of Charles. He knew he could make the battery work with his Na-22 invention and thought it might save the company if Charles turned out to have the right business acumen. Any discussions of money at that time, however, would just confuse the circumstances. They agreed over lunch that they would build and test a battery with Cédric's invention and that, if it worked, Charles would pay the legal expenses for a patent, and Cédric would be compensated down the road through royalties. This arrangement was fine with him. He didn't need the money. He was excited to get the chance to do something useful with his developments at Villa Chandellepont. He had told

Charles that the Na-22 was made by one of his friends at a laboratory in Grenoble and did not disclose that he had been making it in his own shop. The small amounts of the liquid he was able to make himself would suffice to build a prototype, but ultimately, Charles would need a proton beam of his own to make the sodium isotope at NaPiles.

The two began to collaborate on the task of constructing a prototype battery, working three days a week initially. Cédric was able to demonstrate his acumen in the laboratory very quickly, and Charles gave him the door code so he could come and go at will. Cédric completed the prototype in a couple of weeks and arranged to give Charles a demonstration.

"Where is the battery?" Charles asked, looking around the lab.

Cédric said "Follow me. It's in the breakroom." Charles went with him, and Cédric said with a broad smile, "It's in the freezer." He opened the door and retrieved the battery prototype. "It's been in there all night," he said, checking the thermometer, "Minus ten Celsius. Without any Na-22 to generate a little bit of heat, ordinary sodium would be frozen solid."

Cédric placed the battery on one of the tables and connected the leads from a battery tester to the terminals. Looking up at Charles, who needed no explanation, he said, "See? It works." This successful demonstration signaled the end of Cédric's temporary employment status and the beginning of a twenty-year career at NaPiles.

Thereafter, Cédric took charge of the battery laboratory, while Charles went on the road in search of customers. Charles would often return disheartened. Cédric had thought that solving the freezing problem with liquid sodium batteries would lead to immediate acceptance of this revolutionary innovation. But he was mistaken. Electric vehicles continued to experience explosive growth, but Li-ion was proven technology that worked well enough, and no one was willing to take the risk of a replacement no matter how good. It would be necessary to find a new application outside of the realm of automobile batteries, where his batteries might enable applications not adequately served by lithium-ion.

Cédric had developed the habit of riding his electric scooter to the train station in Montmélian. One morning, he tried to turn it on, and the battery was dead, even though he had left it charging overnight. He checked all the connections and concluded that the Li-ion battery, itself, had failed. He had no reason to go to NaPiles that day, so he removed the battery and took it with him on the train to Valence, where the dealer was located, to see if he could obtain a new one. At the service department, he was told that the factory was unable to procure batteries and that no one knew when this situation was going to change. Cédric immediately recognized that this was exactly the opportunity Charles was looking for. When he returned home, he sent an anonymous email to the manufacturer of his trottinette suggesting there might be a company in Saint-Michel-de-

Maurienne called NaPiles, run by a gentleman named Charles Gilbert, that just happened to have a battery technology particularly well suited for e-trottinettes. He suggested that this company might be able to solve their supply problems.

A week later, a beaming Charles Gilbert emerged from his office with a well-dressed man. "Cédric, I would like to introduce you to Monsieur Gardner. He owns an electric scooter company in Valence that might be interested in our sodium batteries. Do you think you might be able to build a couple of prototypes?"

Charles handed Cédric the spec sheet, and he studied it carefully, as if he was seeing it for the first time. "Perhaps," he said skeptically, feigning a frown. "Give me a couple days to see what I can come up with." Cédric had already built a compatible battery in anticipation of that moment, and he had been testing it every day in his own trottinette. He already knew that it surpassed the performance of the lithium-ion battery it was replacing in every respect. He waited until he got home that evening to let out a celebratory shout. His anonymous email to the trottinette company and the existence of his laboratory at Villa Chandellepont would remain a secret for the rest of his life.

The NaPiles sodium batteries with Cédric's Na-22 innovation were practically an overnight sensation. All the field trials had been coming in with glowing reviews, and everyone wanted to get their hands on one of these miraculous batteries, which fit in the same space with the same electrical connections as the Li-ion batteries they replaced. There was no noticeable difference except the NaPiles batteries had doubled the watt-hour capacity, doubling the range between charging. Charging had also been greatly improved. One of the risks with Li-ion batteries was the potential for overcharging, which created heat and was known to cause the battery to catch fire. It was impossible for the NaPiles battery to overcharge because once all the sodium ions in the electrolyte were converted back into sodium metal inside the porous bulb, no further charging was possible. Thus, expensive control circuitry in the charging station was no longer required.

The only real problem was that making Na-22 was a slow process, and Cédric had run out of production capacity at Villa Chandellepont. He had initially built a proton beamline with a current of ten milliamperes, which could generate only a fraction of the Na-22 required. A thousandfold increase in production would be required to meet the surging demand, and Cédric focused his attention on constructing new proton beam lines at NaPiles, which had gone from being a business on the brink of bankruptcy to operating three shifts, seven days a week, and was overwhelmed by orders that were piling in. They had outgrown the facility by the beginning of fall, and it became necessary to expand the business rapidly. This would require a great deal of cash that Charles did not have.

Charles had entered discussions with Mr. Gardener to form a joint venture for manufacturing the batteries. It was recognized that, although Saint-Michel-de-Maurienne was a lovely place to live, it was not a good place to build a ten-thousand-square-meter factory. Mr. Gardener owned a plot of land adjacent to his trottinette factory in Valence, which would be the most logical location for the new production facility. The battery factory was completed early the next year, and the NaPiles joint venture had become fully operational by spring, when all the production equipment was transferred from Saint-Michel-de-Maurienne to the new facility on the Rhône. The commute by train for Cédric was about the same.

Cédric went to work every day for several months in Valence to help with the technology transfer, but he soon realized that working in a large corporation with all the red tape was not for him. He had had free rein when he was the only one working for Charles in the lab at Saint-Michel-de-Maurienne, who trusted him completely, but at the new plant, he was required to justify every purchase. Work had ceased to be a challenge and was no longer interesting. He had been looking for an opportunity to resign, but he had not been aware that Charles had been having similar thoughts.

Charles and Cédric had not interacted much since the move to Valence. One afternoon after work, Charles invited Cédric to join him for coffee to let him know that he had been negotiating to cash out of his share of the joint venture and was in the process of buying back his abandoned laboratory in Saint-Michel-de-Maurienne. “The first time we met,” Charles said, “you told me you would work for free as long as we could build a neutron star in a bottle once the battery business was successful. Well, Cédric, that time has come. I just purchased my laboratory back, and I would like you to come along with me. But you need to know there is no way I can pay you as much as you are making now."

Cédric rejoiced at this unexpected turn of events and said, "Nothing could possibly make me happier than going back to work for you, Charles. Don't worry about the pay. The royalty payments on the Na-22 invention are more than enough compensation. I'm in. When do we start?" He sipped his coffee and looked intently at Charles. "So, tell me about your interest in neutrons."

Charles said, "You know, Cédric, my technical background is rather limited, but I have studied how technology works, and energy technology in particular, and how technology has evolved with civilization. Technological advances almost always occur slowly over time by a series of small improvements to preexisting innovations. Incremental improvements come about by judicious application of known scientific principles in new and clever ways, resulting in things with slightly greater utility than their predecessors. This is assured by the pressure to follow scientific orthodoxy and established engineering discipline as passed down from generation to generation by academic institutions." Charles paused and said, "Please forgive me. I didn't mean to launch off into a lecture on the philosophy of technology."

"No, please continue," said Cédric. "This is all very interesting to me." Cédric was just soaking in every word.

Charles continued, "Radical departures from conventional wisdom about how things should work are vigorously opposed. I have been studying the development of heat engines from the first steam engine built by James Watt. The development of propulsion by heat engines—from steam engines in the beginning capable of generating a few horsepower to high-efficiency diesel engines capable of delivering twenty thousand horsepower—took place over the course of two hundred years. With only a handful of truly disruptive innovations, heat engine development followed a very methodical path. Each new engine followed a logical progression from its antecedent. By the time I was born in 2011, the physical limits of generating energy by burning hydrocarbon fuels had been reached. Unless something new came along, the forward progress of human development would be halted. The dream of safely harnessing nuclear energy was widely viewed as the only option, but nuclear fission, which had been practiced in submarines for decades, had had a difficult time being adapted to commercial applications. From the dawn of civilization, humankind looked up at the sun, wondering how to unlock the mystery of its unimaginably huge energy source on earth. The dream seemed within reach when the first hydrogen bomb was detonated in 1951, because it seemed that the very mechanism of the sun's furnace had been demonstrated. Scientists knew that if they could only somehow figure out how to capture the hydrogen fusion reaction of the sun in a confined space, nearly limitless energy could be harvested on earth. For almost a hundred years, scientists struggled to confine the reaction, which requires temperatures of hundreds of thousands of degrees, with huge magnetic fields and powerful lasers. At one point, some researchers in the United States claimed to have achieved fusion at room temperature, but this turned out to be a hoax. Tens of billions of euros and dollars were spent in university research centers and government labs on the various projects. What was termed *breakeven* was finally reached when sustainable fusion reactions were achieved that generated at least as much power as was required by the magnets and lasers to sustain them. The dream of bringing the power of the sun to earth was in sight. The engineering models all predicted that commercial power plants based on the technology could be built. The reality was that the costs for scaling such devices for commercial deployment were daunting. The technology could only be carried out in large, isolated facilities that were not suited for distributed power generation. The plants would need to be tens of gigawatts in power output—costing many billions of euros each to construct—and would require extensive augmentation of an already feeble and vulnerable power distribution network. The dream of virtually limitless fusion energy had become a nightmare of spiraling costs and regulatory squabbles."

Charles paused to drink the last of his coffee. "You want to know why I am interested in neutrons," he said. "This will sound crazy, but I am convinced that people have been looking to model the energy of the wrong type of star. For sure, the energy of fusion in stars like our sun is impressive, but it pales in comparison to the energy generated by neutron stars. That's because the energy is really in the mass. Einstein made this clear. I believe that unlimited amounts of energy can be generated by clusters of neutrons with the mass density found in neutron stars, if we could just figure out how to fabricate them."

Cédric sat quietly at this last remark, as if these were completely new ideas to him. In fact, it was all he could do to remain seated. He wanted to scream, but he knew it was not the appropriate time to unload his theories on Charles. He restrained himself, knowing that the right time and place was yet to come. He was now convinced that Charles was the right person, and the laboratory in Saint-Michel-de-Maurienne was the right place to develop his microfusion ideas.

Chapter 20: Neutrons

Occasionally, scientific progress takes an unexpected twist, and this is what happened at that time of growing pessimism about the prospects of having fusion power become commercially viable. The remarkable story of the invention of microfusion began in that small, privately operated research laboratory located between Lyon, France, and Torino, Italy, in the small mountain village of Saint-Michel-de-Maurienne on the French side of the Western Alps. It would not be possible to imagine that such a breakthrough could take place in such a nondescript eighty-square-meter warehouse a block from the train station. The unexceptional sign over the front entrance reading "NaPiles" provided absolutely no evidence of the world-altering breakthroughs that would one day be taking place inside.

Over the course of the following eight years, Cédric focused his attention on assembling neutrons into larger and larger clusters. This involved a great deal of trial and error, as no one had ever attempted such a thing before and there were no textbooks on the subject. He was guided in his research by the expectation that sufficiently slowed down, the small attractive magnetic field of free neutrons would be sufficient to bind them together and keep them from disintegrating. Ordinarily, a cloud of neutrons had enough combined kinetic energy to keep them bouncing off one another, so Cédric thought it would be necessary to make them nearly motionless, which required extremely low temperatures close to absolute zero and a strong, confining magnetic field to focus the neutrons into proximity without allowing them to speed up. This way, their internal magnetic fields would take over. Much of the sophisticated equipment required to carry out such advanced research was left over from the development of sodium transmutation. In addition to the proton beam source, Cédric had assembled a wide assortment of sophisticated analytical equipment, such as a mass spectrometer, scanning electron microscope, and radiation detection equipment, in addition to the fully equipped machine shop. For Cédric, no challenge was too great. He could build anything, and his imagination was so vast about how to make things that really worked that Charles would often leave the lab at night wondering which alien galaxy Cédric had come from. If anyone could build a neutron star in a bottle, Cédric was the man to do it.

Charles was not a trained scientist, so he did not need to be concerned about his professional reputation. All the work at the lab was self-funded from cash generated from the sale of his stake in the battery joint venture, so there was no need to justify his decisions or report the results to anyone. Most scientific research at the frontiers of knowledge had become so costly that government-supported laboratories had to compete vigorously for every dollar. The result was that only cautious experiments with a high probability of success ever got funded, and those scientists who did succeed in winning research grants spent most of their time writing new proposals to prolong the research or reporting on their prior work. This all had the unintended consequence of channeling research into diverging programs with narrower and narrower scope of specialization, increasingly isolated from other disciplines.

On the other hand, scientific breakthroughs often take place in the nexus of the incongruent fields where cross-fertilization of ideas can occur. The work of Charles and Cédric with neutrons was well outside of the scientific mainstream and went completely unnoticed. They were never hindered by orthodox views of what was, or was not, possible. Their work with neutrons was motivated by curiosity. They merely wanted to fabricate neutron nanoclusters—a preposterous idea at the time.

The apparatus that Cédric constructed was not all that complex. An aluminum tube about one centimeter in diameter and ten centimeters long was positioned inside a vacuum chamber surrounded by a huge magnet and maintained at a temperature of nearly absolute zero. A polyethylene plug was inserted into the leading end of the tube, and the proton generator was positioned to fire a collimated beam of low-energy protons into the polyethylene plug along the central axis of the tube. The polyethylene had been specially fabricated using heavy hydrogen, or deuterium, rather than ordinary hydrogen. The deuterium nucleus contains a proton plus a neutron that may be dislodged with relative ease when struck by another proton. Protons striking the nuclei of the deuterium atoms in the polymer caused the ejection of some neutrons, which proceeded down the tube.

The magnetic field kept the resulting slow-moving neutron cloud focused into the center of the tube. A detector at the far end measured the proton flux of the beam, and the number of neutrons produced was deduced as the difference between the entering and exiting proton flux.

Individual free neutrons are unstable, so when they decay after a few minutes, they produce beta particles with a characteristic energy that can be easily detected. It was generally known at the time that clusters of just a few neutrons, perhaps as few as six, were stable. Cédric was interested in getting neutrons to clump together into clusters. He suspected, based on the absence of beta decays and the difference in proton flux, that some neutron clusters were forming. The proton beam current was one milliampere, and about 10 percent of the protons were absent at the far-end detector, so he expected that about a thousand neutrons per second could be joined into clusters. A sample port in the reaction tube permitted the contents to be passed to a high-resolution mass spectrometer, where the number of neutrons in each cluster was easily determined by atomic mass. In this fashion, he was able to generate clusters containing up to about ten thousand neutrons, at which point the clusters tended to break apart. This was certainly interesting and groundbreaking research, but such neutron clusters seemingly had no practical application. Cédric had reached a plateau where it had become unclear what the next steps would be.

One morning, he approached Charles. “Charles,” he said, “I think I have accomplished about as much as I can for now. I am pretty burned out, and I think I need a break.”

“What kind of break do you have in mind? A couple of days perhaps?” Charles asked.

Cédric replied, “I am missing something. I know it is right in front of my nose. I am just too close to the work, and I think if I walk away from it for a while, I may gain some clarity. There is a matter I need to tend to in Paris next week, and I may be gone for a while, if you don’t mind.” Cédric could sense Charles’s alarm.

“How long do you expect to be gone?” Charles asked.

“I don’t know—probably not more than a couple of weeks,” Cédric replied. “Don’t worry, Charles. I will be back. I have been seeing some interesting effects recently in the experiments, and I just need a change of scenery to sharpen my mind.”

“What kind of effects?” asked Charles. “Can you give me a hint?”

Cédric paused to consider the wisdom of disclosing any more. “The neutron rest masses are off, way off. That’s all I can say at this time.”

Chapter 21: Sweet Sixteen

Cédric scanned the crowd anxiously from his position at the base of the Eiffel Tower where he had arranged to meet Julia. She was fifteen minutes late, and he began to worry that they had gotten crossed up on the rendezvous. He was about to phone her when he finally picked her out of the crowd and waved. She waved back and ran to meet him, giving him a big hug.

"Uncle Cédric," she said. "This is such a treat. You have rescued me from that dismal school in the dead of winter."

Cédric replied, "It's not my fault that your birthday is in February. We have a dinner reservation at Le Jules Verne on the second level. Let's take the private elevator," he said, indicating the entrance. "They are expecting us."

Once out of the dark and bitter cold night of Paris and into the bright lights of the elevator, Julia removed her wool cap. Her blonde hair flowed under her scarf and disappeared into the fur collar of her emerald-green coat.

"Julia," he exclaimed. "You are far more lovely than I imagined. The video camera on Annie's computer has not done you justice."

Julia blushed.

"Sixteen! I just can't believe it," exclaimed Cédric. "Has it really been nine years since I kidnapped you and took you to America?"

"They have been nine wonderful years," she replied. "How will I ever repay your kindness?"

Cédric smiled as the elevator door opened and the two were greeted by the host. This was the first time he had worn a suit since his father's funeral. It was also the first time he had been back to Paris since he and Julia departed for the United States.

"Yes, Mr. Rothschild," said the host, turning to head into the crowded restaurant. "We have prepared your table next to the window as you requested, overlooking the Seine. It is a magnificent evening to see the lights of Paris."

They were seated, and the waiter uncorked a bottle of champagne that Cédric had prearranged. They tapped their crystal flutes across the table, and Cédric said, "Happy birthday, my dear." The lightshow of the fountain across the river in front of the Trocadero caught their attention momentarily. "Tell me, how is school going?"

Julia continued to take in the lights and then turned to Cédric and replied, "School is fine. Thanks to you, I am fluent in French, but whatever you do, don't tell the headmistress that I am happy, or she will lose her *raison d'être*. She is committed to cheering me up." Julia looked back out the window for a while and then turned back to Cédric with a more serious expression and said, "You know, Uncle Cédric, I still have no memory of Armenia. God in His mercy has wiped my memory clean. Of course, I know the details of what happened, but it is as if I read about it in a newspaper. My earliest recollection is chasing Sassy around Villa Chandellepont."

"How is Sassafras?" asked Cédric.

"Sassy turned into a formidable predator at Peach-Eze," she replied. "She learned to place her trophies of dead, and almost dead, mice on Nico's pillow for approval." They both laughed. "I assume you know about my grandad?" she inquired.

"Bits and pieces," Cédric replied. "I know he interfered with the adoption."

"It's not all that bad," she replied. "As it turns out, I am his only grandchild. Once he got over me being illegitimate, he grew to like me. Nico and Annie were in a bind. They also wanted to adopt me, but this required disclosures that brought my grandfather into the picture. Once he discovered where I was, an army of lawyers got into the act to battle over custody. It worked out for the best, though. Grandad was concerned over what was taking place in the United States with the pending civil war and wanted to get me out of the country for safekeeping. That's how I ended up at the school in Lausanne."

The waiter handed them menus and refilled their champagne flutes. Cédric handed his menu back to him and said, "Will you kindly order for us?"

"With pleasure," he replied. "The beef tips Bourguignon would be my choice for you, sir. And for the lady, I highly recommend the filet of sole." They nodded agreement. An asparagus appetizer with Hollandaise was placed in front of each.

Cédric asked, "What can you tell me about what is going on in the United States? I don't have much interest in politics, and I haven't been paying all that much attention."

"It's all about the chip," Julia replied. "Nico and Annie have been keeping me up to date." She lowered her voice and said, "They are part of the resistance, you know."

"You are talking over my head now," Cédric said. "I am hopelessly ill-informed. I have no idea what you are talking about."

"Surely you know about the chip? The biometric implants?" Julia queried.

"I don't think we have those in France," replied Cédric.

"It won't be long, I can assure you," she replied. "So the president has enacted an executive order requiring every US citizen to have a biometric chip implanted by the end of this year. Without it, no one will be able to buy or sell anything. Annie calls it the mark of the beast. It's pretty scarry stuff. The bureaucrats in Washington insist that it is the only way they will be able to track people's exposure to diseases from pandemics. They say it is for the common good of society, but a lot of Americans, particularly in the south and west, think it's a lot more sinister and don't buy into the rhetoric. Texas has already declared its independence, and several other states are following suit. Nico and Annie think the country is on the brink of civil war."

"I fear you have been radicalized, Julia, my dear," Cédric said.

Julia smiled and said, "Why don't you tell me what you have been up to."

Cédric could tell the instant he spoke the word *neutrons*, Julia had lost interest. She had become a most charming young woman, full of excitement for life, but mathematics and science had no part in it. She was attending the leading private secondary school in Europe, and she was receiving an excellent liberal arts education, but her passion was for international affairs. She had developed a burning desire to return to Armenia to help with the reconstruction of that country. Julia talked about all the excitement of her studies and a pending internship at the United Nations in Geneva. As he sat quietly listening to her, Cédric reflected that he was watching the little girl who, just nine years earlier, he had taken to America and Disneyland. The adorable child who he had hoped to adopt as his own daughter was now sixteen and in an entirely different world. Her life had followed another trajectory altogether that did not include him. The impression was bittersweet. He was reminded of the dinner conversations with his father and brother when he was growing up that excluded him and always came back to discussions of business, investments, and international law. Cédric had learned to retreat into himself to carry on the one-sided conversations demanded by his innate curiosity about the nature of things.

They didn't leave the restaurant until well after midnight. He escorted Julia to her hotel by taxi and then went to Gare de Lyon to catch the late train home. He had planned to spend a week in Paris, but the yearning to be back in his laboratory overruled him. By the time the sun broke the eastern horizon while his train pulled into the station in Montmélian, he had his answer, and he had a clear vision of the next steps. Cédric was more convinced than ever that deuteron fusion would never be practical in free space because the Coulombic repulsion of the positively charged protons in the deuterium nucleus would present an impenetrable barrier to bringing them together. He had a keen sense that neutron clusters would provide the environment where deuteron fusion could take place. He was now energized to discover how, but the neutron clusters would prove to give up their mystery begrudgingly. The year was 2052. Cédric was forty-two years old and in the prime of life. He could sense that a breakthrough was immanent, but it would take several years before he would realize it.

Chapter 22: Clusters

Cédric was glad to be back home at Villa Chandellepont. The brief visit to Paris had brought back bittersweet memories that he had thought were long gone. As he trekked up the footpath from the train station in the fresh snow that had fallen the previous evening, he saw some children in his yard fashioning a snowman. The stream of Armenian children had been replaced by refugees from Romania and other Eastern European countries where rampant government corruption and fiscal mismanagement had made it nearly impossible to live there. The mission at Villa Chandellepont was being managed by the Brothers at the l'Abbey Montmélian, who once again were using Cédric's place to stage the overflow of refugees on their way to permanent destinations. Cédric relished the happy sound of children coming in and out, but he avoided becoming personally involved in any of their lives. The heartbreak he had experienced over his failure to adopt Julia had left him with a scar that had hardened him.

Cédric's daily routine began by attending Mass and sharing breakfast with the brothers at the Abbey. A sack lunch was prepared for him in the kitchen, and off he would go to catch the 7:25 train east for the forty-five-minute commute to Saint-Michel-de-Maurienne. He was typically the first to enter NaPiles, turning on the heat and lights in anticipation of Charles's arrival, who had been coming in later and later each day and was showing signs of growing edginess. Cédric suspected that he was running out of cash, and it was only a matter of time before he would shut the lab. The enthusiasm over making neutron clusters had worn off, and as interesting as their research was, it was unclear if these supermassive entities had any real practical application. The dream of microfusion was more elusive than ever. Charles would typically check up on Cédric's progress before disappearing into his office for the rest of the day. More and more frequently, Charles did not come into NaPiles at all. In the event that he decided to close NaPile, Cédric was planning to purchase the equipment and move it to his own workshop at Villa Chandellepont. After ten years at NaPiles, Charles still had no knowledge of Cédric's scientific background or his private life. All he knew was that Cédric shared his passion for assembling neutron clusters. Cédric kept his past as a well-guarded secret. He knew the time would come to divulge it, but this was not that time.

After his trip to Paris, he went to work with renewed enthusiasm, making larger and larger neutron clusters each day. He spent many months modifying the mass spectrometer at NaPiles to detect clusters with up to about one million neutrons. This was something no one else had ever attempted because there was no known state of matter with anywhere near that many nucleons—at least not on earth. He knew he was dealing with something that had never been seen before, but the clusters were much too small to observe directly, making it difficult to measure properties, such as their rest masses.

He had an unexpected breakthrough one day when he observed a strange signal on the oscilloscope he had been using for troubleshooting an electrical problem with one of the circuits of his mass spectrometer. He had noticed an anomalous high-frequency resonance appearing on the screen every so often that would last for a few microseconds. The mysterious signal would start out as a resonance of a few kilohertz and accelerate in frequency to megahertz before vanishing in a jumble of electrical noise. After some investigation, he concluded that the source was coming from inside the reaction chamber, and he had originally suspected that it was coming from the field coil. But the mysterious signal was intermittent and only occurred a couple of times an hour, necessitating that he set up the oscilloscope to trigger on the event and store the resulting waveform in memory. He studied these signals for long hours in the evening at home. He noticed that they had an uncanny resemblance to what occurs when stars collide. In the course of time, he arrived at the conclusion that the signal was being generated when two neutron clusters came into close enough proximity so that their gravitation attraction began drawing them inward. A spiral dance ensued as the two massive clusters circled each other until they finally joined together, and the dance ended in a burst of energy. Cédric continued to investigate the phenomenon for several months before he convinced himself that it was real.

When he had completed the theoretical calculations over and over, there was a problem, however; the frequencies were several orders of magnitude lower than they should have been for counter-rotating masses based on the expected number of neutrons and their assumed rest masses.

Cédric realized that he had finally discovered the elusive dark matter particle. By analyzing the evolution of frequencies in the spectrum of the signal, he could quantitatively establish the apparent masses of the neutron clusters. The apparent masses were orders of magnitude greater than what the rest masses would predict. He had essentially created the very same conditions inside his reactor that existed in distant galaxies when neutron stars collide. He knew that the difference between the apparent masses and the rest masses of the neutron clusters was the very same "dark matter" observed from the celestial mechanics of distant galaxies. As he had predicted in his 2029 manuscript, "Dark Matter and Time-Dependent Speed of Light," he now had just the evidence to prove that he had been right all along. This would change everything. He now had a new way to measure the decreasing speed of light in the vicinity of supermassive objects. It was a scientific triumph. He could hardly wait to see the look on Professor Hendriksen's face when the discovery was made public.

But the discovery still did not lead to a practical application of the NaPiles research, and certainly nothing resembling microfusion. Cédric knew his discovery would make him famous, but his sense of loyalty to Charles required that he hold off on the disclosure until just the right moment. Disclosure at that time would have required him to divulge secrets about his life as a physicist, but he was not sure how long he could get away with pretending to be just the simple lab assistant.

Charles had always said that no matter how well the ground was prepared and the seeds of innovation planted, scientific breakthroughs generally required an element of serendipity. The discovery of microfusion was no exception. He was home one evening after dinner, watching his son, Vincent, play with a puzzle consisting of a clump of magnetic buckyballs that he had received as a birthday gift from a friend. These were neodymium iron boride magnet spheres that could only be assembled into certain shapes by following a sequence of prescribed procedures. Charles watched as his son pulled a single strand of balls from the clump. The balls stuck together because of the permanent magnetization that gave each ball a north and south pole. Any attempt to attach the north pole of one end of the strand to the north pole of another strand caused the ends to repel each other. The ends could only be connected when the magnets were aligned. He observed his son reassemble the balls by carefully folding the strand into groups and then forming a perfect cube. Individually, the balls behaved as single magnets, but collectively, they behaved by a complex set of rules that required the sum of all the individual magnetic fields to cancel out. This meant that only certain shapes could be made, and the trick of the puzzle was to figure out how to keep the balls in the right places during the various steps while the desired shape was being formed.

Charles took notice when his son formed a circle consisting of eight balls joined together around the circumference. He then continued to wind the strand in a helical pattern to form a perfect tube—a stable shape that seemed to be compatible with all the magnets. Vincent showed his father how he could form a tube with any desired number of balls around the circumference and handed the puzzle to him so he could give it a try.

Charles looped the first eight balls into a circle and proceeded to wind the rest of the balls along the wall of the tube with ease. His imagination did the rest. He realized in a rare flash of genius that neutrons also have north and south poles. If he could figure out how to assemble them into a strand, he could begin winding them into neutron buckytubes.

The next morning, after a nearly sleepless night, Charles went into the lab early. Cédric was already hard at work. The men reasoned that, in addition to the magnetic field that was designed to keep the neutrons centered in the tube, a second magnetic field in the axial direction was also needed. Furthermore, it would be necessary for this new magnet to rotate in order to wind the strands of neutrons into tubes. Building such a magnet was no small challenge, but Cédric had the details worked out within a week. The entire modification was operational within a month.

When they fired up the reactor again, the first thing they noticed was that the clusters were easily exceeding the previous million-neutron limit—considerably in some cases. They also began noticing that the number of neutrons in each cluster seemed to exhibit certain integral multiples of numbers, unlike with the random clusters they'd been getting before the axial magnet was installed. This led them to the conclusion that the new clusters possessed certain ordered shapes, suggesting that the idea might actually be working.

Day after day, they succeeded in fabricating larger and larger clusters, limited only by the thousand neutrons per second they could generate from their one-milliampere proton beam—some twenty-five million neutrons in a workday. They estimated that they would need to make clusters containing more than one billion neutrons before they could detect measurable weight in the most sensitive balance. More importantly, it would take a hundred thousand seconds, or twenty-eight hours, to produce that many neutrons. After a brief consultation, the two men agreed to leave the reactor running overnight. By that point, they were confident that the risk of malfunction was small.

When Cédric arrived the following morning, everything seemed to have been working properly during the night. The mass spectrometer had detected at least three clusters exceeding one million neutrons. This was a scientific triumph, and as soon as Charles arrived at the lab, the two men rejoiced exceedingly. But neither was quite sure what the next step should be. After carefully checking that everything was working properly, they finally decided to go home early on that fateful Friday and leave the reactor running over the weekend.

Early Monday morning, after checking that the reactor was still working properly, Cédric checked on the mass spectrometer to see the histogram of the cluster sizes produced over the weekend. The clusters had steadily increased in size until, suddenly, no more clusters were detected after three in the morning during the previous night. Cédric checked the proton generator and the polyethylene plug and looked for signs of beta decay. Having found nothing amiss, he concluded that the detector in the mass spectrometer had burned out. He installed the spare detector, and still no clusters were showing up.

By the time Charles entered the lab, Cédric had concluded that the clusters had just gotten too big for the spectrometer to measure. They decided to reduce the field strength on the axial magnet to return to the point where they expected to see smaller clusters, but still there were no clusters detected. It was hugely disappointing that they were not able to reproduce the experimental results from before.

Charles and Cédric were having lunch when the alarm went off, signaling a burst of beta radiation and automatically shutting down the reactor. With the lead shielding around the reactor, this posed no threat to the men, but they would have to open the reaction chamber, which needed to be done carefully, while wearing protective clothing.

When Cédric inspected the aluminum tube, it was no longer straight but sagged noticeably downward in the middle. He removed it from the reactor, and to his amazement, it was quite heavy, weighing more than five kilograms. The original aluminum tube had weighed only one hundred grams. He removed the polyethylene plug and looked down the barrel, seeing what appeared to be several deep scratches that looked more like tiny black fibers upon more careful inspection. He estimated the fibers to be about a millimeter in length and about one micron in diameter.

Inverting the tube and tapping it into a porcelain crucible, some of the fibers tumbled out, and the crucible weighed more than three kilograms. The two men stared at each other in wonder and amazement. They were hoping to someday make neutron clusters, but neither expected that they would be able to see these tiny neutron tubes in the bottom of a crucible. As far as they were aware, this completely new state of matter had never been observed before.

Cédric had suspected that magnetic forces were responsible for bringing the neutrons together initially, but gravitational forces would take over at about one million neutrons. The evidence for this was that the clusters would drop out and get deposited on the walls of the reaction tube. He could detect these increases in the weight of the tubes on his microbalance. But there was a problem; the increase in weight exceeded what the weight should have been based on the number of neutrons generated, and the increase in weight was many orders of magnitude more than he could explain. The current of the proton beam was one milliamperes, so the maximum number of neutrons that could possibly be generated in one hour was about fifty million. The clusters should have had a rest mass of only a few picograms, at most, but Cédric's neutron clusters had been weighing too much by hundreds of grams.

He had been placing the clusters in a beaker of water to keep from losing them and make it easier for him to track their weight. He had noticed a very curious behavior one day when he observed that the weight of the beaker decreased when he stirred the water. The weight would return to the constant value after a few seconds as soon as he stopped stirring. The weight change was dramatic and seemed to depend on how vigorously he stirred the liquid. This was the first clear evidence that mass and velocity were related and would serve as a guidepost for much of his subsequent work.

Cédric began preparing a specimen for the scanning electron microscope, while Charles was furiously writing every detail in his laboratory notebook.

"Cédric, we have a problem," said Charles, looking up at last. "According to the meter on the proton generator, the reactor ran for a total of 121 hours. At one milliampere, we would have produced a total of 42 billion protons, or no more than 4.2 billion neutrons. That's assuming a 10 percent yield. And 4.2 billion neutrons should only weigh 7×10^{-14} grams. That's fifteen orders of magnitude less than what you just weighed it at!"

Cédric simply straightened up and smiled.

"Don't you see? It's impossible. We did not generate anywhere near enough neutrons to fabricate clusters this massive. We have obviously done something wrong." Charles stared at Cédric, waiting for some sort of response, and got nothing.

Cédric merely exhibited the countenance of profound satisfaction.

Finally, Charles said, "You understand what's going on, don't you?"

Cédric nodded and replied, "I have a theory. Would you like to hear it?"

"Yes. Please," replied Charles.

Cédric began, "How is the rest mass of a neutron determined? You can't just plop one down on a scale. The rest mass is determined by measuring the kinetic energy of neutrons in a particle beam. The neutrons are traveling rather fast in this case. In fact, neutrons in all ordinary matter are moving around rather quickly. But I believe there is a relationship between mass and velocity that requires the mass to depend on the velocity. As crazy as this sounds, I have some evidence that proves it. The so-called neutron rest mass is not the rest mass at all. The measurement just assumes that the mass is invariant with velocity. When we assemble neutrons into clusters, what we are doing is effectively freezing them into stationary states where they manifest their true rest mass."

Charles stared at Cédric in disbelief. "Cédric. How in the world do you know this stuff?"

Cédric grinned. "Perhaps the time has come for me to explain some things about my past. Excuse me for a minute. I need to get something to show you." Returning momentarily, he handed Charles a manila folder with a document inside.

Reading the title page and thumbing through the pages quickly, Charles asked, "Did you write this?"

"Yes, sir," replied Cédric. "I think you will find all the answers in there."

Chapter 23: The Manuscript

Cédric had suggested that Charles head home and curl up in front of his fireplace to read the manuscript. Cédric had warned him that it wasn't exactly casual bedtime reading. It would take some time to digest it. Charles took his advice and headed home, which was a good thing because there was a light drizzle and it was expected that it would start to freeze, making driving hazardous. He was greeted enthusiastically by his black Labrador retriever in the front yard. The house was empty, as his son was still at school and his wife had gone shopping in Chambery. He stoked the pellet stove, poured a glass of wine, and made himself comfortable in his favorite recliner. He then opened the folder from Cédric and began by reading the abstract.

Dark Matter and Time-Dependent Speed of Light

J. Cédric Rothschild

July 28, 2029

Abstract

It is proposed that dark matter is an artifact left over from the early stages of galaxy formation resulting from the intrinsic time dependence of mass. Decreasing mass gives the impression that stars are more massive than they otherwise would be based on their luminosity. In order for total energy to be conserved during expansion of a galaxy from a super massive black hole, if apparent mass is decreasing with time, then the speed of light must be increasing with time. Observations of relative motions of stars in galaxies reflect the inertial mass of interbody gravitational forces, which are communicated at the speed of light. Star luminosity, on the other hand, reflects the mass of the light-emitting star itself. A hypothesis is proposed that models these effects, providing an alternative to the conventional explanation of the nature of dark matter.

Charles reread the abstract and dove into the introduction. The connection between galaxy formation and neutron clusters was not yet clear, and the mathematic derivations in the manuscript were over his head. He put the paper aside and grabbed his computer tablet to see if there was anything he could find about Cédric online. As it turned out, there was a great deal of information about him of which Charles never had the faintest inkling. He had never had any reason to investigate him, and Cédric was a very private individual who had never talked about his past. He was born in Paris in 2010. His father had been a successful investor, and his mother a socialite. Both were apparently now deceased. Cédric had been raised mostly by governesses and had attended the top Parisian schools. He'd been an unexceptional student, in and out of trouble for spouting contrarian views. He had generally been considered spoiled and strong-willed.

It was during his time at Candlebridge University that he had begun to embrace the notion that the speed of light was not actually constant. He vehemently defended the premise of cold fusion, writing, as an undergraduate, the only published paper that Charles could find. In this paper, Cédric tried to make the case that deuteron fusion in a palladium metal lattice really did occur, as evidenced by the generation of a small amount of helium, but the rate was too slow to be conclusive. He proposed that the rate of the fusion reaction would be enhanced by slowing down the speed of light. This idea was widely ridiculed.

For his PhD, Cédric could find no support for any research having to do with theories involving variable light speed, so he financed his experiments out of his own pocket. He had built an ingenious apparatus for measuring the time of flight of a laser pulse fired through a hole in a block of depleted uranium, the densest substance he could get his hands on. The laser beam was split, with part of the beam going through the small hole in the block of uranium in a vacuum chamber and the other half just passing through the vacuum of space. By recombining the two beams, Cédric was able to demonstrate that the arrival of the pulse passing through the block of uranium was retarded at the detector compared with the pulse passing through only vacuum using the interference fringes of the two pulses. He was able to show to a high degree of accuracy that the longer the tube, the more retarded was the light pulse.

This was when the scandal had begun. Charles read all about the story as covered in the Candlebridge and London newspapers. Cédric needed longer and longer tubes of depleted uranium, which he was unable to procure from any source in England. Although depleted uranium was a controlled material, it was available in limited quantities from facilities processing nuclear fuels for power plants. Cédric had wanted a tube ten centimeters long, but his supplier had told him that it would take two years to obtain that much depleted uranium. Cédric was impatient and impetuous to the point of recklessness. He circumvented the university procurement system and found a supplier who could make his tube out of unprocessed uranium. Although the uranium tube was slightly radioactive, Cédric planned to insert it into an outer lead shroud, according to the news reports.

More importantly, however, procuring contraband radioactive materials was a serious violation of school policy. Cédric had supposed that no one would ever find out. His plan had been to sneak the tube into his lab in the middle of the night. He was unaware that the physics building, where his laboratory was located, was equipped with an assortment of radiation detectors; should any of the numerous experiments in the building experience a spurious radiation leak, the facility manager would detect it. The following morning, the police showed up and took Cédric to jail in handcuffs. He was brought before the university disciplinary committee and expelled from the school. Thus, Cédric's light speed investigations came to an abrupt termination.

Charles scoured the internet for follow-on stories but found nothing except an anonymous op-ed piece in a London paper claiming that the Rothschild affair was a whitewash. It said the true reason for his expulsion was that the school was receiving tens of millions of pounds each year to discover the mysterious particle responsible for dark matter and that the school was uncomfortable having a graduate student claiming that dark matter was merely an artifact of increasing speed of light.

Charles was sitting in the dark when his son and wife returned. They were both surprised to see him home early. He had totally lost track of time and was buried in thought. He restoked the pellet stove and let the dog out. The temperature had dropped, and already there were five centimeters of snow on the lawn.

At the dinner table, Charles asked his wife, "Gabrielle, how well do you know Cédric at the lab?"

She thought for a minute and then said, "He's a very quiet and reserved fellow, but he's pleasant enough. I'm not sure he ever said a word other than '*Bonjour, Madame Gilbert,*' and '*Au revoir, Madame Gilbert. Bonne journée.*' Why do you ask?"

"He has worked for me for ten years, and I am embarrassed to say I hardly know the man. It turns out that he has a rather colorful past," replied Charles.

"We used to play two-handed bridge when I stopped by the lab sometimes after school," said Vincent. "He told me he had learned how to play the game at a country day school in Paris for spoiled aristocrats. I know he was just kidding." After dinner, Charles stoked the pellet stove and returned to his recliner, the dog at his side, to finish reading Cédric's manuscript.

The following morning was cold and gloomy. Low-hanging clouds sputtered a few snowflakes. Twenty centimeters of snow had already accumulated on the ground, and Charles could hear the annoying *beep-beep-beep* of snowplows in the distance. Gabrielle dropped their son off at school and then drove Charles to work. Cédric came out of the lab to meet him as he entered the door and handed him a micrograph, acting like it was just another ordinary day.

"I was able to get this image of one of the fibers," he said. "You can see it is totally black and amorphous. It appears that the electron beam just can't penetrate it." Cédric then pointed to the near end of the fiber in the micrograph. "You can see a slight indentation at the end, so I think this indicates that the fiber must be hollow, but I was hoping to get better resolution so we could estimate the number of neutrons in the wall."

Charles looked intently at Cédric for a moment, noticing that he had on the same clothes he had been wearing the day before. "You never went home last night, did you?"

Cédric, responded without emotion, "No, sir. By the time I finished the micrographs, it was snowing very hard. I didn't want to trudge through the snow to the train station just to discover that the trains were not operating."

"So, you spent the night in the lab?" inquired Charles.

"Yes, sir."

"Cédric, I think we have a few things to discuss," said Charles, looking into Cédric's red and weary eyes.

“I suppose you read the manuscript then?” said Cédric.

“Yes, and a good deal more.” Charles fished in his pocket for the folded printout of the op-ed from the London newspaper. “Do you have any idea who wrote this?” he said, handing the paper to Cédric.

On seeing it, Cédric grinned broadly. “I did,” he replied nonchalantly. “So, I guess you have been checking up on me?”

“Why didn’t you ever tell me any of this before?”

Cédric stared at his feet for a moment to collect his thoughts. “It just never came up.”

Charles remained silent.

Cédric could tell that he was expecting to hear a lot more, so he said, “I haven’t had anything to eat this morning. Would it be okay if we go to the café down the street? Then I will tell you everything.” Not waiting for a reply, he turned to grab his coat and scarf.

Charles followed him out, locking the door to the lab as the two headed down the freshly plowed sidewalk.

The café next to the train station was a popular meeting place for locals. On this particular cold day, it was nearly full. A roaring wood fire radiated welcome warmth into the room. Charles selected a quiet table in the corner, and the familiar waiter brought them their usual coffees and croissants out of habit. Cédric ordered a breakfast omelet as well. The two sat quietly savoring their coffees without speaking. After a few moments, Cédric said, “I was so close.”

Charles gave him a puzzled look.

"I was so close. That last experiment would have settled the light speed issue once and for all." Cédric paused and looked up with a grin, adding, "And also would have made me famous."

"What experiment?" queried Charles.

"At Candlebridge," responded Cédric. "I could measure the changes in the speed of light to one part in a million with my apparatus. I have improved the experiment since then and more recently found a way to correlate the speed of light to the half-life of isotopes, like Na-22."

"You've lost me," replied Charles.

"I am able to demonstrate conclusively that the speed of light is slower in the vicinity of dense masses."

"I'm still a bit confused. Everyone knows that the speed of light slows down in solids compared to in vacuum," said Charles.

"Ah," replied Cédric with delight, "but the beam was not passing through the uranium in my Candlebridge experiment; it was only passing through the vacuum of the hole passing through it. The light pulse was slowed down by the mere proximity of the mass of the uranium surrounding the hole through which the light pulse passed."

"Surely you are not the first one to observe this," responded Charles dubiously.

"You wouldn't think so. But ever since the experiment of Michaelson and Morley, it has been a sacred tenet of physics that the speed of light is constant in vacuum. I had clear evidence that this is not the case, and as far as I know, I am the first one to ever observe this."

Cédric's omelet arrived. "If that's the case," said Charles, "then you should have received the Nobel Prize in Physics."

Cédric did not respond for some time while he enjoyed his breakfast and freshly squeezed orange juice. "Well, that's when the story took an interesting turn. After the police showed up the next morning to cart me off to jail, my lab was sequestered as a crime scene—a crime scene! Can you believe that?"

"Cédric," Charles interrupted, wanting to steer the direction of the conversation, "There must be a lot more to the story that you are not telling me."

Cédric paused to regather his thoughts. "The manuscript I gave you to read yesterday, the manuscript on dark matter?"

"Yes," replied Charles. "I searched for a published version but found nothing."

"That's just the point," replied Cédric. "I wrote that manuscript in the months prior to my arrest. It had been rejected three times by the leading astrophysics journal. It turned out that one of the reviewers was a professor at the university, who, incidentally, oversaw a substantial government contract to study the nature of dark matter. My claim that dark matter is just a manifestation of gravity—that it is a relic of black holes and galaxy formation—well, that was very threatening to that guy."

“It’s not all that uncommon among scientists to have disputes, is it? Where was your adviser in all of this?” asked Charles.

Cédric looked down at his empty plate while he considered how to respond. “I guess that’s when the dark matter—pun intended—got the best of me. You see, Charles, I was very spoiled as a child. I always got my own way. I was strong-willed to the extreme. So, after my incident with the police, I decided to take on the university. There was a tribunal. A simple scolding would have sufficed, but I took the matter personally and made a very public stink. In reality, what I did by smuggling unprocessed uranium into my lab was serious but in no way deserving of expulsion from the school. Expulsion was a self-inflicted wound. I expected my father to come to my rescue and put the school in its place, but he was deeply embarrassed by the incident and would not even talk to me. I was expelled, the school confiscated my lab books and apparatus, and I was finished as a scientist.”

Cédric waved to the waiter for another round of coffee. “I slipped into a time of deep despair and depression. This was a very dark time for me. I began reading some books written by a twentieth-century Oxford professor named C. S. Lewis. Originally, I picked up the books to learn English, but ultimately these books saved my life. In particular, the book *The Screwtape Letters* became my faithful companion everywhere I went during the following couple of years. My parents had divorced by then. My mother had developed Alzheimer’s, and my father had placed her in a nursing home. He was about to marry his gold-digging paramour when she murdered him in a squabble over a prenuptial agreement. There was no place for me at home in Paris, so I moved to Val d'Isère to try to put my life back together. I just spent time in a machine shop for a couple of years learning the machinist trade. I built a steam engine from scratch. Someday I was hoping to show it to you." Cédric paused for a long time to sip his new cup of coffee and then said, "My father left me a sizeable fortune." He looked up at Charles to see his reaction.

It took Charles some time to digest this last comment.

"I guess you are wondering why I kept working at NaPiles as your lab assistant for the past ten years," said Cédric.

Charles said nothing. His eyes spoke volumes.

"I don't normally read newspapers, but on this one particular occasion, someone had left a copy of the *Grenoble Matin* on my table at a café, and I shoved it in my backpack. I had a near fatal motorcycle accident on the way home that day, and as I was recuperating in the hospital, I pulled out the copy of *Grenoble Matin*. I was ready for a change and began surveying the help-wanted ads just to see what kinds of things people were doing. When I saw your ad, something just clicked. I finally decided to check you out. It took me a couple of years, but the minute I met you, I knew that I wanted to make a career at NaPiles."

"Why didn't you tell me all of this at the beginning?" asked Charles.

"I was afraid you would think I was overqualified for the position. And after you hired me, my past was just no longer relevant."

"But ten years, Cédric! In ten years, you never once revealed a clue," exclaimed Charles.

"Actually, there was one point," responded Cédric, "when I stood outside your office door about to knock. I knew you were out of money and contemplating closing the business. We were very close to perfecting the Na-22 breakthrough. I knew it would revolutionize the sodium battery business. I was worried that my work would be for nothing, and I nearly approached you to see if you would accept an investment in the company from me. I decided at the last minute not to do it because I so valued our relationship."

"But, Cédric, you never got any credit for that invention," said Charles.

"My name is on the patent, and that is sufficient."

Charles took in a deep breath while he tried to put the pieces together. Then he said, "You are the one who wrote that anonymous email to Mr. Gardener at the e-trottinette company, aren't you?"

Cédric made no reply.

"Why did you stay on after I bought NaPiles back from the joint venture then?" asked Charles. "You could have had a terrific job in Valence."

“Oh, I was considering all kinds of options at the time,” replied Cédric. “I didn’t need the income. That is when you started talking about making neutron stars in a bottle. Who in their right mind would miss out on an opportunity like that?”

Charles was completely flummoxed. “Why didn’t you tell me then and there about your background?”

Cédric paused, staring into his empty coffee cup. “You know, Charles, in the ten years I have worked for you, you never once tried to second-guess me. You trusted my judgment, and I had complete freedom in the lab to build experiments that would work the way I knew they should work. What you routinely brought to the table was your flashes of genius, like the whole business that neutrons would act like strands of magnetic buckyballs. I was confident that a day like yesterday would arrive sooner or later, and there was never any reason for me to interject my own personal baggage into the arrangement.”

Charles sat quietly listening to the crackling fire, saddened by the realization that, in ten years, he had been so self-absorbed that he never had a clue that Cédric was anything more than his faithful lab assistant.

Finally, Cédric said, “You realize that we are on the cusp of unlocking the mysterious energy source in neutron stars, don’t you?”

“I guess I will have to take your word on that,” responded Charles.

The two headed back to the lab. The sun was starting to peek through a few holes in the dissipating storm clouds, and it had warmed up considerably during the preceding hour. Cédric explained to Charles that he had made a slight modification to the reactor by mounting a new aluminum tube on top of a load cell and disconnecting it from the mass spectrometer, which had now become superfluous. He had decided to defer any discussion of his discovery of the dark matter particle until a later date.

"I gather that you did not sleep last night," commented Charles.

"Sleep!" exclaimed Cédric. "Who can sleep at a time like this?" Upon entering the lab, he walked over to the reactor to be sure everything was operating optimally. The idea behind the load cell was to determine when one of the neutron fibers became too heavy to be levitated by the magnetic field and dropped down onto the inside of aluminum tube. He set it up so that the computer would log the proton current and the weight of the aluminum tube at the same time.

Just as he was watching, the load cell recorded a sudden jump in weight of 1.87 kilograms. "Charles!" he shouted. "You have got to see this." The elapsed time of the proton generator was 7.18 hours, so he calculated the number of neutrons produced to be about 250 million. Charles looked on with interest while Cédric did the calculations, explaining the steps as he went.

"See, 2.5×10^{8} neutrons weighing 1.870 kilograms suggests a neutron rest mass of about 7.5×10^{-9} kilograms. That's eighteen orders of magnitude greater than the accepted value of 1.67×10^{-27} kilograms." Cédric looked up at Charles to be sure he was following. "We have apparently created a supermassive object with properties not too different from what exists in a neutron star. The only real difference is that we have done it at a temperature slightly above absolute zero."

Going on excitedly, Cédric said, "Now we know that the total energy of the ensemble of neutrons in the fiber has not changed appreciably. If it had, we would be detecting copious beta emissions. This means that mc^2 based on Einstein's equation has not changed. For energy to be conserved, the ratio of the masses must equal the reciprocal of the ratio of the speed of light squared. Here's the point: the mass ratio of the measured weight, 1.87 kilograms, divided by the rest mass of the neutrons generated, 4.18×10^{-19} kilograms, is about 4.5×10^{18}." Cédric looked at him with a huge grin, as if everything he had ever thought or done seriously in his life had finally fallen into place. "There is one, and only one, possible explanation for this: the speed of light inside the fiber is slower than the free space value—in fact, by the square root of the mass ratio." Cédric typed some numbers into his calculator. "That would be about 2×10^9 times slower, which means the speed of light inside the fiber must be just fourteen centimeters per second." Cédric walked around the reactor again to recheck the readings while a shocked Charles stood motionless. "You realize, Charles, if this is not the biggest scientific discovery in human history, I can't imagine what is."

Charles said, “Even if what you are saying is true, I’m not sure I completely grasp the implications.”

Cédric replied excitedly, “The implications are truly mind-boggling, but I am really worn out. I didn’t know that triumph could be so taxing. After fifteen difficult years, I am finally vindicated. If you don’t mind, I would like to head home now to celebrate with a bottle of Bordeaux wine I have been saving for this very occasion. I am going to take a hot bath and sleep for twelve hours. I will be back in the morning with a plan of action for the next step.” He departed without saying another word.

Chapter 24: Microfusion

The following morning, Charles went to the lab earlier than normal to catch up on some paperwork. He was expecting Cédric to be late, but the lab was open, and Cédric was already hard at work. "How was your celebration last night?" Charles inquired.

"Oh, the jubilation lasted about as far as the train station. My brain is in overdrive, and I just can't turn it off. I decided to save the wine for another occasion and just went to bed early instead." Cédric went to his desk to fetch some printouts. "Here, I have something interesting to show you. By the way, we made three more neutron fibers during the night. It is curious that each one seems to weight about the same, between one and a half and two kilograms."

Cédric handed Charles the beaker containing the neutron fibers he had collected from the previous two days. "I have kept this beaker isolated, surrounded by lead bricks with a scintillation detector. Look!" he said to Charles. "They are still in there, and I never detected a single beta decay! This is a real mystery. I had expected them to decompose by now. Neutrons are not stable, as you know, but it seems these clusters are very stable. Their weight has not changed at all—at least when they are at rest. I have been giving a lot of thought to the reason for this, and I have a hypothesis. But I warn you, it's very far out there."

"Tell me," Charles said eagerly.

"Well, the rate of nuclear decay is time dependent. That is, the half-life of a decay process is given per unit time. But what is time, really? It is inextricably linked to the speed of light. When we say, for example, a star is one hundred light-years away, what do we mean? We mean it takes a light beam traveling three hundred million meters per second one hundred years to get here. The distance traveled per unit time is assumed to have a fixed value. Everything we measure that is time-dependent presumes this constant value of the speed of light—nuclear decay rates, for example. But what if this is not actually the case? The accepted half-life of a free neutron is about ten minutes. But what is it in a reference frame where the speed of light is nine orders of magnitude slower? It's one hundred billion seconds! That's more than three thousand years." Cédric got up from the table to let the reality sink in while he fetched a cup of coffee from the espresso machine. "Espresso, Charles?"

"Yes, please." Charles was looking at the notes Cédric had scribbled. "How can you be sure?"

Cédric continued as he operated the espresso maker. "This explains the stability of our neutron fibers. I don't think we would see a single neutron decay in our lifetime. Everything in the fiber is slowed down. What's even more interesting is that everything within the gravitational influence of the fiber is also slowed down."

Cédric handed Charles his coffee and sat back down. "There's more," Cédric continued with a jubilant smile. "This morning, I noticed something odd. You know, in a big government lab, something like this would go unnoticed because everyone's work is so compartmentalized that no single individual ever gets a chance to see the big picture and correlate seemingly unrelated events. I've been noticing that the power required by the cryo-cooler has been increasing. This would be an indication that we were generating some heat inside the reaction chamber. I had attributed it to the heat generated by protons crashing into the detector. But this morning, I saw something quite startling. Every time a new neutron fiber was detected by the load cell, there was a sudden increase in the power consumption by the cryo-cooler."

"What do you think that means?" asked Charles.

"It means the heat is coming from the neutron clusters, not protons in the detector." Cédric let this news sink in while he fetched a printout from the mass spectrometer. "I had disconnected the mass spectrometer once we stopped seeing massive clusters appear. In hindsight, I regret doing this, but I turned it back on yesterday." Cédric handed the printout to Charles. "I had only been looking for high atomic mass clusters. I never bothered to look at the low atomic mass peaks until yesterday. Well, here's the data from one to twenty amu that I never bothered to check. You will see a peak at amu 1 for single neutrons and some stray protons, as expected, and a small peak at amu 2. That would be due to some deuterons. I expect that every once in a while, when a proton from the beam strikes a deuterium nucleus in the polyethylene target just right, it might knock out a deuteron rather than just a neutron. But this is a one in a million event, so the peak in the mass spectrograph is small."

"What's this rather large peak at amu 4?" inquired Charles.

"Ah, yes. I was hoping you would notice. That's helium."

"Is that unusual?" asked Charles.

"Totally," responded Cédric with glee. "That is the fingerprint of nuclear fusion."

Cédric led the way to a small conference table in the lab and spread out his papers. "Yesterday afternoon on my way home on the train, it struck me that we might be making little nuclear bombs. It probably wouldn't play well in the press if we wiped Saint-Michel off the map." He looked up at Charles with a wry grin. "Don't worry, Charles. That will never happen. The level is miniscule, but I think it explains why the cryo-cooler is working harder. When I started doing my PhD research, I was captivated by a paper published in 1989 by a couple of scientists in Utah by the names of Pons and Fleischmann, claiming the discovery of cold fusion. They were ridiculed mercilessly and ultimately disgraced. I think this made them my kindred spirits. They were a sort of role model for rogue scientists like me. Anyway, many experiments conducted over the following years could not generate enough heat to be conclusive. There was ample evidence, however, for the production of small amounts of helium by deuterium-deuterium fusion. As a scientist, spouting support for cold fusion was like believing in the Tooth Fairy, so I kept my opinions to myself. But I never stopped pondering the prospects. I concluded that cold fusion was real, but the reaction rate was just too slow to be definitive."

Charles brightened. "I think I may know where you're going with this."

"Indeed," replied Cédric. "Any two deuterons that come into contact with a neutron fiber have three thousand years to decide if they want to join together, rather than picoseconds, as in a normal cold fusion cell.

"There is something else," said Cédric. "When we were only making unstructured neutron clusters, I didn't see any helium or other unusual low amu species. That's why I stopped checking. I didn't start seeing the helium signature until we started making neutron tubes. The random clusters did not produce measurable helium. I think this is because deuterons are repelled by the magnetic field of the neutron clusters. The magnetic field of neutron tubes, on the other hand, vanishes on the inside. Any deuterons that happen to find their way to the opening at the ends will slip inside and remain essentially unperturbed forever."

Cédric stood up and clapped his hands. "Charles, we have unlocked the secret of microfusion."

Charles sat stunned. "You realize, Cédric," he finally said, "you have now ventured into a fantasy world. No one would ever believe this."

"But no one needs to know. Nor should they know," replied Cédric. "This discovery has nothing to do with becoming famous.

My scientific reputation is not on the line. All the evidence points to the discovery of microfusion. With just a few small modifications to the reactor, I believe I can prove it. If not, there isn't much downside. We can just keep this between us. We won't ever have to face the public humiliation Pons and Fleischmann faced. That's the beauty of privately funded research."

"I think it would be wise to begin preparing a patent disclosure, in any case," said Charles.

Cédric replied, "By the time you have something ready to submit to the patent attorney, I will have all the supporting evidence you'll need—that is, unless I am just delusional and living in a fantasy world." Cédric chuckled in such a confident manner that this was clearly not going to be the case.

Chapter 25: Cédric's Pea

Cédric had convinced Charles to get out of his hair and spend a few days at his ski chalet in Breuil-Cervinia. This also gave Charles a good opportunity to work on the patent disclosure and study Cédric's light speed theories more carefully. He had received a call from his wife a couple of days later that there had been an explosion and fire at the lab—nothing too serious, but Cédric requested that he come back immediately. Charles was expecting some sort of catastrophe. Instead, he was greeted at the lab by a jubilant Cédric.

"What's all this about a fire?" Charles asked.

"Oh, it was nothing," replied Cédric. "I just ignited some insulation, and the smoke detector alerted the fire department. They had it out in just a couple of minutes. Look! You are not going to believe what I have to show you."

Charles was surveying the damage to the scorched wall behind the reactor, while Cédric was holding up a printout from the thermocouple inside the reactor.

"I actually melted the reactor tube!" Cédric exclaimed.

"Okay, Cédric, why don't you start at the beginning," Charles suggested.

Cédric explained, "I had substituted the hydrogen tank we were using to supply the proton generator with a tank of heavy hydrogen to generate a beam of deuterons, and I removed the polyethylene plug that we used for generating neutrons and replaced it with a gold foil to slow the deuterons down. Before I did this, I made a single neutron fiber, as I had done several times before, which was lying on the bottom of the aluminum reactor tube. I verified this by the weight detected on the load cell. A few seconds after I switched on the deuterium beam, there was a blinding flash of light. The back end of the reactor was blown out, and the wall was on fire!" Cédric was beaming. "Don't you see, Charles? I just carried out the very first controlled fusion experiment. This is a triumph!"

"This is not exactly what I would call *controlled*," Charles replied, looking again at the scorched back wall. "It's a wonder you weren't killed!"

Cédric just smiled and held up the mass spectrometer printout showing a huge spike of helium. "Charles!" he said. "Don't you see? We just built a neutron star in a bottle! As soon as I get this mess cleaned up, I will rebuild the reactor and adjust the beam current so the result is less dramatic."

Charles stared at him and said, "Cédric, have you lost your mind?"

Cédric replied, "Don't worry. I know what went wrong. I fed the reactor with too much deuterium. I didn't expect all of it to fuse at once. I basically created a miniature hydrogen bomb."

This last comment was no comfort to Charles, who stood and just shook his head.

"Okay," said Cédric. "At least let me rebuild the reactor. I don't think it is damaged beyond repair. It will take me a couple of weeks. Then we can discuss where to go from here."

While Cédric was rebuilding the reactor, Charles was busy documenting every detail in anticipation of the patent that needed to be filed on the microfusion invention. Safety aside, Charles and Cédric had a pretty good idea of the commercial potential of their discovery. They collaborated closely on every detail in preparation for a public announcement.

Charles had been developing a growing sense of concern over the potential implications for national security in that it was probable that the ability to fabricate miniature hydrogen bombs was at least something the French government should be aware of. He visited the French nuclear directorate in Grenoble several times to arrange confidential briefings on the technology. Their conclusion after a series of meetings was that Charles was certifiably insane. Since there was no working reactor at that moment and no way to demonstrate the experiment, Charles grew increasingly impatient with the whole process.

Meanwhile, Cédric was on track to be able to restart the reactor under more controlled conditions using a much lower deuteron beam current. Cleaning up the mess inside the reactor after the explosion consisted of scraping hundreds of tiny molten globules of aluminum from the reaction tube that had gotten stuck on the inside walls of the chamber. Most of these globules were just ordinary aluminum, but there was one—about the size of a pea—that was different, being very heavy and weighing more than a kilogram. He surmised that it contained the neutron fiber in which the reaction had taken place. One of the mysteries was why the neutron fiber—if it really was the original hollow neutron fiber—had not been blown apart by the blast. The pea-sized globule, which had a glassy appearance, was nearly spherical. He placed it in a plastic vial and spent some days trying to decide how he would go about analyzing it.

One day, he was rolling the pea around in the palm of his hand when he observed that it seemed to get lighter and lighter the faster he moved it around, just like he had observed previously with the fibers in the beaker of water. That was when he made the most remarkable discovery of his entire life. The pea accidently rolled out of the palm of his hand and started to fall to the floor. Cédric let out a shriek, fearing he would destroy or lose the specimen. But it didn't fall. It simply drifted to the ground like a feather. He repeated the action several times before placing the pea back in the vial and carefully putting it on the shelf. That freak observation would become the motivation for everything he would do for the rest of his life.

Cédric succeeded in getting the reactor working again with numerous improvements, where he began assembling neutron fibers with ease. He also made the new reactor robust enough that, should he have another accident like before, the reactor vessel would be able to withstand it. He developed a protocol for creating a neutron fiber in the chamber and very slowly increasing the beam current to produce heat and a constant and controlled flux of helium. The reactor was fully instrumented with calorimetry sensors and a radiation detector, so he was able to establish complete control over the process.

Meanwhile, Charles had completed all the patent disclosures and turned them over to his patent lawyer in Grenoble. He had finally succeeded in arranging for one of the scientists from the nuclear directorate to visit Saint-Michel-de-Maurienne for a demonstration. That skeptical scientist watched carefully as Cédric demonstrated his reactor and tried to explain how it worked. Once the poor French scientist got over the shock of what he had seen and reported it back to the directorate, NaPiles was overrun by an army of government people and national police. Thereafter, the entire project was sequestered as top secret due to national security concerns, and Cédric and Charles were not allowed to reenter the lab. Soldiers packed up all the equipment and cleaned out the lab, relocating everything to Grenoble. Cédric was instructed to set up the new lab and undergo weeks of debriefing. Had it not been for the invention disclosure Charles dropped off with his patent lawyer, that might have been the end of it. As it turned out, they wrote NaPiles a check for €1.5 million for the equipment and gave Charles a stern warning never to discuss this with anyone under penalty of law.

As the last truck was departing from the parking lot with the remaining contents of the NaPiles laboratory, Cédric reached in his pocket and handed Charles the plastic vial containing the little magic pea. He said, "Charles, this vial contains the most important thing you will ever see. Don't ever show it to anyone and don't lose it. Put it somewhere safe. It has been a joy to work with you. Stay in touch." They embraced, and Cédric headed for the train station for the last time. Charles went home, placing the vial on the bookcase in his office. He subsequently forgot all about it in the chaos of the following months.

Chapter 26: The Mathematician

Microfusion was being considered as perhaps the most important discovery of all time, but due to the secrecy involved, no one had any knowledge about it outside of a small cadre of scientists and administrators at the Nuclear Directorate. Cédric had been assigned to work in a building called the General Research Laboratory, or GRL. The agency that oversaw the work was typical of almost any government bureaucracy trying to carry out top secret research. The highly classified work was compartmentalized, and each person assigned to the project typically knew very little about the activities of anyone outside of their own specialized work cell. Simple tasks that Cédric was accustomed to doing himself got parceled out to various groups. Every design iteration required mountains of red tape to obtain engineering approval and multiple signatures. He was not allowed into the machine shop, and he needed to obtain a work authorization just to tighten a screw, and then, once the screw tightening was authorized, another worker authorized to tighten screws was required to carry out the work. Nonetheless, development of microfusion proceeded rapidly. It was quickly discovered that winding neutron strands into tubes was unnecessary. In fact, Cédric's discovery that deuterons were able to get packed into the hollow space inside the neutron tubes was deemed too unpredictable and dangerous. It was found that deuterons could just as easily occupy interstitial sites between unstructured neutron nanoclusters. The concentration of deuterons could be tightly controlled so that the resulting material, mistakenly termed *powder*, produced a constant flux of heat. This material was easy to make, and megawatt-scale generators were being produced in just a matter of weeks.

Cédric had been treated like a celebrity at first, but it wasn't long before he had been reduced to irrelevancy. The rigid constraints of the work environment quickly became tedious for him, and he slowly disengaged mentally from the project. He had been granted a provisional secret clearance, but the permanent clearance was being held up due to his drunk driving arrest in Colorado, which he had failed to disclose during screening interviews with the security officials. Working at the GRL had become a type of house arrest. His contract prevented him from publishing papers or disclosing anything. Management had not wanted to run the risk that the microfusion technology would ever get tainted by what they considered to be Cédric's bizarre variable light speed theories. The bigger problem, however, was that he was being treated as a second-class scientist. He was looked down upon by the senior scientists who held multiple degrees from prestigious universities and had authored textbooks and hundreds of peer-reviewed scientific papers. Cédric had none of these credentials, and his colleagues had subtle ways of reminding him of this fact. He had been assigned to a working group consisting of some of the best and brightest scientific minds in all of France. At question was the issue of variable light speed.

The reality of microfusion was never in doubt, but the senior scientists in the group insisted on finding an alternative explanation to Cédric's claim that the speed of light slows down in the presence of supermassive neutron clusters. They needed an explanation that did not require them to discard three hundred years of scientific orthodoxy.

Things came to a head when the matter of the strange whistling signal observed when two neutron clusters collided was being discussed. Cédric was certain that he had resolved the question satisfactorily, but his explanation required acceptance of his theories regarding the time dependence of both the light speed and the mass. In the end, the other scientists rejected his theories. One day, Cédric had reached his breaking point and stormed out of the conference room in a rage. He went into the breakroom to fix himself a cup of coffee and sat down in the corner to stew.

"May I join you?"

Looking up, Cédric recognized one of the other scientists who had just joined his work cell. He pointed to the chair across the table and said nothing.

"My name is Magdalena," she said, extending her hand in greeting. Her smile melted Cédric's hostile countenance in an instant. All he could manage was an embarrassing stare.

She said, "I believe you, Dr. Rothschild."

"I'm not a doctor," was his response.

"Formal degrees mean nothing to me," she said. "I have been listening carefully for the past couple of days to you expositing your light speed theories. Certainly, you know how threatening these ideas are to the others in our group. They can't permit themselves to believe for one instant that everything they ever thought about light speed is wrong. Surely you understand this."

"Tell me, Magdalena, what is your field of expertise?"

"I am a mathematician," she replied. "A modeler, to be exact. I develop ultrafast algorithms for complex simulations that typically cannot be treated by any other means."

"Like many-body mechanics problems?" asked Cédric, perking up.

"Yes," replied Magdalena.

"Would you by any chance know how to simulate galaxy formation from a black hole?" he asked.

The commute from Montmélian to Grenoble by train took only thirty minutes, but it was becoming increasingly difficult for Cédric. His back had started bothering him, and the trek up and down the hill to Villa Chandellepont had become a struggle for him. He had come to the realization that no one at the GRL cared whether he showed up for work, and he began showing up later and later, and sometimes not at all. He had entered a season of melancholy. When he was working at NaPiles, he had the daily challenges of problems to solve that kept him going, but no such challenges were coming from work at the GRL. He had become increasingly introspective and spent much of his time alone in his office, writing religious and scientific reflections in his journal. His intellectual energies had become focused on gaining a better understanding of gravity in the context of variable light speed. But generally, he was feeling isolated and lonely.

One day, Cédric overheard some people in the cafeteria discussing recent data that had been collected on binary stars nearby in the Milky Way galaxy. He perked up and slid his chair to join their table. This resulted in hushed silence because their project was highly classified, and they should not have been talking about it in the open.

"It's okay," said Cédric. "I have a secret clearance."

The people at the table—none of whom Cédric knew—were looking at one another in astonishment. One finally said, "I am pretty sure your clearance doesn't go high enough to eavesdrop on what we were just talking about."

Another said, "Hey, aren't you the variable light speed guy?" This brought a chuckle. Cédric withdrew and returned to his own table.

It took some time and a fair amount of bribery for Cédric to unravel what those people had been discussing. But even in a highly compartmentalized institution like the Astrophysics Directorate, once one was on the inside, even things shrouded in secrecy could be obtained, given the right resources and some sense of what one was looking for. As it turned out, there was some sort of top-secret installation on the back side of the moon. He was unable to determine the purpose, but there was apparently a high-resolution gamma imaging system sending huge amounts of encrypted data back to the GRL. They had apparently been monitoring some sort of anomalous celestial event, the nature of which no one seemed to know. What Cédric was able to find out, however, was that detailed tracks of moving objects in the galaxy were being recorded. He wondered if there might possibly be new data on the motion and collisions of binary neutron stars. If such data were to contain sufficient fidelity, it could prove very interesting. With Magdalena's assistance, he managed to gain access to certain subsets of the data that were considered "uninteresting." Those images may have been uninteresting to whoever was obtaining them, for reasons buried deep in secrecy, but they were a gold mine for Cédric because they contained the tracks of several binary neutron stars in the background.

Classical mechanics dating back to the time of Sir Isaac Newton provided the framework for how the force of gravity would determine the motion of stars as they approached one another on a collision course. Conservation of angular momentum would draw them into a spiral dance, requiring them to circle around one other in smaller and smaller orbits with faster and faster velocities until they finally collided with an enormous flash of gamma radiation. Then they would disappear into a black hole from which no more radiation could escape. This phenomenon had intrigued Cédric from childhood, but no one had actually observed it taking place in real time because the event often took place over centuries. Bits and pieces of the process had been discerned from the many such snapshot images that had been photographed at different times and places capturing the various stages of the binary system evolution. Cédric had thought that, if the resolution were high enough, images obtained over weeks or months might provide the detailed trajectories necessary to determine whether the motions actually behaved according to Newton's prediction. Space-based telescopes in orbit around the earth had brought a huge improvement over celestial telescopes, but their relative velocities with respect to the earth made data deconvolution difficult. A telescope based on the back side of the moon was quite another matter. The stable platform offered by the moon, absent the background interference from the earth, and having a fixed position in space relative to the earth should offer unprecedented details not previously available. Cédric could hardly contain his excitement.

The problem was that the amount of data that needed to be processed was daunting—well beyond anything in Cédric's ability to handle and requiring the GRL's fastest computers. He had submitted a proposal to the authorities to study the data. After some consideration, they concluded that such a project might get Cédric out of their hair and eliminate the trouble he had been stirring up over his explanation of the strange signals detected when neutron clusters collided. They also assigned Dr. Magdalena Roberts to the task, knowing that she was sympathetic to Cédric's bizarre theories and was becoming a liability to the program.

Magdalena had arranged for a small conference room within a secured area, called a SCIF for sensitive compartmented information facility, where secret information was handled. Once the images were determined to be "harmless," they were released for study but only within the secured area. It was fortuitous that a pulsar from a particular binary star system was being used for synchronizing the images collected once each day at exactly the same time. This provided a precise three-dimensional location for every object in the galaxy. Cédric could not have hoped for more than what was provided by these images obtained in the x-ray and gamma ray spectrum over the course of the proceeding twelve months—378 time-sequenced images, to be exact. The data provided about one arc-second of space, which was sufficient for Cédric and Magdalena to identify several binary neutron star systems and begin fitting the trajectories. After a while, the security officer in charge of the area concluded that they were not spies and began permitting them some liberty to remove certain of their work from the secured area.

Magdalena said one day as they were reviewing the sequence of the images, "Cédric, there's really not much to go on."

Cédric replied with confidence, "Each day, the data gets better and better. We already have nearly enough data to see whether the stars are following classical orbits. We should be able to observe that the magnitude of the effect is increasing. The classical model predicts that the force of gravity between the two neutron stars is the product of their masses divided by the square of distance separating them, times the universal gravitational constant. Look." He pointed to the track representing what the classical model predicted. "Already there is a deviation beyond the statistical error."

"Is it significant enough?" she asked.

Cédric replied, "This is the point where I need your model. We can't really predict what the trajectories should be without it. My hypothesis, based on variable light speed, predicts that the speed of light is not the proportionality constant between the square root of the energy divided by the masses. I claim that the speed of light is slowing down in the vicinity of the neutron stars due to the enormous masses involved, and that the speed of light should be decreasing exponentially as the stars move closer and closer together. We should be able to detect this, but I can't estimate the magnitude of the effect without the ability to model the system with variable mass and variable gravity at the same time. Every dependent variable in the problem needs to be treated as having time-dependency. You are the only one I know who can do this."

Magdalena sat back in her chair. "Cédric. Do you have any idea how much work is involved in writing the code for such a model?"

Cédric just smiled and said, "Who else do you know who is better equipped for such an undertaking?"

In order to have a place to stay when the weather was bad, Cédric had rented a small apartment on the west bank of the Isère in Grenoble, close to the city center and not far from the GRL. He had started to like Grenoble more and more, as he enjoyed being surrounded by people. Grenoble was charming. It was a laid-back city, not too big but with all the big-city advantages and less hustle and bustle than most big cities. He loved to stroll along the river to think and reflect while frequenting the numerous cafés and bistros. He finally decided to move his office from Villa Chandellepont to his Grenoble apartment and informed Brother Andrew that the upstairs rooms would be available as needed. The timing could not have been better. The demands of the mission to Eastern European refugees had become overwhelming, and every bed was a blessing.

There was something more subtle that was drawing Cédric to spend more time in Grenoble: Magdalena. The relationship had started out simply as collegial. They would meet in the cafeteria at the GRL for lunch a couple of times a week to discuss his gravitational theories. This turned into spending time together on weekends. Cédric started experiencing a range of unfamiliar emotions. All he could think about was Magdalena. He had tried to explain what he was experiencing one day to Brother Andrew, who chuckled and said, "Cédric, I think you are falling in love." The prospects of such a thing had not crossed his mind. He had grown up in a totally dysfunctional environment with a philandering father and a mother ill-equipped to deal with the stress of a failed marriage. His brother had always had an entourage of girlfriends. The only love that Cédric had ever received growing up was from his American nanny, Annie. He had always been awkward and uncomfortable around girls. He had assumed that falling in love was something others experienced—not him. Anyway, he was quite sure that Magdalena did not share his feelings, until one lovely day in spring, when they were strolling along next to the Isère, she took his hand in hers and intertwined her fingers with his. He nearly passed out. They walked on for some time without saying a word. Cédric knew he had begun a new chapter of his life.

Chapter 27: Gravity

Magdalena was British. She was ten years younger than Cédric. At age thirty-nine, she was radiant. All Cédric wanted was to be around her and spend as much time together as possible. She had grown up in Manchester and knew all about Chandellepont University and the "Rothschild scanal". In fact, her uncle, Cecil Edwards, had been Cédric's thesis adviser. She had demonstrated unusual aptitude in mathematics from childhood and was considered a geek in school. She had jumped at the chance to earn her PhD in the United States at Princeton University. It came as a big surprise to him to discover that she was also a thrill seeker. She had always liked jumping off things and had originally come to Grenoble to take up paragliding. This led to skydiving, technical mountain climbing, and a couple of fast descents from the summit in a wing suit. Cédric, on the other hand, liked to study about gravity but did not care much for experiencing its effects. A broken leg from a failed attempt on a snowboard to make a jump as a child and a more recent broken wrist from a crash on a trottinette that hadn't fully healed served as reminders that gravity was not Cédric's friend. Magdalena had been trying without success to get him to try paragliding. That was more thrill than he cared to take on at his age. Anyway, his chronic back pain would have prevented it. His chiropractor had cautioned him to avoid high-impact sports. He reached a compromise of sorts with Magdalena. She had never ridden a horse, and Cédric promised to take her riding once the weather improved. He had assured her that the experience would still be thrilling without the associated risk, because the distance to the ground was a great deal less than with paragliding.

That winter in Grenoble had been unusually cold. Snow from several storms had piled up everywhere, making getting around challenging. The work at the GRL entailed endless hours for Magdalena writing computer code and validating the models and fitting the images to them. There wasn't much that Cédric could accomplish by going into the lab, so he stayed in his apartment, where he worked on his gravitation theories. The initial indication from the trajectories of the binary neutron star system that they had been studying supported his hypothesis that the mass of the stars was increasing with time. He knew this flew in the face of Newtonian mechanics, but the data was still not sufficiently compelling. The traditional model of the force of gravity attracting two bodies was based on the presumption that the masses were constant. Isolated neutron stars could gain mass by vacuuming up interstellar debris, but Cédric did not believe it would be possible for the stars to gain as much mass as the data was suggesting. He was confident that each of the neutron stars was subject to the law of conservation of energy, which meant that the observed increase in mass of the rotating stars had to be offset by a corresponding decrease in the square of the speed of light, according to Einstein's formula, $E = mc^2$. The time-sequenced gamma ray images that he and Magdalena were able to study were beginning to tell this story in a convincing manner. Almost all other methods for measuring celestial events relied on the assumption that the speed of light is a universal constant, and the interpretation of observations depended explicitly on the fixed speed of light in some way. Cédric;s and Magdalena's method relied, instead, on inertial observations of the stars, which did not directly depend on the speed of light, fixed or otherwise. It was the discrepancy between the inertial mass of stars in the distant galaxies and the assumed mass based on their luminosity that had led Cédric to hypothesize thirty years earlier that the dark matter that was proposed to explain the discrepancy was really an artifact of increasing light speed. Galaxy formation from a black hole involved increasing speed of light and decreasing effective mass as the galaxy expanded. What they were observing with the binary neutron stars was the process in reverse. Cédric hypothesized that the masses of the two stars would continue to increase, and the speed of light in their vicinity would continue to decrease as they drew closer and closer together—until they collided to form a black hole, where the light would be frozen into a stationary state at close to zero velocity. The cycle of galaxy formation could then repeat for eternity.

Cédric had made plans to meet Magdalena for dinner. She had told him earlier in the day that she was working on a particularly demanding section of computer code and not to interrupt her, so it came as a surprise when he received a text alert to call her as soon as possible.

"Cédric!" she exclaimed when she answered his call. "You are not going to believe what I just discovered. How quickly can you come to the GRL?"

"What is it?" he asked.

"I can't explain it over the phone," she replied. "You need to see this for yourself, but it means joining me in the SCIF."

Cédric bundled up and headed across the bridge to the tram stop on the other side of the river. In ten minutes, he got off at the front entrance of the GRL and went through the mandatory security screening for entering the facility. Magdalena was waiting for him in the SCIF.

"So, what's all the excitement?" he said, sitting down next to her in front of the video screen mounted on the wall. She had arranged the enhanced gamma ray images in sequence for the past year and a half to run like a movie clip that took about fifteen seconds. The motions of the two neutron stars circling each other could be observed over the course of about a quarter of a revolution. Magdalena had superimposed a disc showing the equatorial plane of the two stars and a line showing the axis of revolution.

She ran the clip. "Watch this," she said.

Cédric observed the sequence of images he had seen several times before. "I've already seen this," he said.

She rewound the sequence to the beginning and paused at the first frame, pointing to another star just off axis below the equatorial plane of the neutron binaries. "Keep an eye on this star in the southern hemisphere," she said, starting the sequence again.

"I see," said Cédric. "It moved slightly in the direction of the axis. It looks like it is being pulled in by the gravitational field of the binary. Nice work! Let's go grab coffee."

Magdalena started the sequence again from the beginning. "Now watch this other star," she said, pointing to a star along the axis in the northern hemisphere. When she ran the sequence again, Cédric stood up and walked up to the screen.

"Run that again," he said. He watched carefully to be sure. Turning, he asked, "Are you absolutely positive about the position of that star relative to the binary?"

"I have checked it and rechecked it," she replied.

"Run it one more time," he said. After some reflection, he sat back down. "That star is moving away from the binary, isn't it?"

"Yes," she answered with delight. "Do you think it is some sort of antigravity effect?"

"Possibly," he replied. "I have been grappling with the concept of gravity for years. Some things just didn't add up. Why is the force of gravity always attractive? Until now, I assumed, like everyone else, that it's just the way it is. Gravity is simply an intrinsic property of mass, and masses attract one another for some unknown reason. Magdalena, I think you just discovered that this may not always be the case!" He looked intently at her and asked, "Who else has seen this?"

"No one," she replied. "You are the first to see it."

"Good," he replied. "Let's just keep this between the two of us. Some things are finally starting to fall into place, and I need time to think about this."

"Are you going to give me a hint what's on your mind?" she asked.

"We have been operating under the assumption that gravity is an intrinsic property of mass that is somehow communicated between masses by some wave phenomenon at the speed of light—gravity waves, if you will. Your analysis of the neutron binary has been confirming that the masses of the neutron stars are increasing as they draw closer and closer together, and we have been attributing this to decreasing light speed, which retards how long it takes for the gravity information to be communicated between the two stars. I observed this effect in a most remarkable way some years ago when I accidently dropped a piece of aluminum with a neutron cluster encased inside. I told you this story, didn't I? The sphere drifted to the floor like a feather. I have been trying to understand what I saw ever since without success. But what you just showed me—the possibility that gravity could be repulsive—changes everything." Cédric paused to try to articulate some wild thoughts he had been turning over in his brain for years—ideas he had not allowed himself to pursue until that moment.

"Tell me more," she said.

"Are you sure?" he responded. "These ideas are nascent and not very well formulated in my mind at this point."

"Cédric," she said, taking his hand, "when was the last time I gave you a hard time for having crazy ideas?"

He smiled. "Okay, but bear with me. This is sort of off the cuff. It has always troubled me that gravity and magnetism are not related in some way."

"You are not the first one to be troubled by that," said Magdalena. "Einstein spent his final years at Princeton trying to find a unified field theory. There is a whole wing of the library there dedicated to that pursuit."

Cédric continued, "I am convinced that Einstein would have found it if he had been willing to abandon the Lorentz hypothesis that the speed of light is a universal constant. Had he done that, he would have realized that the universal gravitational constant was also not really a constant. There is only one type of matter that we know of—antimatter notwithstanding. Matter consists of roughly equal numbers of positively and negatively charged particles. When charges are separated and isolated from one another, then like charges repel each other and unlike charges attract each other by the strong Coulomb force. There is no analog for this with gravitation." Cédric pointed at the video screen. "Until now."

"Stationary charges attract or repel one another by Coulomb's law, but they must be moving to produce a magnetic field. Scientists since Newton have been treating gravity like a static phenomenon, like electrostatics without the charges, rather than like magnetism, which is a dynamic phenomenon. Static charges produce no magnetic field. For that, they must be in motion. Magdalena, gravity is not a consequence of the product of two masses. Mass has no intrinsic sign, but velocity does. Gravity is a consequence of the product of their momenta, a vector quantity that depends on both their mass and velocity. If you place two wires side by side and pass a current through them in opposite directions, the wires will be attracted by the induced magnetic field, and if you pass the current through them in the same direction, the wires are repelled. The attraction or repulsion has nothing to do with the sign of charge carriers—they are electrons in both wires. It depends on their relative velocities."

Cédric had become more and more excited as he explained this idea, which in hindsight had become patently obvious to him by that time. He stood up and pointed to the disc on the video screen containing the two neutron stars they had been studying. "Imagine if those stars were rotating charges. They would produce a magnetic field that would attract or repel other charges in the vicinity, depending on their sign. Gravity is no different, Magdalena. The rotating neutron stars are generating an enormous gravitational field that is attractive in the southern hemisphere and repulsive in the northern hemisphere."

Magdalena asked, "If that's the case, why has no one observed this before?"

Cédric replied, "For two reasons, I suppose. First, no one has had the kind of precision image sequences we have at our disposal, and the second is that no one was looking for this phenomenon because they assumed, like me, that gravity is always attractive. It is a miracle that you saw this. Do you have any idea of the consequences of this discovery?"

Magdalena was beaming. The look on Cédric's face was all the reward she had ever hoped for. Finally, she said, "It's nearly eight. Don't you think we should head to dinner and order a bottle of champaign to celebrate our discover of antigravity then?"

Cédric said, "We shouldn't call it antigravity. That's the wrong term. Antigravity belongs in science fiction. It would be like calling the north pole of a magnet the magnet and the south pole the 'antimagnet'. Just like with magnetism, gravity is a field phenomenon determined by the motion of masses rather than the motion of charges."

"What do you propose we call it then?" Magdalena asked.

He paused to reflect on the answer. "How about *gravitrons*? I just made that word up," he said with satisfaction.

"*Gravitrons.* Gravitrons is catchy. I like it," Magdalena said, "Let me put a few things away then, and we can go celebrate."

Chapter 28: The Trail Ride

Magdalena and Cédric worked feverishly on the Gravitron treatise throughout the winter and spring. Fleshing out the complex theory demanded a level of vector calculus that was beyond Cédric's math skills, but fortunately it was something Magdalena was comfortable with. The manuscript was nearing completion by her birthday on May 4. Cédric had invited her to celebrate her birthday with him at a very posh restaurant at the Bastille on the Chartreuse Mountain overlooking the city. They took the Grenoble-Bastille cable car up to the restaurant for their moonlight reservation at eight. Once they were seated and had ordered their dinner selections, Cédric removed a folder from his vest pocket and handed it to Magdalena with a big smile.

"What is this?" she asked, removing the contents while he watched expectantly, waiting for her reaction.

"It's your birthday present," he said. "I finished it yesterday."

She began reading the title aloud, "*Gravitron Theory and the Dynamics of Gravitational Fields Induced by Supermassive Objects in Motion*." She stopped reading momentarily. Then, without looking up, she continued, "By J. Cédric and Magdalena R. Rothschild." She raised her head slowly to engage Cédric's smile. He was holding up a huge diamond ring. "I don't understand," she said.

"Will you marry me?" he asked.

She was caught completely off guard. They had never discussed marriage, and the possibility had not even crossed her mind. She finally managed to say, “Cédric, this is very sudden.”

He replied, “I love you, and I want you to be my wife.”

“I don’t know what to say,” she said.

“Just say yes,” he replied. “Neither of us is getting any younger, and we need to continue the family legacy.”

“Family legacy? Children? Cédric! Have you lost your mind? I just turned forty.” Tears flooded her eyes as she stood up from the table and excused herself to go to the ladies’ room.

When she returned, she sat quietly for a while, then said, “Cédric, I love you dearly. I was just not prepared to have you propose marriage. We never discussed this.”

“I’m sorry,” he said. “I imagined that you would be thrilled.”

“The answer is not ‘no’,” she replied, “but I just need some time to consider it. We are such good friends. The idea of marriage just never crossed my mind.”

Cédric held up the ring. “Will you at least accept this as a birthday gift?”

Magdalena responded softly, “It would not be proper for me to wear an engagement ring before we are formally engaged. I am just going to need some time to think about this.”

Several days later, they went to dinner again, and Magdalena handed the folio containing Cédric’s manuscript across the table. “I made a few editions and some comments. You know, Cédric, you are a terrible speller,” she said with a giggle.

"So, what is your overall opinion?" he asked.

"It's truly brilliant," she replied, "but you already knew that."

Cédric had been staring at the cover page. "You crossed out your name," he commented.

"You mean as your wife?" she said.

"No, as my coauthor," he replied.

"I can't be your coauthor, Cédric."

"Why?" he replied. "You have made an essential contribution to this paper, and you are the only one between us with any publications to their credit. Without you, we would have no chance of getting through the peer review."

"Publications, yes, but in applied mathematics journals, not astrophysics." Magdalena picked up her menu and stared at it blankly. Then looking intently at him across the table, she said, "Even if you had Albert Einstein as a coauthor, this manuscript would never pass peer review."

Cédric looked back at her bewildered and somewhat hurt. "You have known all along my intentions to publish this paper," he said.

"I'm sorry, Cédric. No journal would ever accept this manuscript for publication. You know I believe your theories and consider them brilliant beyond imagination." She took his hand across the table. Looking at him lovingly, she said, "Your ideas are just too radical."

"Okay," he said. "We will simply self-publish the paper then."

"Without any experimental evidence?" she asked.

He shot back, "What do you consider the observation of the gravity effect from the neutron binary we have been studying to be?"

"You can't publish that. It's classified!" she shot back.

"Who cares?" he asked.

"I do!" she exclaimed. "I would lose my job and maybe be fined or go to prison."

He replied, "If you were to marry me, it wouldn't matter. You would never have to work again." A long silence prevailed. Having been sent away several times, the server stopped coming by their table to take their orders.

Cédric finally brightened and said, "I just had an incredible idea. What if we were to create a pseudonym? Then no one at the GRL would know."

"That's insane, Cédric," Magdalena replied.

He was deep in thought. "Consider this," he said enthusiastically. "We create a woman scientist with an exotic-sounding name. We fabricate her curriculum vitae, make up a bunch of scientific publications in nonexistent foreign journals." He looked up at the ceiling with a mischievous grin. "Sonya," he said. "A Romanian *femme fatale*. Dr. Sonya ... Dumitescu!" he blurted out. "It's perfect!"

"Cédric, now you have completely lost your mind."

"It's either that or you agree to marry me and be my coauthor." They both broke out laughing.

Cédric pulled up in a rental car in front of Magdalena's apartment where she had been standing as previously arranged. It was an unusually beautiful day in June, without a cloud in the sky. Magdalena slipped into the passenger seat.

"So, where are you taking me?" she asked.

Cédric kissed her on the hand and replied with a smile, "Val d'Isère."

"What's in Val d'Isère this time of year?" she asked.

"It's a surprise," he said. "I told you that I spent a lot of time there when I was a boy. I am taking you somewhere very special."

Once they started up the steep, windy road of the mountain pass, he asked, "Do you mind if I pull off the road where I had my motorcycle crash?"

"Of course not," she replied.

"I have not been back since the accident, so I hope I will recognize the spot. Ah, yes," he said, pointing to the road sign that was still bent sightly from when he had jumped from his Harley at the last minute before going over the edge.

They got out of the car, and Magdalena whistled when she peered over the edge of the two-hundred-meter sheer drop-off. Cédric stood back from the cliff, deciding not to relive the experience.

Back in the car, he asked, "Did you see my Harley down there?"

She answered, "If it's still down there, I didn't see anything. Perhaps the vegetation has overgrown it."

Back on the road, he said, "I used to drive this way a couple of times a week when I was living at the family compound in Val d'Isère. I have only been back once since my father was murdered."

Magdalena sat quietly to allow Cédric to reflect on his past. "Those were very dark days," he finally said, "But everything changed when I met you. Those dark days are long gone now."

The car pulled into a driveway in the outskirts of Val d'Isère and into a parking space next to a large barn. Horses and riders were coming and going in all direction.

"What is this place?" Magdalena asked.

Cédric replied, "Do you remember that I promised to take you horseback riding when the weather improved? This is the riding stable where I rode horses as a child. I have reserved two horses for us to go on a trail ride." He went to the back of the car to fetch the supplies for their picnic lunch at a lake a few kilometers up into the mountains.

Magdalena said with apparent apprehension, "You do remember, don't you, that I have never been on a horse."

"Don't worry," said Cédric. "I have arranged for you to have a lesson before we head out."

She learned quickly and soon seemed to be comfortable on horseback. Once she was checked out to the satisfaction of the instructor, she and Cédric headed out for a gentle ride along the service road of the ski area that led to the lake where they were planning to have lunch. The sky was brilliant blue in the crisp alpine air. The surrounding mountains still blanketed with snow created a bright backdrop for the emerald meadows covered with wildflowers. The thunder of late spring runoff cascaded down the slopes over waterfalls and echoed through the valleys. Numerous small streams intersected the trails, requiring the riders to be vigilant when crossing.

Magdalena yelled joyfully ahead to Cédric, "This is the most fun I have had in years."

Cédric looked back at her with a nod to confirm the shared exhilaration.

Then she said with a playful laugh, "The only thing lacking is speed." She kicked her heels into the side of her horse to go faster. "Catch Sonya if you can!" she shouted as she sped past Cédric on the trail.

"No, slow down!" he yelled. "You are not ready to gallop." But Magdalena had rounded a bend and was out of sight by the time he was able to catch up to her. Magdalena's horse was stopped and munching on the grass with reins dangling down, her body on the ground nearby.

"Magdalena!" he called out as he dismounted his horse. "Are you okay?"

She did not respond. She was lying motionless face down in some mud on the far side of a stream that crossed the trail. He ran up to her and gently rolled her over. Her eyes were closed tightly, and Cédric thought she might be unconscious. He took out his mobile phone and pressed the emergency button.

The response came immediately. "This is the Val d'Isère Dispatch. What is your emergency?"

Cédric replied in a panic, "I am horseback riding. My companion got thrown from her horse. She has a large gash on her head, and she is unconscious. It appears to be very serious. Please come quickly."

There was some rustling at the other end, followed by a long pause. "Okay. I show your transponder location as the west side of the Col du Santon. Is that correct?"

"Yes!" cried Cédric.

"The helicopter is on the way," replied the dispatcher.

It seemed like an eternity before Cédric heard the sound of helicopter blades. He jumped up and waved his arms to catch their attention as the craft feathered and settled on the meadow fifty meters away. Two people jumped out as the ambulance helicopter was about to touch the ground and the rotor began powering down. One of them ran toward Cédric, kneeling down next to Magdalena to feel her pulse.

"Is she dead?" Cédric asked.

The EMT shook his head and signaled to the other person to bring a gurney. He checked her vital signs and gave her an injection. The two EMTs carefully slid her onto a hard board and strapped her down, gently supporting and immobilizing her head before transferring her to the gurney and racing back to the ambulance helicopter.

"Where are you taking her?" Cédric demanded.

"To the Val d'Isère central hospital," one of them said. "Do you know it?"

"Yes," replied Cédric. He was in shock by that time and barely noticed the helicopter shooting into the sky with a roar. The horses had been spooked by the noise, but Cédric saw them grazing in the distance.

Cédric paced back and forth in the waiting room at the hospital for hours. Each time he asked the receptionist for a status update, she assured him that he would be notified as soon as possible. He had provided as much information about Magdalena as he knew, which wasn't very much. She had a sister in England, but he had no idea how to contact her. He had sent a message to her uncle who had also been his thesis adviser at Candlebridge but only received an automated response saying, "Greetings. This is Dr. Cecil Edwards. I have retired from the university, and I am out of the country. I will get back to you as soon as I am able." Otherwise, the hospital had succeeded in retrieving Magdalena's medical records.

At last, a doctor entered the waiting room. His countenance was grave as he flipped through the pages on his clipboard. "What is your relationship to the injured party?" he asked.

Cédric replied, "She is my girlfriend. Is she going to be all right?"

The doctor replied evasively, "Tell me about the accident."

"When can I see her?" Cédric asked.

"She is heavily sedated and cannot have any visitors. How did the accident take place?" he asked.

"I didn't see her actually fall," Cédric replied. "We were riding horses. It was her first time. Suddenly she took off in a gallop, and when I caught up with her, she was lying on the ground unconscious. She was bleeding heavily from a gash on her head. Everything else is just a blur."

"Can you confirm the patient's name and date of birth?" the doctor asked.

"Yes. Magdalena Roberts. May 4, 2020. When can I see her?" he asked pathetically.

The doctor looked at him carefully and finally said, turning, "Come with me."

Magdalena's head was bandaged and swollen. A ventilator tube extended from her mouth. Cédric hardly recognized her. She was confined to the bed with straps to prevent her from moving. Cédric gently took her hand, which lay limply at her side, and looked up at the doctor without speaking.

The doctor said, “She has apparently suffered a spinal cord injury. She is unable to breathe on her own. We are not equipped to treat her in this hospital, so we are in the process of arranging to transport her to the hospital in Grenoble.

The seriousness of Magdalena’s injuries dawned on him at that moment. He squeezed her hand reassuringly and felt a faint squeeze back.

Chapter 29: Independence

Magdalena's recovery was slow and painful. Two weeks in intensive care was followed by several surgeries and weeks in the hospital. Cédric sat by her bedside almost every day as the doctors held out hope that she would regain the use of her legs. But in the end, it had become clear that she would remain a paraplegic for the rest of her life. This realization led her into a deeper and deeper depression. Cédric had arranged to have her transferred to a private rehabilitation hospital where she could undergo physical therapy to prepare her for life in the world, but otherwise there was not much he could offer in the way of comfort. The Nuclear Directorate had placed her on long-term disability with full salary and benefits.

Cédric continued to be employed at the GRL and received a regular paycheck even though he rarely went into work. His absence was not noticed, however, as it was clear that the only reason they kept him employed was to enforce the conditions of his confidentiality agreement, which prevented him from publicly disclosing any of his work. Nevertheless, it did not keep him from sharpening his *gravitron* theories, even though he knew that if he were to try to publish his manuscript and go public with his theories, he would be fined and maybe sent to prison. Work on his manuscript had been progressing, but at more than fifty pages, it had turned into more of a manifesto than a simple journal article. He retained Sonya Dumitescu as a coauthor as a means of disguising Magdalena's involvement in the work. Anyway, she had mostly lost interest in the collaboration.

Periodically, he travelled to Montmélian to spend time with the brothers at the abbey and check up on Villa Chandellepont. Brother Andrew asked him on one occasion if Magdalena had reconsidered his marriage proposal.

Cédric replied with a sigh, "I don't think she will marry me. At least not now that she is convinced that I would only be asking her out of pity and guilt. The very best thing I could have offered her is myself, but I guess she will have to settle for the next best thing. I set up a trust fund that should cover all her needs for the rest of her life. I haven't told her yet. She has made it clear that she has no interest in any of my money. I also purchased a place in Grenoble for her. It is in the process of being renovated to be completely wheelchair accessible."

"How does she like it?" asked Brother Andrew.

Cédric replied, "I haven't told her about it yet either. She is stubborn and will probably refuse it, but I hope that once she figures out that there is no one out there willing to carry her up the three flights of stairs to her apartment, she will give in. Anyway, I put the title of the property in her name. She can do whatever she wants with it."

"What are your plans for Villa Chandellepont then?" asked Brother Andrew.

"That is one of the things I wanted to discuss with you," Cédric replied. "The property in Grenoble has an outbuilding that is perfect for my new workshop. It has an unfinished space on the second floor that I turned into an apartment for myself. Magdalena, if she agrees, will have the main house to herself. At least I will be nearby if she needs assistance. I am planning to relocate the equipment from here to this new workshop. I have basically solved most of the last remaining issues of my gravitron theory, and it is time to start building a prototype device to demonstrate the effect."

"What is it?" asked Brother Andrew as Cédric unlocked the door of the workshop that had been sitting idle for more than two years.

Cédric replied with a grin as he opened the door and switched on the lights, "I am planning to build a hovercraft wheelchair for Magdalena. But I won't know if the idea will even work until I try it. For this, I will need the neutron filament winder in my workshop here."

"I thought you disassembled it when you went to work for the Nuclear Directorate," Brother Andrew said.

"Disassembled, yes," replied Cédric, "but I stowed away all the pieces, and no one at the directorate will ever know that I reassembled it somewhere else."

Cédric pulled back the tarp covering his steam engine that had not been operated for almost twenty years and smiled proudly. He took a mental inventory of the work benches, machine tools, and crates containing the neutron generator and filament winder to confirm that there would be enough space in his new shop for everything. Then turning to face Brother Andrew, he confided, "I have been having chronic back pain that has been getting progressively worse for the past year. The walk up to Villa Chandellepont from the train station has become excruciating."

"What does your doctor think is wrong?" asked Brother Andrew.

"I haven't actually seen a doctor," Cédric replied. "My chiropractor is afraid that something more serious than a misaligned spine is at the root, but I hate doctors, and I have been putting off seeing one. Once I start down that path, they are sure to find something wrong with me. Doctors are just hammers trained to look for nails. Anyway, Magdalena needs me in Grenoble. It's time for me to give up this property and move on."

Brother Andrew responded, "Does that mean you will be putting Villa Chandellepont up for sale?"

Cédric looked intently at his friend who had been an anchor for him since the day they met after his motorcycle accident. "No," he said. "I am thinking of donating it to the abbey."

Brother Andrew stood speechless.

Cédric said, "I don't need the money. This place has served a useful purpose over the years for housing refugees. I am proud to have had a part in that. Maybe you can sell it to purchase another place somewhere more suitable to your needs."

The two walked quietly out of the workshop. Cédric took one more look around before switching off the light and taking down the Chandellepont sign over the door. "I have arranged for a trucking company to come clear out the lab and move everything to Grenoble. Do you mind meeting them and letting them in when they arrive? They will also be taking the walnut office furniture that Oskar and Johann made, but otherwise, I plan to leave everything else behind."

Cédric brought Magdalena red roses, which he had done almost daily to cheer her up. He was feeling particularly happy that day and was hoping it was contagious. "I have been making some significant headway on our gravitron manuscript," he said.

"You mean your manuscript," she shot back.

He sat down across from her wheelchair and took her hands, saying, "You know I would never have recognized that gravity is a vector field without your help." After a long pause, he smiled broadly and said, "They told me you are ready to be released from the hospital."

She pulled her hand back and wheeled away from him, tears streaming down her face. "Cédric, what am I supposed to do? Where will I go?"

He stood up and left the room, momentarily returning with a nurse in tow.

"I just signed your discharge papers," he said. "They are finally letting you go home."

"That's ridiculous," she replied. "There are three flights of stairs up to my apartment."

Cédric said cheerfully, "I have a big surprise for you."

A shuttle van was stationed at the front door, with the ramp deployed and the driver standing by to help her get inside. She had mastered the joystick of her electric wheelchair and could maneuver it almost anywhere she wanted as long as it didn't involve stairs. She pivoted around at the base of the ramp and started to head back inside. "I can't do this," she exclaimed.

"Can you trust me?" said Cédric reassuringly. "There is something I want to show you."

After some coaxing, Magdalena consented to get into the van. Cédric sat quietly next to her as they passed through familiar neighborhoods in the eastern suburbs of Grenoble and headed up a driveway lined with horse chestnut trees. A white stucco house with red tile roof stood at the end.

"Where are you taking me?" she asked.

"Just wait," he said as the van drove around to the right and up a slight incline to the back of the house and came to a stop. The driver deployed the ramp and signaled for Magdalena that it was safe to exit the van. Several workmen in coveralls came out of the house upon their arrival and, waving to Cédric, piled into a fleet of trucks and work vans parked along the back retaining wall.

"Is this your house?" Magdalena asked, admiring the place.

"No," replied Cédric. "It's yours." He did not wait to see her reaction but raced inside, hoping she would follow. A new concrete ramp led from the driveway into the house. Magdalena positioned her wheelchair on the ramp and slowly entered, observing that there was no sill in the doorway to overcome. She did a pirouette in the kitchen to take in the countertops that had been lowered to chair height, then followed Cédric into the living room. She stopped at the base of the staircase and stared at the landing above.

"You are not going to believe this," he said excitedly, opening a hall closet that revealed an elevator door. "Why don't you try it," he said, turning to dash up the stairs to meet her on the second floor, where the elevator opened into a large salon containing all the furniture from her apartment. Upon seeing the familiar things, she felt like she was home. She looked up at him with tears in her eyes and quietly said, "Thank you, Cédric."

Magdalena adjusted quickly to her new surroundings. Before long, she was calling for a shuttle van to take her into town to shop. She was cooking in her kitchen and doing some gardening in back with the help of a caretaker Cédric had hired to maintain the grounds. She also returned to work at the GRL. This came as a big surprise to Cédric because he had imagined that she would not want to work again now that she did not need to. He never appreciated how much Magdalena cherished her independence.

As time went on, they gradually drifted apart. He accepted the reality that she had never loved him the way he had loved her. He managed his heartbreak by pouring himself increasingly into his work. He had become reclusive and passed almost all his time either in his workshop or writing in his journal. He rarely went out. He was eating less and less, sometimes going all day without eating at all. He began sleeping only a few hours each night, and when he did sleep, it was often sitting at his desk. He was obsessed with his work. Once he had gotten his neutron filament winder operational, he was able to carry out experiments that had been in the back of his mind ever since he had observed the mysterious pea-sized aluminum globule that he had accidently created when he blew up the reactor at NaPiles years earlier. He knew that there was a lot more to supermassive neutron clusters than just microfusion but until then had no way to investigate the effect. His scientific instincts had assured him that his neutron filaments held the key to testing his gravitational field theories. He had also come to the realization that the commercial value of his discovery would be unimaginably profound.

He reluctantly settled on the term *antigravity* to describe the effect. He had demonstrated it in a compelling way when he wound a strand of a few billion neutrons several times around the rim of a wheel that had an axle passing through the center. His intention was merely to mimic the counterrotation of two neutron stars by creating a spinning top with the mass distributed around the circumference. He had anticipated that the increased angular momentum of the spinning top would be substantial and that it would become lighter, but he had not been sure what would happen when he spun the device for the first time on his workbench. It floated into the air and continued to spin against the ceiling of his lab until it finally slowed down before gently drifting back to the ground. He repeated the trial, but this time he spun the top clockwise instead of counterclockwise as he had done before. The top spun with difficulty and, after a couple of seconds, toppled over on its side and came to a stop. Cédric performed this experiment many times to confirm that it was repeatable. The effect was consistent with his new theories but observing it in his laboratory for the first time still came as a surprise. His theories on paper were one thing but seeing the effect in action was quite another.

Cédric had hypothesized the existence of a fundamental particle he called a *polatron*, which is the product of mass times velocity. It is a vector quantity by virtue of the velocity vector. Ordinarily, the product of mass and velocity is known as momentum in classical mechanics. When the velocity approaches the speed of light, relativity comes into play, but Cédric's polatron theory considered the case of nonrelativistic velocities of large masses—planets and stars, for example. A body of mass, m, moving with a velocity, v, has momentum p. What Cédric had realized was that the masses in the Newtonian gravitation law refer to the effective mass, not the rest mass. In the case of ordinary matter, there's not much difference between the two. But in the case of a supermassive cluster of neutrons moving with a velocity perpendicular to the earth's gravitational field, the effective mass decreases as a function of the velocity because of the time lag resulting from the movement of the position vector between the polatron and the center of the earth. For ordinary matter, the displacement of this vector with time is of no consequence, but when the speed of light is retarded by nine orders of magnitude in the vicinity of the neutron cluster, he knew that the effect would be profound. Cédric hypothesized that the effective mass depended on the velocity and direction of that body. Big G in Newton's formula could not possibly be constant. Rather, it depended on the speed of light inside the neutron cluster. Albert Einstein had spent the last years of his life in a futile attempt to come up with a unified field theory that incorporated gravity based on the presumption that *G* was a universal constant. His instincts that gravity and electromagnetism had to be somehow linked were correct, and Cédric had suspected he would have discovered that *G* was not a constant had he not held so tenaciously to his belief that the speed of light was constant. Cédric had recognized that gravity depended on time, making *G* an explicit function of the speed of light, which, in turn, is a function of time. The velocity term needed to be incorporated into this new function. A polatron is a body moving with velocity, *v*, that has a variable effective mass. A polatron is described by a vector just like with ordinary momentum, but the bookkeeping of the effective mass and velocity are taken care of by a time-dependent function, *G(t).*

Cédric knew that the masses could not be negative, but the velocities certainly could be. The gravitational force was not just the scalar product of the momenta but turned out to be the cross product of the vector velocities, $v_1 \times v_2$. This discovery by Cédric was simple and elegant. For one thing, it meant that the gravitational force is a vector quantity that is orthogonal to the respective velocities of the supermassive bodies and obeys the right-hand rule. It meant that gravity and force are orthogonal to the velocity and that the force due to gravity has a direction. It points up or down depending on the relative motion of the bodies. When it points down, the effect is attractive, but when it points up, the gravitational force is repulsive. No one ever thought to measure the force between ordinary masses moving past each other at a high velocity because, even if one could carry out such an experiment in a laboratory on earth, the effect would be undetectable because the relative velocity of the two bodies would be eclipsed by the much greater velocity and mass of the earth in orbit around the sun. Cédric recognized that in order to observe any such effect, much greater masses would be required.

His spinning top was certainly interesting and demonstrated compellingly the antigravity effect. But it was still just a toy. He enclosed the top in a metal sphere about the size of an orange and built a wooden case for it. The problem was that it didn't actually do anything useful. It just went up and came back down. He recognized this shortcoming and began experimenting with counterrotating rotors. He started constructing concentric rotors, with an inner rotor inside another rotor. If the outer rotor were spinning counterclockwise while the inner rotor was spinning clockwise at just the right speed, the device levitated. By adjusting the relative rotor speeds, the device would ascend and descent on command. He also discovered that the direction of the gravitational force vector could not only be switched from up to down, but also it could be moved around with respect to the vertical axis, by quickly changing the speed of the inner rotor relative to the outer one. This produced a lateral torque that made the device steerable like a helicopter. Thus, the basic design for Cédric's first practical device was taking shape—an antigravity, levitating wheelchair.

Chapter 30: Requiem

Magdalena had occasionally stopped by Cédric's laboratory after work to hear about his most recent inventions. She had become a believer in antigravity after seeing the demonstration of the spinning sphere drifting up to the ceiling and started paying more attention to his breakthroughs that came almost daily. Her enthusiasm grew in anticipation of the promised test flight of her new hovercraft wheelchair. A new challenge had surfaced, however, that consumed Cédric for several weeks. The simple antigravity sphere could not be steered. Three degrees of operating freedom would be required to deploy the technology in a wheelchair or any other practical mobility device. His plan was to mount a joystick to the arm of the chair. He had demonstrated that steering could be accomplished by altering the speed of the inside and outside rotors, and thus the direction of the gravitational field with the rotor-inside-a-rotor design, but he was having difficulty controlling the motors that determined the rotor speeds from the outside. It proved impossible to use ordinary electrical connections or electromagnetic signals because these were blocked by the strong gravitational fields surrounding the rotors. He made a monumental breakthrough when he realized that polatrons could communicate the control information without being blocked by the gravity field. This involved constructing a small polatron transmitter inside the joystick. By mounting a rotating spindle inside the handle, consisting of a spinning toroidal coil of neutrons that generated a uniform gravitational field along its axis, the speed and direction of the spindle provided the signal directly to control the levitating rotors. Cédric had considered this device as his greatest invention. He knew that it would be necessary to control the rotor speeds and direction in order to construct any useful device. He considered this invention so secret, in fact, that he chose not to describe it in any of his daily journals. He planned, instead, to document the device in a patent disclosure when he got the time.

Cédric had become so engrossed in his work that he had been remiss in checking his tablet for mail, and Magdalena had become concerned when she had not heard from him for a while. She finally asked the caretaker to check in on him to see if everything was okay and tell him to read his mail. She wanted to see if he would join her for dinner with some friends from the GRL. His mailbox mostly contained pages of junk mail from people trying to sell him something he didn't want, but he happened to notice a message from Julia that was already a week old.

Dear Uncle Cédric,

Believe it or not, I finally graduated with a law degree from George Washington University. I landed my dream job with the UN Mission in Geneva working on the refugee problem in Eastern Europe. I just arrived in Geneva with Nick and Annie. They came to help me get settled. We were hoping to find a time to pay you a visit.

Also, I have been working with a guy who claims he knows you. He says he has been trying to get in touch with you but is getting no response. His name is Joel, and he is the pastor of a church in Bucharest. What should I tell him? We are all looking forward to seeing you soon. Annie and Nick will be here for a couple more weeks, and then they are heading back to Grand Junction, so I hope to hear from you soon.

Much love,
Julia

Cédric searched through his inbox for messages from a guy named Pastor Joel and discovered several that he had assumed were junk. He received countless pleas for money and generally did not take them seriously.

Dear Mr. Rothschild,

Through a mutual acquaintance in Montmélian, Brother Andrew, I was made aware of your unprecedented generosity to the plight of the Romanian people. The refugee crisis is overwhelming, and I am forced to beg for help.

My country is being taken over by a sinister group called the Syndicate. What we are dealing with is one of the darkest elements of the entire human race. The saddest thing is that most of the people who do their bidding are just ordinary farm boys and girls who have been pressed into service as a consequence of the corrupt systems operating right under our noses. If it weren't true, I would think it was fiction. First, the Syndicate takes over the central banks, which is ponderously easy in poorer countries. Next, they finance political candidates to gain control of the governments. Of course, this is all accomplished under the guise of freedom and democracy. These elected officials grow the size of government, which means they need more and more money to perform the duties they claim the people they pretend to serve think they need. It all looks very legitimate, and no one complains because these elected officials stay in office by dispensing favors to the very people who keep them in office. Then they slowly ratchet up taxes, such as property taxes on subsistence farmers. These farmers don't have any cash, per se, and the government won't take payment in goat cheese, so they begin selling assets to raise cash for the taxes. There is never enough, so they are forced to borrow from the banks—the very banks responsible for bankrolling the politicians in the first place. Then, the loans are secured by the value of the farms, and when the farmers can't keep up with the usury interest rates, the bankers show up one day with foreclosure documents and threaten to kick the farmers off the land that in many cases was in their family for generations. If the farmers happen to have healthy teenage sons or daughters, the bankers offer to defer the loan payments in exchange for what they call "community service," which means being pressed into service of the Syndicate.

What several prominent members of my church in Bucharest are proposing is to establish a private bank to provide low interest loans to cash-strapped farmers and small businesses without the need to use their farms and businesses as collateral. Brother Andrew suggested that I contact you. He said that you may know people in the banking community who can help in this endeavor.

I had the pleasure recently of meeting a charming young woman in Geneva you know, by the name of Julia, who was herself a refugee as a child. She is trying to get the United Nations involved in this banking crisis. It is not too late, but the hour is getting late. Julia has told me of your generous support for refugees. We have an opportunity to defeat the conditions that are creating the refugee crisis in the first place. I hope you will seriously consider my plea.

Best regards,
Pastor Joel

Church of the Risen King,
Bucharest, Romania

The taxi pulled up to the end of the driveway. Nico, Annie, and Julia got out and went up the staircase leading to the front door to ring the bell. There was no answer, and they thought perhaps they had come to the wrong place when the caretaker appeared from the side of the house and said, "Miss Roberts is at work. May I be of assistance?"

Annie replied, "We are looking for Cédric Rothschild. This is the address he gave us."

"Cédric's place is the building in the back. You will know it when you see the sign 'Chandellepont' over the door," the caretaker said. "I talked to him this morning, and he said he would be expecting guests today."

The three took the footpath around to the left. Nico beamed proudly when he saw the sign that he had made for Cédric's workshop in Val d'Isère. He pushed the doorbell, and they waited expectantly for Cédric, who failed to arrive at the door. Nico tried the handle, but it was locked. He went looking for the caretaker while Annie began peeking in the windows. She saw Cédric sitting at a table motionless and wrapped on the window to get his attention.

"I think something is wrong," she exclaimed as Nico returned with the caretaker, who fumbled with his keychain before finding the right one for opening the door.

Upon entering the workshop, they saw Cédric slumped down in his chair. Annie felt his forehead, which was warm and clammy. Then she instinctively felt for a pulse. Nico and the caretaker had rushed outside to call for an ambulance.

Julia took his limp hand. “Is he dead?” she asked.

“No,” replied Annie, “I don’t think so, but he is totally unresponsive. Cédric, It’s Annie. Can you hear me?”

Cédric uttered a muffled groan at the welcome sound of her voice.

Cédric lay in his hospital bed in the intensive care unit with a respirator and assortment of diagnostic devices. Magdalena had been summoned from work and sat by his side, stroking his hand. “The last time I saw him, he was very gaunt. I was worried about him,” she said, looking up at the others.

Several nurses were busy checking the instruments and monitoring his vital signs. He was badly dehydrated, and some color was returning to his face as the glucose water from his IV began to take effect. A doctor entered the room flipping through pages on a clipboard. “I can’t find any medical history for this patient,” he said.

Magdalena said, “He was seeing a private concierge doctor. He found out that he had pancreatic cancer about six months ago.”

The doctor replied, “Then why was he not hospitalized?”

Magdalena replied, “He said he had work to finish. He feared that once he went into the hospital, he would never be able to leave again.”

“Okay then,” said the doctor. “I will order a PET scan.”

The scan turned out not to be needed. Cédric never regained consciousness and stopped breathing within an hour.

Chapter 31: Epilogue

Cédric had known that his cancer was terminal and untreatable. In anticipation of his death, he had put most of his affairs in order. He had created a foundation to manage the assets from his estate and appointed Sonja Dumitescu as the executive director when Magdalena had refused the role. He had thought that by the time his estate was settled in French probate court, the fact that Sonya did not actually exist would not matter because by then the bulk of his estate would have transferred to the private bank in Bucharest that Pastor Joel was helping to establish.

He had printed out a hardcopy of the final draft of his gravitation manuscript and deleted all the earlier drafts, including the final version from his computer. The single printed version was all that remained of his work. He had sealed it in an envelope and placed it in a fireproof safe along with his laboratory notebooks. Everything of importance from his entire life's work went into the safe, and he destroyed all noncritical documents so that a clean trail of invention could be established when the patents were filed. His instructions to Magdalena were to safeguard these documents and donate the proceeds from the patent royalties to his foundation.

Cédric worked feverishly in his final days to complete Magdalena's levitating wheelchair, but at last, it was left unfinished—the various components were spread out unassembled on his work benches. The antigravity sphere was tucked away in its nondescript wooden case in a supply cabinet against the far wall of his laboratory. Karl, the caretaker, helped her tidy up the workshop. The tools were returned to the hooks on the wall or put away in the toolboxes. The various components of the wheelchair were placed in plastic tubs and stored away on shelves, leaving all the workbenches bare except for the steam engine. Magdalena paused next to it and turned the flywheel manually for a few strokes of the piston, reflecting on how Cédric had said that the steam engine combined all the elements of mechanics and thermodynamics. She remembered how he would fire it up when he was stuck on a problem and stare in wonder at the little machine, which he said never failed to give him inspiration.

Karl brought in a hydraulic lift to give Magdalena access to Cédric's studio apartment on the second floor. She had never visited it while he was still alive. She was surprised to see how simply he had lived. The apartment had no superfluous adornments whatsoever. She and Karl packed away the books from his library to be donated to the local university according to Cédric's wishes. The heavy fireproof safe was moved to the main house along with the C. S. Lewis anthology that she had heard about but never seen.

After cleaning up, all that remained in Cédric's studio were a few items of furniture. She pushed aside the swivel desk chair and maneuvered her wheelchair up to the walnut desk that

Cédric's Armenian friends in Montmélian had made for him. His journal lay open to the final entry from the day before he died. She switched on the reading light and began to read.

> I have accomplished only a fraction of the things I set out to do, and, sadly, the things I would have accomplished had I lived to one hundred will never be done. Since I received my cancer diagnosis, I have worked with an urgency in a futile attempt to complete as many of the things I started as possible. But the biggest tragedy of all is that I now fear that Magdalena's wheelchair will go unfinished. If I were to be totally honest with myself, I would have to admit that most of the things I have done in my life were done selfishly for me only. Magdalena's wheelchair is different. I have been building it out of love for her. I never loved anyone so much and never pursued anything so passionately with the solitary objective to make someone else happy. Perhaps, in the end, the greatest reward of all is that I was able to love someone else more than I loved myself. I long to hear my Master say, "Well done, good and faithful servant."
>
> June 12, 2062

www.ingramcontent.com/pod-product-compliance
Lightning Source LLC
LaVergne TN
LVHW020537100826
845148LV00010B/1510